Danger of Defeat

By Edward Marston

THE HOME FRONT DETECTIVE SERIES

A Bespoke Murder • Instrument of Slaughter
Five Dead Canaries • Deeds of Darkness
Dance of Death • The Enemy Within
Under Attack • The Unseen Hand • Orders to Kill
Danger of Defeat • Spring Offensive

THE RAILWAY DETECTIVE SERIES

The Railway Detective • The Excursion Train
The Railway Viaduct • The Iron Horse
Murder on the Brighton Express • The Silver Locomotive Mystery
Railway to the Grave • Blood on the Line
The Stationmaster's Farewell • Peril on the Royal Train
A Ticket to Oblivion • Timetable of Death
Signal for Vengeance • The Circus Train Conspiracy
A Christmas Railway Mystery • Points of Danger
Fear on the Phantom Special • Slaughter in the Sapperton Tunnel
Tragedy on the Branch Line
The Railway Detective's Christmas Case • Death at the Terminus
Murder in Transit • Mystery at the Station Hotel
Inspector Colbeck's Casebook

THE OCEAN LINER MYSTERIES

Murder on the Lusitania • Murder on the Mauretania
Murder on the Minnesota • Murder on the Caronia
Murder on the Marmora • Murder on the Salsette
Murder on the Oceanic • Murder on the Celtic

THE MERLIN RICHARDS SERIES

Murder at the Arizona Biltmore
Homicide in Chicago

a&b

Danger of Defeat

EDWARD MARSTON

Allison & Busby Limited
11 Wardour Mews
London W1F 8AN
allisonandbusby.com

First published in Great Britain by Allison & Busby in 2023.
This paperback edition published by Allison & Busby in 2024.

A CIP catalogue record for this book is available from
the British Library.

10 9 8 7 6 5 4 3 2 1

ISBN 978-0-7490-2975-3

Typeset in 11/16 pt Adobe Garamond Pro by
Allison & Busby Ltd.

By choosing this product, you help take care of the world's forests.
Learn more: www.fsc.org

Printed and bound by
CPI Group (UK) Ltd, Croydon, CR0 4YY

In fond memory of my grandfathers,
both of whom fought in the Great War as young men
and who were profoundly changed by the experience

CHAPTER ONE

February, 1918

When the telephone rang in the middle of the night, Harvey Marmion was immediately awake. He jumped out of bed, shivered in the cold, grabbed a dressing gown, then pulled it on as he hurried downstairs to pick up the receiver in the hall. Superintendent Claude Chatfield barked orders into his ear. Marmion barely got a word in. When the line went dead, he ran upstairs, dressed quickly and quietly, then left his wife still sleeping soundly in bed. Ellen would understand. An absent husband meant that there was an emergency. Living with a detective inspector had made her accustomed to his sudden disappearances. Marmion was effectively on duty around the clock.

While he waited for the police car to arrive, he tried to

process the information that Chatfield had given him. There had been an incident somewhere in Limehouse. A policeman had been shot. Marmion knew the area well. When he had first joined the Metropolitan Police Force, he had pounded the streets of Poplar and Limehouse. Memories of that period in his life flooded back into his mind – bad memories for the most part. It had been hard, unremitting, often dangerous work but he had come to see that it was a good apprenticeship for him. Going back there, however, was bound to generate mixed feelings.

When the police car picked him up, it was driven to the house where Joe Keedy now lived. Marmion used the knocker to rap out a summons. The sergeant responded at once, leaping out of bed, dressing at speed, then tumbling out of the front door before diving into the back seat of the car beside Marmion. The vehicle drove off. Keedy was angry.

'I hope there's a bloody good reason to get us up this early,' he said.

'There's the best reason possible, Joe. A police constable has been shot dead.'

'Oh, I see. That's different.'

'He and his partner disturbed burglars in Limehouse.'

'Did they get away?'

'No,' said Marmion. 'They were tracked to their house. You ought to be grateful to Chat for calling on us. It sounds serious. In any case,' he joked, 'what could be nicer than hearing the superintendent's voice at four in the morning? It was music to my ears.'

Keedy stifled a response. He could think of something far

more satisfying to do at that hour of the night, but it involved Marmion's daughter, Alice, to whom he was engaged. What would be typical police banter with any other colleague was impossible with his future father-in-law.

'Why did the superintendent pick on us?'

'We've got form, Joe. Don't you remember that you once persuaded a man not to commit suicide by jumping into the Thames?'

'That was ages ago.'

'And I once stopped a drunken husband from slitting his wife's neck when she dared to argue with him. I simply talked to him quietly until he eventually dropped the knife and burst into tears. Unfortunately,' said Marmion, ruefully, 'it doesn't always end so happily.'

'More's the pity!'

'Something tells me that we're facing a much bigger crisis this time.'

Keedy closed his eyes. 'Wake me up when we get there.'

Superintendent Chatfield had reacted to the situation with speed and efficiency. He arrived at the scene to find dozens of uniformed policemen watching a small, terraced house from a safe distance. Inside, he was told, were the three suspects. One of them, at least, possessed a gun and had already shown his readiness to use it. Chatfield had no wish to see another policeman killed so he proceeded with caution. Men had already been deployed to the rear of the house in case the burglars tried to escape that way. He checked on them to see if they had spotted any movement inside or outside the house. Chatfield then returned to the front of the house with his megaphone. Before he could use it to begin negotiations, however, he saw a police car turn into the street and come to a halt. Marmion and Keedy jumped out and ran across to him. Chatfield was glad to see the detectives.

'Three men are holed up in that house,' he told them, pointing a finger. 'I'm hoping to persuade them to come out, but they may have other ideas.'

'Blimey!' exclaimed Keedy, looking around. 'You've got plenty of manpower here, sir. It's like the Siege of Sidney Street.'

Chatfield shook his head. 'It's not a bit like it, Sergeant,' he argued. 'In that instance, there was a huge police presence, bolstered by officers from the City of London Police and sharpshooters from the Scots Guards. Also, it was three years before the war broke out, so it was easy to rustle up reinforcements. We can't do that now.'

'There's another difference, sir,' observed Marmion, looking up and down the dark street. 'Most people are still asleep in their beds. The sound of gunfire in Sidney Street brought everyone out of their houses. The police had a job to control the crowds.'

'I'm hoping for a peaceful solution,' said Chatfield. 'I'll try to lure them out.'

'Do we have any idea who they are?'

'We have a name for one of them. According to a next-door neighbour, he's Dan Haskins. He rented the house a month or so ago and, apparently, gets on well with everyone. He told the neighbour that he works as a nightwatchman in a factory in Ben Jonson Road.' Chatfield rolled his eyes. 'In fact, as we've now discovered, he's a burglar and so are his associates. That's the other difference between this situation and the one in Sidney Street,' he went on. 'In the latter case, we were up against a murderous gang of Latvians. At least the burglars inside this house will understand English.' He raised the megaphone. 'It's time to have a conversation with them.'

When Alice Marmion came downstairs, wiping the sleep from her eyes, her mother had been up for some time. Ellen had lit a fire in the living room and was now making tea in the kitchen. She was pleased that her daughter had spent the night at home for a change. Ordinarily, Alice lived in a rented room several miles away.

'I'm sorry if the noise woke you up,' said Ellen.

'What noise?'

'The telephone rang.'

'I didn't hear it.'

'You must have heard the police car screeching to a halt outside. That's what brought me awake. I expect there's been an emergency of some sort. Your father had to charge off somewhere.'

'I was fast asleep, Mummy. Never heard a thing. I know that being in the Women's Police Force can't compare with what Daddy and Joe do, but spending all day on your feet is very tiring. I was really exhausted last night.'

'You'll have to get used to this, Alice.'

'Used to what?'

'Waking up and finding there's nobody in the bed beside you.'

'I see what you mean.'

'When you and Joe are married, he's going to be hauled out in the middle of the night from time to time.'

Alice sighed. 'I suppose that it's the price I pay for having a husband who is a Scotland Yard detective. Ah well,' she added with a smile. 'There are compensations.'

Crouching in the doorway of a nearby house, megaphone in hand, Chatfield tried to persuade the burglars that there was no escape. Armed policemen stood ready to storm the building, but the superintendent hoped that it would not be necessary. He had persuaded criminals once before that they had no option but surrender. This time, however, his words were having no visible effect. Not a single sound came from the house where Dan Haskins lived.

'Perhaps they've hopped it, sir,' suggested Marmion.

'Impossible,' said Chatfield, tetchily. 'We've got the place surrounded.'

'Are you quite sure that someone is inside it?'

'Of course, I am.'

'Have you seen anyone at the window, sir?' asked Keedy.

'No,' admitted Chatfield, 'but they were spotted entering the building. A light was switched on in the front bedroom. It went off soon after I arrived. They can hear me perfectly well. Why don't they answer me?'

'They must have sneaked off somehow, sir,' said Keedy.

'They're still there, Sergeant. I'd stake my pension on it.'

'Then what do we do?'

'We bide our time and make them sweat,' replied Chatfield.

'When they least expect it, we'll batter the door down and catch them napping.'

'Can I go with them?' volunteered Keedy, excited by the prospect.

'You've no means of defending yourself.'

'I'll have the advantage of surprise.'

'Leave it to those with firearms,' advised Marmion.

'I don't want to miss all the fun,' complained Keedy. 'I'll take a gun, if you insist. I've been trained to use one. The superintendent tried to persuade them to come out and they ignored him. Brute force is the only answer.'

'It's too dangerous, Joe.'

'You know me. I never run away from danger.'

'Then that's settled,' decided Chatfield. 'After ten minutes, the door will be smashed open, then in you go.'

He summoned two burly policemen, each holding a shotgun. While the superintendent gave them their orders, Marmion was trying to persuade Keedy to reconsider. The last thing he wanted was for his future son-in-law to take such a risk. His words went unheard. Keedy was poised for action. Nothing would stop him. When he was offered a bulldog revolver, he checked to see that it was loaded. Keedy felt invincible. Ten minutes ticked past, then he and the two policemen braced themselves. On a command from the superintendent, the three of them crept forward. One of the policemen used the butt of his shotgun to batter the door open, then Keedy led the way inside.

A gunshot was heard and Keedy howled in pain. Marmion gasped in horror.

* * *

After breakfast with her mother, Alice Marmion was about to leave the house and go to work when the telephone rang. Ellen lifted the receiver and spoke into it. Pleased to hear her husband's voice, she was soon aghast. Alice could see that she was hearing dreadful news. As soon as the call was over, Ellen put down the receiver with a trembling hand.

'What's happened, Mummy?' cried Alice.

'It's Joe . . .'

'What about him?

'He's been shot and rushed to hospital.'

Alice shuddered. She felt as if her whole future was suddenly in doubt.

CHAPTER TWO

Everything happened so quickly. As soon as the three of them rushed into the house, Keedy had been stopped in his tracks by a bullet. It had been fired by a man at the top of the stairs. Before the two policemen could return fire, the burglar had fled the scene. They were torn between pursuing him and helping Keedy to safety. In the event, it was Marmion who came to his friend's aid. Rushing into the house, he saw Keedy at the bottom of the stairs, lying on his back and groaning in agony. Marmion then became aware of flames crackling in the living room and threatening to spread into the hallway. To confuse the police and cover their escape, the burglars had set the house alight. Getting Keedy out of the building was now of paramount importance. Marmion tried to move him as gently as he could, but he was inflicting more pain on the sergeant. Chatfield stepped in to lend a hand and the two of them eased Keedy out into the street.

A fire had also been lit upstairs so there was no possibility of chasing the occupants of the house. It seemed impossible for them to escape. Did they prefer to be burnt alive than hanged for murder? He looked down at Marmion who was trying to comfort Keedy and stem the bleeding from his wound.

The sound of gunfire had awakened the whole street. It was suddenly filled with anxious people, desperate to know what was going on. Those who lived close to the burning house feared that their homes would soon be engulfed in flames. Panic set in and they demanded action from the police. Chatfield's attempts at reassuring them fell on deaf ears. Inhabitants of nearby streets came out to swell the numbers. Controlling the baying mob was impossible. It was not long before the clang of fire engines and the noise of an ambulance added to the cacophony. The whole street was in uproar.

Finding a taxi at that time of night was virtually impossible so Ellen Marmion had to try another way to reach the hospital. She and Alice ran to the grocer's shop and banged on the door. The bald head of Geoffrey Biddle soon appeared through an upstairs window that suddenly opened.

'We don't open until eight o'clock,' he snarled.

'It's an emergency,' cried Ellen. 'We have to get to Mile End Hospital.'

Biddle's tone changed at once. 'Is that you, Mrs Marmion?'

'Yes – we need a lift. We're so sorry to call on you like this, but I can't think of any other way. My daughter's fiancé has been shot. They've rushed him to hospital.'

'Say no more. I'll come at once.'

Ellen and Alice stood beside the van parked outside the shop. Geoffrey Biddle's name was painted on the side of it with the claim that he was a Purveyor of Fine Groceries. To the two women, he was something else at that moment. Biddle was a blessing. They were overwhelmed with gratitude. When he came out of the side door of the house, the grocer, a tall, skinny, red-faced man in his fifties, was wearing pyjamas, dressing gown and slippers. As he unlocked the doors of his van, he apologised that one of them would have to travel in the rear with a collection of empty cardboard boxes. Alice was a willing volunteer.

'I don't mind doing that,' she said. When it had been unlocked, she clambered in through the rear door of the van.

'We're so grateful to you,' said Ellen.

'Tell me what happened when we're on the way, Mrs Marmion,' said Biddle. 'In a situation like this, I'm glad to help you.'

'Thank you.'

'Yes,' added Alice. 'Thank you, Mr Biddle.'

'Get in and don't apologise. You did the right thing.'

The van was soon shooting away from the kerb.

Mile End Hospital had been built in 1859 as the infirmary for the local workhouse. It was rebuilt some thirty years later and a training school for nurses was added in 1892. Constructed with Victorian solidity, it had an essentially functional air. After the outbreak of war, it had been converted into a military hospital to cope with the constant supply of wounded soldiers brought home from the battlefields. Ambulances arrived there day and night.

Harvey Marmion was pacing up and down in the waiting room, blaming himself for allowing Keedy to go into a place of danger. While he admired the sergeant's courage, he wished that it had been tempered by discretion, but that would be asking for the impossible. There was a daredevil streak in Keedy that had made him such a fearless detective. His luck had finally run out.

Marmion was still praying that Keedy was out of danger when his wife and daughter were shown into the waiting room. As they ran to him, he put a consoling arm around each of them. Questions poured out of the women.

'What exactly happened to Joe?' asked Alice.

'How badly is he wounded?' said Ellen.

'Is he in danger?'

'What have the doctors said?'

'Tell us, Daddy,' pleaded Alice.

After calming them, he took them across to a row of chairs and made them sit down.

'They think that Joe will pull through,' he told them.

'Thank God!' exclaimed Alice, eyes filling with tears.

'But he's going to be out of action for a while – a long while, possibly.'

'Why bring him here?' asked Ellen.

'This was the nearest hospital. He may not be a soldier, but he was wounded while fighting in another war, the one against

20

crime. They were happy to accept him. By the time we got here, Joe had lost a lot of blood. He's in the operating theatre right now. I daresay they'll need to remove the bullet first.' Marmion forced a smile. 'Don't fear the worst. Joe is a fighter. He'll come through this.'

Alice exchanged a look with her mother. They were both quietly terrified.

Keedy lay on the operating table, subdued by an anaesthetic that had removed the pain instantly. The bullet had hit him in the stomach, but the surgeons had yet to establish the full extent of his injuries. One thing was in his favour. He was an unusually fit, strong young man. Also, his limbs were still attached to his body. To surgeons who routinely operated on men with missing arms or legs, it was a welcome change. They knew that Keedy had been injured while trying to arrest one of the burglars involved in the murder of a policeman. Their patient was a hero.

'Mr Biddle?' said Marmion in surprise. 'You came here in the grocer's van?'

'It was Mummy's idea,' explained Alice. 'I'd never have thought of asking him.'

'We've been customers there for donkey's years,' said Ellen. 'I felt that he was bound to help us in an emergency – and he did. Even if it meant that Alice had to spend the journey rolling around in the back of the van.'

'I didn't mind that, Mummy. It was transport. That's all that matters.'

'Where is Mr Biddle now?' asked Marmion. 'Is he waiting outside?'

'No,' said Ellen. 'I sent him back home. He has a shop to open. I hoped that we might have a lift back from a police car. You can arrange that, can't you?'

'I'll do my best. We only have a limited supply of vehicles at our disposal, or I'd have sent one to pick you both up.'

'I'm not going anywhere until I've seen Joe,' said Alice, firmly. 'I don't care how long I need to wait. My place is here. Joe would expect it.'

Ellen nodded. 'And quite rightly.'

Before he could make a comment, Marmion noticed that Claude Chatfield was hovering outside the door. He excused himself and left the room.

'I blame the superintendent,' said Ellen. 'He should never have allowed Joe to go into a house when there was an armed man inside.'

'Knowing Joe, I fancy that he insisted on going in.'

'You may be right, Alice.'

'He'd never turn his back on a challenge. It worries me sometimes.'

'Yes,' said Ellen, face puckering with anxiety. 'Joe Keedy is far too brave for his own good.'

Unaware of what was happening, Keedy was in a world of his own. He didn't feel the tweezers that were carefully inserted into the wound to extract the bullet or hear the sharp clink as it was dropped into a metal dish.

* * *

The two of them had withdrawn to a quiet corner of the entrance hall. When Marmion had given Chatfield the latest news about Keedy, the superintendent told him what had happened back in Limehouse. He spoke through gritted teeth.

'They got away,' he admitted.

'How?' asked Marmion in amazement. 'The house was on fire. When the flames were finally doused, I thought that you'd find three charred bodies.'

'You underestimate them. Dan Haskins – or whatever his real name was – had not been idle. During the time he and his accomplices were staying there, they went up into the attic and carefully removed some of the slates. The gap was covered by a tarpaulin. That was their emergency exit. When they realised that they had to get out of there quickly, they went through the hole, climbed along the roof to the end house and attached a rope to its chimney. While the rest of us were watching the fire blaze away, Haskins and his two friends were shinning down that rope in turns before making a run for it.'

'The cunning blighters!'

'Worst of all,' said Chatfield, 'they escaped with a substantial haul.'

'How do you know that?'

'We've had a spate of burgled jewellery shops in the East End. The modus operandi is always the same. Someone saws through the grille on the front window and removes it. They cut out a pane of glass big enough to allow them to climb in. While one of them empties the cheaper items in the window display, the others open the safe and snaffle the expensive stuff. Last night,' Chatfield went on, 'they were disturbed. As a result, we have a dead policeman, a wounded detective and a house burnt to a cinder. We'll also have the press tearing us to pieces for failing to catch any of them. All in all, it was a disaster.'

'These men were professionals, sir.'

'Yes, and they made us look like rank amateurs.'

'Haskins did say that he worked at night. Now we know what he was really doing.'

'I want them,' growled Chatfield. 'This case takes priority from now on. I want all three of those devils caught and trussed up like Christmas turkeys. You can have as many officers as you need. Catch them – and do it soon!'

'I'll do my best, sir.'

'The search starts right now.'

'It started the moment one of them shot Sergeant Keedy. God willing, he may survive, but I owe it to him to spend every waking hour on the trail of those men. They're more than criminals to me,' said Marmion, grimly. 'I'll find them. It's a promise.'

CHAPTER THREE

Left alone in the waiting room, Ellen and Alice began to realise the full implications of what had happened. As a result of being shot, Joe Keedy – even if he survived – might be a permanent invalid, unable to continue as a detective or to take on any other job. Only weeks earlier, he and Alice had finally chosen a house where they could begin married life together. It was small, dowdy, and needed a lot doing to it, but they could see its possibilities. They were thrilled when given the key and undaunted when they made a list of the more immediate repairs necessary. In the time that Keedy had been living there alone, he had already made improvements, working feverishly whenever he could snatch a free hour or two.

'How much will Joe be able to do now?' asked Ellen, worriedly.

'There's another problem, Mummy,' said her daughter.

'How can we afford the rent if he is forced to give up his job? I'll have to go back to teaching. I'd hate that.'

'But you used to love the work, Alice.'

'That was before the war. Things are different now. It would take me away from home all day. Who would look after Joe while I was at school?'

'I could help.'

'I'd feel so guilty if that happened. I'll be Joe's wife. It's my duty.'

'You're not getting married until June,' Ellen reminded her. 'Until then, it would be wrong for you to share the house with him. What would people say?'

'We'll have to change the date of the wedding, Mummy. I'm determined to do that. I want to marry Joe as soon as I can,' she insisted. 'I've waited long enough to become his wife and I'm not waiting any longer. I'll speak to the vicar as soon as I can and arrange another date.'

'Won't you have to discuss it with Joe first?'

'He'll agree with me.'

'You sound very certain of that.'

'I am, Mummy. What worries me is who will look after him meanwhile.'

'They're bound to keep him in hospital for a time. Every bed here is needed for wounded soldiers so he may not be able to stay long. I'll see if your father can get Joe transferred somewhere much nearer to us.'

'That would be wonderful.'

Ellen heaved a sigh. 'Oh dear! What a dreadful night this has been!'

'It could have been worse.'

'What do you mean?'

'Mr Biddle might have refused to give us a lift in the middle of the night. What would we have done if that had happened?'

'We'd have walked all the way here,' said Ellen, thrusting out her chin.

'It would have taken us ages.'

'It doesn't matter. We'd have done it gladly.'

'Yes,' said Alice, embracing her warmly. 'We would.'

Iris Goodliffe had arrived early for her daily shift in the Women's Police Force. As she chatted with her colleagues about how cold it was, she kept wondering where her beat partner could be. Alice Marmion was usually the first person there, her uniform immaculate and her sense of purpose evident. None of the other constables was as efficient or as committed as Alice. She set the standard for everyone. Iris was grateful to be able to spend so much time with her. That morning, however, there was no sign of her friend. She was still looking around in dismay when she heard a sharp voice behind her.

'You'll be on duty with Constable Porter today,' announced Inspector Gale.

'Where's Alice?' asked Iris, spinning around.

'I've no idea and no time to speculate on why she is not here. What I can tell you is that she will receive a stern reproof when she does finally deign to appear.'

'Only something serious would keep her away. I'm worried.'

'Control your anxiety and find Constable Porter. She is still relatively new and needs someone who knows the ropes as well as you do.'

'Yes, Inspector – if you say so.'

'I do say so,' rasped the other.

Like all the other women, Iris was afraid of Thelma Gale, a cold, humourless martinet who treated those beneath her so bossily that she had earned the nickname of Gale Force. It was important to get away from the inspector before she was roused. Foolishly, Iris lingered.

'There's five minutes to go,' she pointed out. 'Alice might still turn up.'

'Can't you obey an order?' snapped Gale.

'Well, yes but—'

'Get on with it, woman!'

'I'm sorry, Inspector. I will . . . Excuse me. I'll find Jessica at once.'

And she fled as quickly as she could.

When he came back into the waiting room, Marmion found that his wife was alone. He was glad to have a quiet moment with Ellen.

'How is Alice coping?' he asked.

'She's doing her best,' replied Ellen, 'but the news has been shattering. She's worried to death – so am I, for that matter. It seems so unfair, Harvey. They're a young couple on the verge of getting married and this happens.'

'It's a risk that every policeman must take, love. Joe knew that when he joined the Met.'

'Alice was ready to accept that risk – the same way that I did.'

'I've been lucky. So has Joe – until today. Anyway,' he added, 'I'll have to go back to Scotland Yard with the superintendent now. I did ask about transport for you both and he was happy to provide it. All you need to do is to contact me at the Yard when you need a car.'

'It may not be for some time. Alice won't leave until she has definite news about Joe.'

'What about her job?'

'She's forgotten all about that. There's only one thing on her mind.'

'Inspector Gale needs to be told what's happened. I'll take care of that. I don't want her thinking that Alice has let her down deliberately.' He saw his daughter approaching him. 'I was just telling your mother that I'll get in touch with Inspector Gale.'

'Oh, my God!' exclaimed Alice. 'I'd forgotten all about her.'

'She certainly won't have forgotten about you.'

'Gale Force will be livid with me.'

'That's because she doesn't know that you're here,' said Marmion. 'I'll explain it to her and smooth her ruffled feathers at the same time.'

'Thank you, Daddy!'

'I must be off.'

After giving both women a farewell kiss, he went swiftly out of the room.

Alice was anxious. 'Did you ask about a lift home?'

'Your father will arrange it. All I need to do is to ring him when we're ready.'

'The car is for your benefit, Mummy. I'm not moving from here until I've talked to one of the surgeons and seen Joe with my own eyes.'

'That may not be allowed.'

Alice folded her arms. 'Then I'll stay here until it is.'

Thelma Gale was both angry and mystified by Alice's failure to turn up that morning. The two of them had had clashes in the past but she still believed that Alice was the best policewoman under her command. When she looked through her records, she could find ample evidence of that. To some extent, she accepted, Alice had distinct advantages. As the daughter of a detective inspector and the future wife of a detective sergeant, she was steeped in the processes of crime prevention. Whenever she had given lectures to those at her command, Thelma Gale knew that the most intelligent questions would always come from Alice Marmion. It did not excuse her absence that morning. When she did finally arrive, she would get a roasting from her superior.

The inspector was still thinking about the encounter when the telephone on her desk rang. She snatched the receiver up and gave the caller a curt welcome.

'Inspector Gale here,' she snapped. 'Who is it?'

'Detective Inspector Marmion,' came the reply. 'I have an apology to make.'

She was flustered. 'I'm the one to make an apology,' she

said. 'I'm sorry to be so brusque with you.'

'I didn't notice.'

'Oh . . . I see.'

'I just wanted to explain why my daughter was unable to turn up this morning,' he said. 'Sergeant Keedy and I were called out in the middle of the night to arrest some burglars who had shot dead a policeman. They'd taken refuge in a house in the East End. When it was stormed, the sergeant led the charge inside. His bravery was his undoing, I'm afraid. He was shot.'

'Goodness!' she cried. 'Was he killed?'

'No, but he was seriously injured and rushed to Mile End Military Hospital. My wife and daughter are still there. It's the reason that Alice was unable to turn up for duty this morning.'

'Thank you for telling me, Inspector,' she said. 'I'm very grateful.'

'Please forgive Alice if she is unable to resume work for . . . some time.'

'Yes, yes, of course. Tell her not to worry about us. She has more than enough on her hands. And please give her my best wishes. I do hope that everything turns out well.'

She put the receiver down and tried to absorb the impact of what she had just been told. Alice Marmion was in distress, uncertain if the man she was engaged to marry would survive. She would be on tenterhooks. Thelma Gale felt ashamed of the unseemly haste with which she had blamed Alice for failing to turn up. She was full of sympathy for her now. Sergeant Keedy had been shot in the execution of his duty. If he died as a result, the effect on Alice would be devastating. Even if she did return to work, she would never be the same confident, dedicated policewoman again. Something would have perished inside her.

CHAPTER FOUR

The death of a serving policeman was an event of such importance that it was reported to the commissioner of the Metropolitan Police Force. When he entered his office at 8 a.m., Sir Edward Henry found the details in a report on his desk. Having read it, he summoned Claude Chatfield. The superintendent responded immediately.

'This is sad news,' said the commissioner. 'I hate hearing of a policeman being murdered.'

'It's particularly tragic in this case, Sir Edward. Constable Meade was on the point of retiring when the war broke out. He saw how badly we'd be depleted by losing so many men to the army, so he volunteered to stay on.'

'That was very commendable.'

'This is a poor reward for all those years of service he gave us. His family and friends will be shocked by the news.'

'As indeed am I,' said the commissioner. 'But I'm alarmed to hear that Sergeant Keedy was also shot. Meade's career was in the past, but Keedy's lay before him – until today.'

'He may yet recover and return to duty, Sir Edward.'

'That's my dearest hope. It must have come as a terrible shock to Inspector Marmion. He is in danger of losing both his sergeant and his future son-in-law.' He lowered his voice. 'What's the latest news from the hospital?'

'Keedy is still in the operating theatre. Marmion's wife and daughter are in the waiting room, praying that he will make a complete recovery but . . . the sergeant was shot from close range.'

'He would be a great loss to us.'

'We can but hope, Sir Edward.'

'Quite so.'

'Meanwhile,' said Chatfield, 'I have the problem of replacing Sergeant Keedy. It is not easy when we are at full stretch. Scotland Yard has nobody available, so I have had to accede to Marmion's request.'

'Oh?'

'He wants a detective constable to be promoted to the rank of acting sergeant.'

'Does he have a particular individual in mind?'

'Yes, he does. It's someone who has worked with him and Keedy before.'

'What's his name?'

'Clifford Burge,' said Chatfield. 'I must say that I have my doubts about him.'

'No disrespect to you,' said the commissioner, 'but

I prefer to rely on Marmion's judgement. Besides, I seem to remember good reports of Burge. Isn't he the man who helped to break up those gangs of feral youths in Stepney?'

'Yes, he is.'

'Then he sounds the ideal choice. Detective Constable Burge was, as I recall, brought up in the East End. I'd say that he was the obvious man to investigate one or possibly two murders of police officers in Limehouse. You can tell Marmion that I applaud his choice.'

'I will,' said Chatfield, hiding his resentment.

'Has Burge shown any inclination towards promotion?'

'He's been studying with a view to taking the examinations, Sir Edward.'

'Splendid!' said the other, beaming. 'He can have practical experience of the role of sergeant and a chance to show his mettle. In time, of course, we hope that Keedy will be able to return to duty. Meanwhile, we have a good replacement.'

Chatfield forced a smile of agreement.

Alice and Ellen Marmion were still in the waiting room at the hospital, chafing at the absence of information about Keedy. Even though the chairs were uncomfortable, Ellen managed to drift off to sleep. Her daughter's patience was wearing thin.

'How much longer are they going to be?' she demanded.

'What?' asked Ellen, stirring.

'We've been here for hours, Mummy.'

'And we may be here for a few more. We must be patient, Alice. The surgeons are doing their very best for Joe. They can't be hurried. Try not to fret about it.'

'There's surely something they could have told us.'

'Be grateful that Joe was brought here so quickly after he was shot. That must count in his favour. And remember what your father told us. They think he'll pull through.'

'That was just a hopeful guess. I want the truth.'

'I know,' said Ellen, putting a hand on her arm. 'And the longer we wait, the more agonising it becomes.' She stood up. 'Shall I see if I can get us another cup of tea?'

'No, no – I could hardly drink the last one.'

Ellen sat down again and studied her daughter's face. Alice was pale and drawn. Her attractive features were masked by anxiety. Her eyes were dull and there were bags beneath them. Ellen put an arm around her shoulders.

'Whatever happens,' she said, 'we'll manage somehow.'

'Everything I hoped for has suddenly disappeared.'

'You don't know that.'

'Yes, I do.'

'Joe will fight like mad. He'll survive somehow.'

'But what sort of state will he be in afterwards? That's why I'm so worried.'

'I know.'

'You don't,' said Alice, on the verge of tears. 'You don't know about the plans we were making for our life together. We talked about having children. Joe was keen to start right away but I thought we should wait a couple of years. Someone has taken the decision out of our hands now.'

'No, they haven't. Joe will survive. I feel it in my bones.'

'Yes, but what sort of injuries will he have to live with?

He was hit in the stomach. The bullet must have done all sorts of damage. Don't you understand?' she wailed. 'The man who fired that shot might have taken away any chance we had of bringing children into the world.'

Clifford Burge was delighted when he got the summons. Of all the senior officers with whom Burge had worked, Marmion was by far his favourite. Burge almost ran to his office. He was a thickset man in his thirties with broad shoulders and a craggy face. After tapping the door, he went straight into the room.

'You sent for me, sir,' he said.

'I did, indeed,' replied Marmion. 'Take a seat. I've lots to tell you.'

While Burge lowered himself onto a chair, Marmion explained what had happened during the night in Limehouse. His visitor was shocked to hear about the death of a policeman and the wounding of Keedy.

'Will he survive?' he asked, worriedly.

'We hope so.'

'Sergeant Keedy always seemed so indestructible. I can't believe that he's been rushed to hospital. To be honest,' confessed Burge, 'I've always looked up to him. He's exactly the sort of detective that I'd like to be one day – conscientious, fearless, and always poised for action.'

'That day has come sooner than you expected,' said Marmion. 'Because we have a shortage of officers available, I recommended that you might be upgraded to acting sergeant.' Burge blinked in astonishment. 'There's no need to look so amazed. In my view, you are a perfect replacement – and I'm sure that Joe Keedy would agree with me.'

'I'm just so . . . shocked, sir.'

'You're being offered a big opportunity. Seize it with both hands.'

'I certainly will,' said Burge with enthusiasm. 'When do I start, sir?'

'Right this moment.' Marmion reached for a sheet of paper on his desk and handed it over. 'This is an interim report I prepared for the commissioner. You'll see that the murder victim was Constable William Meade. His beat partner was Constable Gerald Foley. I met Foley outside the house where the burglars were hiding. He told me that, when he was shot, Meade insisted Foley went after them as they fled. If he hadn't done that, we'd never have known where they were.'

'I daresay that he would have wanted to stay with Meade.'

'Exactly,' said Marmion. 'He hated having to desert him. But the sound of the gunshot brought people out of their houses, so he was not leaving Meade in the lurch. He raced after the burglars, saw where they went, then called for assistance.'

'Foley did the right thing.'

'That's not the way he looks at it, I'm afraid. He still feels guilty about deserting Meade. I want you to get across to the Limehouse Police Station to interview Foley. He may still be in shock, so handle him with care.'

'I will, sir.'

'Read my report on the drive there.'

Burge was delighted. 'Do you mean that . . . ?'

'Yes,' said Marmion, amused by his response. 'You've moved up in the world. Detective sergeants have access to police vehicles. Off you go.'

Burge leapt to his feet. 'I can't believe that this is happening.'

'Prove to me that I'm not making a terrible mistake.'

'Yes, Inspector.'

'And when you've finished with Constable Foley,' added Marmion, 'get your driver to take you to the jewellery shop that was being burgled. Interview the owner and assure him that we'll pursue the men responsible until we catch them. That's a promise.'

Time dragged slowly by. What made their ordeal even worse was that Ellen and Alice were no longer alone. Other people started to trickle into the waiting room, all transfixed by the clock on the wall that would tell them when visiting had started. It was impossible not to overhear details of how the lives of others had changed dramatically. Soldiers who had gone off bravely to war had come back hideously wounded. Some would spend most of their lives on crutches or in a wheelchair. And it was not only descriptions of their physical injuries that shocked the two women. It was the way that war had warped the mind in some cases.

When she heard a mother complaining that her son had turned from a pleasant, well-behaved young man into an angry, foul-mouthed, self-pitying wreck with a missing leg, Ellen was irresistibly reminded of her son, Paul. Having been invalided out of the army after the Battle of the Somme, Paul had come back home from a military hospital to cause all sorts of problems and had then fled from a family in which he no longer fitted. His mother had no idea where he was. Paul was her war wound. The pain was constant.

A nurse came into the waiting room and signalled to the two women. Ellen and Alice were on their feet at once, rushing across to her. When they pressed for details, the nurse told them politely that they would have to wait until they had spoken to one of the surgeons. She escorted them along a corridor, then showed them into an empty office. They sat there for some time before the tall, imposing figure of Hector Garland came into the room. The grim expression on his face made them start. Had the operation been a failure?

As they rose from their seats, he gestured for them to sit down again. He then produced a semblance of a smile and introduced himself as the person in charge of Keedy's case.

'I am sorry to have kept you waiting for so long,' he apologised. 'Surgery of that kind cannot be rushed. It's a delicate business. We had to move with excessive care.'

'Is Joe still alive?' Alice blurted out.

'Yes, he is, Miss Marmion.'

'And will he make a complete recovery?'

'I have every hope that he will,' said Garland. 'But I must warn you that it will take time. There was severe internal damage so extensive surgery was needed. On the other hand, Sergeant Keedy was lucky. The shot was fired by someone high above him, so the bullet entered at a downward angle. That helped vital organs to escape damage. However,' he added, 'I can't say anything more about the operation itself beyond the fact that I believe it to have been a success.'

'Thank God!' said Alice, clasping her hands together.

'Will it be possible for us to see him?' asked Ellen.

'No,' said Garland, 'I'm afraid not. It will be hours before he even comes around from the anaesthetic, and he will be completely disoriented. I appreciate your desire to see him but the earliest time I would suggest is tomorrow morning.'

'Why do we have to wait until then?' gasped Alice.

'It's because it's necessary,' said Ellen, squeezing her daughter's hand. 'We'll be back tomorrow the moment that visitors are allowed in.'

'I wish that you could see him sooner,' said Garland, softly, 'but we must err on the side of caution. And it's only fair to warn you that you may not be allowed into Sergeant Keedy's room. You will only be able to see him through a window.'

'But I want to speak to him,' protested Alice.

'Of course, you do,' said Ellen, gripping her wrist. 'We all do. But we must take it in stages. It's in Joe's best interests.' She turned to Garland. 'Thank you so much for what you have done. We do appreciate it. You must forgive my daughter for being so . . . well, you understand.'

'I do, Mrs Marmion,' said Garland. 'Of one thing, I can reassure you. The worst is over. You may go home now, happy in the knowledge that Sergeant Keedy is in good hands.'

Keedy had no idea how long he had slept. When his eyelids finally began to flicker and his brain started to function once more, he became aware of the fact that he was in a bed with tubes stuck into him. The slightest movement brought a jab of pain and he let out a grunt. The face of a pretty nurse suddenly came into view. She bent solicitously over him.

'Hello, Joe,' she said, sweetly. 'Remember me?'

CHAPTER FIVE

Clifford Burge was thrilled by his unexpected promotion. Even though it was only temporary, it gave him the opportunity to make his mark. Instead of wallowing in his good fortune, however, he brought his full concentration to the investigation. On the drive to Limehouse, he read Marmion's report three times, impressed by the detail but worried about the absence of any description of the three burglars. They needed to be apprehended as soon as possible. Burge was excited at the prospect of being able to track them down.

When he reached the police station, he learnt that Gerald Foley was still there. Burge was allowed to question him in an interviewing room. Foley was a tall, pale, rather gangly man in his twenties, who was finding it difficult to come to terms with what had happened. He kept blaming himself for the death of his partner.

'I should have stayed with him and tried to stem the bleeding,' he said. 'Bill told me to go after them, but his need was much greater. How will I be able to face his family? His wife will blame me and so will his children. Bill had three grandchildren as well. Those kids will grow up hating me.'

'That's not true at all,' argued Burge. 'You did what Constable Meade ordered you to do and chased those three men. If you hadn't done that, we wouldn't have been able to track them to their house. Now let's concentrate on the burglars,' he went on, taking out his notebook. 'Describe them in turn.'

'It was dark. I hardly saw them.'

'If you chased them all the way to that house, you must have learnt something about each one of them. Were they tall, short, thin, fat? And how old were they? You're young enough to run fast. What about them?' He could see the confusion in Foley's face. 'Take your time. There's no hurry. Think back to the moment when you first became aware of them.'

There was a long pause before Foley spoke. 'Bill saw him before me.'

'Who?'

'Their lookout. He was short and skinny and younger than the others. He could run faster than them, I know that. And one of them was much older. I could tell that because he was struggling to keep up with the others. Also,' said Foley, 'he was the one with the gun. I know because he suddenly stopped and pointed it at me as a warning.'

'What did you do?'

'I ducked into a shop doorway. When I peeped out, they were on the move again. I followed them from a safe distance.'

Burge listened patiently, drawing out information that Foley had not realised he possessed.

'You did well,' he said at length. 'But for your persistence, we'd have had no idea where the burglars went. As for Constable Meade's family, I don't think they'll blame you. They'll have nothing but admiration for the way you reacted. In chasing those men, you risked your life.'

'It was a waste of time,' said Foley, morosely.

'You found out where those men were hiding.'

'What use was that? I heard that they shot Sergeant Keedy, then they set fire to the house and escaped. We've lost them completely.'

'Oh, no, we haven't,' said Burge, tapping his notebook. 'I've got valuable information in here about these devils. You were right about one of them being much older. He rented that house under the name of Dan Haskins, claiming to be a nightwatchman. Clearly, he was the leader and the man with the gun. When we catch him, we'll find out his real name.'

Foley bit his lip. 'I keep thinking about Bill's family.'

'He'd been a policeman all his adult life. The family knew the risks involved. They're also aware that crime has increased rapidly in areas of London like yours, where we have insufficient patrols. You and Constable Meade showed courage in trying to arrest the burglars,' said Burge. 'I think that his family will appreciate that.' He closed his notebook and slipped it into his pocket. 'I've just thought of something,' he added. 'You told me that their lookout was a young man.'

'Oh, yes. He could run like the wind.'

'Then he's fit and active.' Burge frowned. 'Why isn't he in the army?'

Marmion went to the superintendent's office to tell him about the latest development at the hospital. Claude Chatfield was glad to hear that Keedy was finally out of the operating theatre and that his condition was being monitored on a regular basis.

'What about your wife and daughter?' he asked.

'They went back home in the car we provided. Alice took a lot of persuading to leave. If it had been left to her, she would have camped in the waiting room until she could see Joe – Sergeant Keedy, that is.'

'Will she return to her duties in the WPS?'

'Not for a while,' explained Marmion. 'When I told Inspector Gale what had happened, she was very sympathetic. She and Alice have not always seen eye to eye, but she could not have been more supportive on this occasion.'

'That's reassuring.' Chatfield's voice darkened. 'Any news from Burge yet?'

'It's far too early, sir.'

'I think that we took a huge risk in choosing him. He's not ready to take on the duties of a detective sergeant.'

'I disagree. Burge is a quick learner. It won't take him long to grow into the role.'

'Well, don't let him feel too comfortable in it. He's only a stopgap. When Keedy is fit enough to join us, Burge can go straight back to where he belongs.'

'We don't know for certain that the sergeant will come back to us.'

'Then we'll find someone to replace him on a permanent basis,' said Chatfield, slapping his desk for emphasis, 'and it will not be Detective Constable Burge. Where is he, by the way?'

'I sent him off to interview Constable Foley, one of the men who disturbed the burglars. After that, he'll go off to speak to Mr Winckler, the owner of the jewellery shop that was raided last night. Winckler needs reassurance,' said Marmion. 'Burge will be good at offering that. He's an East Ender himself. He talks their language.'

When he reached the shop, Burge found a scene of commotion. With the help of his assistant, a glazier was replacing the plate glass window and two other men were standing by until they could fit a new iron grille in front of it. Pedestrians going up and down the street paused to watch the action and join in the fevered speculation. In the middle of it all was Manny Winckler, the short, skinny, gesticulating owner of the jewellery shop, who kept giving orders at random before throwing his hands up in a gesture of despair. Burge introduced himself to the man. Expecting thanks for coming to speak to him, Burge was instead hit with a torrent of complaints.

'Where have you been?' demanded Winckler, jabbing a finger at him. 'I want to be able to make a full report and all they sent me was a policeman to stand outside the shop until

I could organise the repairs. It's not good, it's not fair, it's not acceptable.'

'I'm sorry to hear that, sir,' said Burge, 'but I was not responsible for what happened. I've been sent from Scotland Yard to find out the full details. You must understand that the attempted burglary was not the only crime committed last night. A police constable was shot dead right here and the burglars were pursued by his companion to a house some distance away. During the siege of that house, one of our detectives was shot at close range and rushed off to hospital.'

'I wish him well,' said Winckler, dismissively, 'but I want my jewellery back. Before the policemen turned up, my till had been emptied and the stock in the window had been stolen.'

'You'll have to speak to the insurers about that, sir.'

'How can I do that when they're not here? I rang them hours ago.'

'Is there somewhere where we can talk in private, Mr Winckler?'

'Do you know how much insurance I have to pay?'

'Let's go inside the property, please. It's far too busy out here for a discussion.'

'Catch these vile thieves, Sergeant Burge!'

'We'll do our best, sir – but we need your assistance.'

'What can I do?' cried Winckler. 'I'm a jeweller, not a detective.'

'You may well have information that could lead to arrests,' said Burge. 'We've had similar burglaries in the last few months. You were lucky. They were interrupted before they could open the safe and take the most expensive items.'

'My grille is destroyed, my shop window ruined, my jewellery stolen – you call that luck?'

'Yes, I do. Constable Meade died in the execution of his duty. He was trying to protect your property. Were you or any members of your family hurt in any way?'

'Well, no . . .'

'Then you should be grateful for your good luck,' said Burge. 'One of the burglars was armed and, as we know, ready to use his gun. Yet a policeman was brave enough to challenge him. Now, can we please go somewhere more private where we can talk about what is, first and foremost, a murder case. It also involved the lesser crime of burglary.' He looked Winckler in the eye. 'A human life is more precious than anything stolen from the shop. Don't you agree?'

Winckler said nothing. Suppressing his anger, he led Burge into the shop.

When the police car had dropped them off at home, the first thing that Ellen Marmion did was to go to the grocery shop to thank Geoffrey Biddle for giving them the lift to the hospital. The grocer was eager to hear the latest news so that he could pass it on to his customers. He was also delighted that Keedy had survived the operation and was likely to recover in time.

'How did you get home?' he asked.

'My husband arranged for a police car to bring us.'

'I'm always here in an emergency.'

'We can't thank you enough, Mr Biddle.'

Ellen left the shop and walked briskly home. She was pleased to find that Alice had already made a pot of tea. After hanging up her coat, Ellen sat opposite her daughter at the table and raised a subject that had been at the forefront of her mind since they first heard the dreadful news about Keedy being shot.

'When are we going to contact Joe's family?' she asked.

'I think that we should wait, Mummy.'

'Why? They have a right to know. Think how hurt your father and I would be if you were rushed to hospital, and nobody bothered to tell us.'

'I'm trying to do what Joe would want.' explained Alice. 'His mother is very nervous and easily upset. If we'd told her that Joe had been shot and that surgeons were trying to save his life, Mrs Keedy would be in a terrible state. Joe would want us to wait until the worst was over so that we had good news as well as bad.'

'We've got good news, Alice. You heard what the surgeon told us.'

'I need to see Joe with my own eyes before I'm ready to contact his family.'

'Get in touch with them right away.'

'No, Mummy,' insisted Alice. 'I'd rather ease their pain. They're going to be very shocked. When Joe told them that he wanted to join the police, he had a terrible row with his parents. His mother was terrified that he'd be killed or badly injured in the course of his duties, and his father was hurt that he was leaving the family business.'

'I remember that. Joe told them that he wanted some excitement in life. I fancy that there's precious little of that in being an undertaker.'

'Yet his elder brother loves the work. That's why Dennis

took over the running of the business when their father was taken ill. Dennis is very religious. He enjoys a job that takes him to a church time and again. Joe is different,' said Alice. 'He avoids church like the plague.'

'Well, he can't avoid the one he's going to get married in. That's another person who ought to be told,' said Ellen. 'It's only fair that the vicar should be warned. You can tell him when you ask if you can bring the date of the wedding forward.'

'I'll do that, Mummy. As for Joe's parents, I'm certain that we should hang on until we know for definite that he's turned the corner. There's no point in causing unnecessary panic, is there? Wait until I've seen Joe myself,' advised Alice. 'That's what he wants most – the sight of someone who loves him.'

Joe Keedy kept drifting in and out of consciousness. His mind and body were telling him that he needed a long rest. When he did open his eyes once more, he tried to speak but his throat was too dry, and he could only manage a croak. The nurse was soon at his side, holding a glass of water to his lips and smiling serenely. When he had taken a few gulps, he studied her for a few seconds.

'You look like Maisie Bell,' he murmured.

'It's Nurse Bell to you, Joe,' she teased. 'That's what you always called me.'

The Winckler family lived above the shop. The jeweller conducted his visitor upstairs and into the living room. When he nodded to his wife, she slipped out at once. After waiting until Detective Sergeant Burge had sat down, Winckler flopped into an armchair and ran a hand through the remains of his hair. He was in his late fifties, but he looked considerably older.

'Now,' he said, 'do you want a list of everything that was stolen?'

'Not just yet,' replied Burge, notepad at the ready. 'First of all, I need to ask about the sorts of customers you deal with.'

'I deal with all sorts, Sergeant. Customers know they can rely on me. I only sell good merchandise.'

'You've obviously been in this business for a long time and built up a good reputation. I don't need to tell you that, before they raid a jewellery shop like yours, burglars will always do some research beforehand.'

'I can spot them a mile away,' boasted Winckler. 'When they come in here and pretend to look at my rings or necklaces, they always ask for the best I have. Sometimes they bring a woman who tries things on to divert my attention, but I know what they are really doing. They never buy anything, of course, because they expect to get it free when they steal it.'

'What do you do with such people?' asked Burge.

'When I'm certain they're crooks, I tell them that I'll call the police. If they stay and argue, I warn them that they've been photographed by hidden cameras.'

'And have they?'

'No,' said Winckler, chuckling, 'Such cameras don't exist yet but they don't know that. It puts the fear of death in them. They can't get out of my shop fast enough. And – this is important – they never come back.'

'Someone came back last night, sir,' Burge reminded him.

'They haven't been here before.'

'I believe that they had. It's just that they fooled you somehow.'

'Never!' exclaimed Winckler, smarting at what he took as an insult.

'Let me finish, please,' said Burge. 'I've dealt with dozens of robberies from shops like yours. Some criminals simply throw a brick through the window, take what they can and make a run for it. The ones who targeted you were not smash and grab merchants. That grille on your window would have deterred them.'

'It's why I had it put there.'

'What we're dealing with, I fancy, is someone cunning enough to get in here and win your confidence. This person would have come alone and taken note of where everything was. To convince you that they were trustworthy, there might even have been a purchase of some sort at a moderate price.'

'You are wrong, Sergeant. I am never tricked. Besides,' said Winckler, tapping his chest, 'I haven't had a male customer in here alone for weeks.'

Burge smiled. 'What about a female customer?'

CHAPTER SIX

As soon as they had drunk their cup of tea, Alice lapsed into a prolonged silence. Her mother could see that she was brooding. Left alone, her daughter would simply agonise about Keedy's fate. Ellen felt that she had to rescue Alice somehow.

'Thinking about it won't help,' she suggested, rising to her feet. 'There's so much to be done and we ought to be doing it.'

'What do you mean?'

'When Joe comes out of hospital, what will he need most?'

'Love and attention,' said Alice.

'Yes, but not here. He'd want them in the comfort of your own house. That's where we should be – doing what we can to improve the place in readiness. If we keep active, there'll be no time to brood.'

'You're right, Mummy,' agreed Alice, getting up. 'And there are dozens of jobs to do there. It would be a real treat for Joe if he came home and discovered that we'd done some of them.'

'Then let's go.'

After putting on their outdoor clothing, they set off. When they waited for the bus, Alice remembered the discussions that she and Keedy had had about the exact location of their new home. While he was ready to be within easy reach by bus of her parents' house, he had been against the idea of living within walking distance of it. Alice had accepted his argument that he did not want his mother-in-law popping in whenever she chose or, by the same token, of watching his wife walking back and forth on a regular basis to the house where she had been born. As a result, the couple had settled for a property that was almost three miles away.

Even though they were only renting the house, Alice had never lost a sense of pride in being there. Because it was their future home, they made light of its shortcomings. Since there was no indoor sanitation, they would have to use the privy at the end of the garden. Whenever they wanted a bath, they would need to heat water in the boiler and bring in the tin bath that hung on a hook on the outside of the kitchen. Damp had darkened one wall in the spare bedroom. One of the upstairs windows needed a new pane of glass. Most of the woodwork was in desperate need of repainting. None of these and other defects daunted them. She and her husband would be together.

The bus arrived and they sat beside each other. Ellen could sense her daughter's excitement slowly building. When they reached their stop, they walked for a few minutes then turned into the street where the house was located. There was no sign of Alice's brooding now. She could not wait to begin to make the place fit for Keedy to come home to.

'What shall we do first?' asked Alice with enthusiasm.

'We could have a cup of tea.'

'No, Mummy – that will have to wait.'

'Why?'

'Because we haven't deserved it,' insisted Alice. 'Let's roll up our sleeves and get busy first. The time for a cup of tea is when we've earned it.'

'It's your house,' said Ellen with a laugh. 'You make the rules.'

Having selected the team of officers for the investigation, Marmion had deployed them in various ways. As he sat in his office at Scotland Yard, he pored over a map of London on which he had marked the locations of the other burglaries. He was still trying to work out why those jewellery shops had been chosen when Clifford Burge returned. There was a smile on the latter's face that suggested his efforts had borne fruit. Marmion indicated a chair.

'Take a seat and tell me how you got on,' he said.

'Learnt a lot, sir,' replied Burge, sitting down. 'Constable Foley was too busy blaming himself for Meade's death at first, but I managed to talk him out of it. He was then able to tell me something of real value.'

Referring to his notebook, he told Marmion every detail that he had gathered and how he had managed to lift Foley's spirits by praising him. After waiting for him to finish a description of the first interview, Marmion picked on a significant fact.

'That was a good point to make,' he noted. 'If the youngest

of the three men was clearly fit, why hadn't he been conscripted? You can hardly claim exemption from national service by saying that it would interfere with your career as a burglar.' Burge laughed. 'I fancy that he either dodged his responsibility or joined the army and then deserted.'

'I agree.'

'We've had conscription for unmarried and married men since 1916. Very few people have managed to escape it. Women have played their part, of course. If they discover someone who is too scared to fight, they send him a white feather and try to shame him into action. Anyway,' said Marmion, 'let's move on to the jeweller. What sort of person is Manny Winckler?'

Burge pulled a face. 'He's one of those people who thinks that the entire resources of the Metropolitan Police Force should be focused on him. Did everything but demand a visit from the commissioner himself.'

'No chance of that,' said Marmion with a chuckle.

'Once we went into the house, he calmed down a bit. Mr Winckler stopped waving his arms like a windmill and had a proper conversation with me. When I told him that burglars always visit a jewellery shop before they rob it, he boasted that he could spot them immediately and send them packing.' Burge referred to his notebook again. 'Then I asked him if anyone had come into the shop alone with a view to sizing the place up.'

'What did he say?'

'No man had been there without a woman in tow but – and I seized on this – he admitted that a woman had come in alone.'

'Who was she?'

'An elderly woman from Bethnal Green – a Mrs Corkwell. It

was obvious from the way that she was dressed that she'd fallen on hard times, but she didn't try to tell him about her problems. Simply wanted an estimate for a piece of jewellery with a view to selling it.'

'What did Mr Winckler do?'

'He could see that it was probably the only thing of value that she had and was sorry that she had to part with it. But – as he told me – business is business.'

'What exactly was this piece?'

'It was a beautiful opal necklace with diamonds around the stone.'

'Did the jeweller give her an estimate?'

'Yes, he did – but only after he'd examined it carefully. She just stood there quietly and watched. Winckler could sense she was sad at having to sell the necklace. When he'd finished, he wrote a figure on a little card he uses for estimates, then handed it to her. She was shocked.'

'Why?'

'Because she had no idea that it was worth so much. She'd had an estimate from another jeweller, and it was less than half the one given by Winckler. When she showed him the card with the earlier estimate on it, he warned her not to sell the necklace to the other jeweller.'

'Where is all this leading us?' asked Marmion with a hint of impatience.

'I'm wondering if this woman might have been working for the burglars, getting inside the shop so that she could take stock of it.'

'Mr Winckler didn't think so and he's been in the trade a

long time. What makes you believe that he was fooled by this woman?'

'It was the jewellery shop she mentioned, sir. When he saw the card, Winckler recognised it immediately. Melrose and Gibb in Bethnal Green. My thinking is this, Inspector,' said Burge, excitedly. 'Did Mrs Corkwell go to the first jewellery shop to get an estimate or was she sent there by the burglars?'

'You're jumping to a highly unlikely conclusion,' warned Marmion.

'Am I, sir? You must have a list of all the jewellery shops that have been burgled recently.'

'I have it right here, as it happens.'

'Does it include the name of Melrose and Gibb, by any chance?'

Marmion ran a finger down the list in front of him, then produced a broad grin. 'I think you may have stumbled on to something,' he said. 'Using an old woman would be a good way to ward off suspicion. You could still be wrong, of course, but it's worth testing your theory.'

Reaching for the telephone directory, Marmion thumbed through it until he found the number that he wanted. He rang it and gave the operator the number. When he got through, he found that he was talking to Edwin Melrose, part owner of the jewellery shop.

'Good day to you, sir,' he said, politely. 'I'm Inspector Marmion from Scotland Yard . . . No, no, we haven't caught the burglars who broke into your property, I fear, but we may have picked up their trail. Can you remember if, in the weeks leading up to the raid, you had a visit from an elderly woman by the name of Mrs Corkwell . . . Oh, I see, you didn't . . . Well, do you recall someone who brought in an opal necklace for valuation . . . ?'

Marmion listened intently as Melrose spoke into his ear. Burge could see from the inspector's reactions that he was being given confirmation of a visit from an elderly woman. When he finally put the receiver down, Marmion turned to him.

'You've just earned yourself another ride in a police car, Cliff,' he said.

'Did Mrs Corkwell go there?'

'She might have done but she wasn't using that name at the time. What Mr Melrose remembered was the opal necklace. He valued it for her.'

'According to Mr Winckler, he told her it was worth far less than its real value.'

'That's as may be. I'm only interested in the coincidence of an elderly woman visiting two jewellery shops that were later burgled. Get over to Bethnal Green at once and find your way to the shop. It's in the High Street.'

Burge was out of the room in a flash.

Braving the cold, they took off their coats and got busy at once. In the kitchen were brushes of all kinds, an array of dusters, cleaning liquids and polishes that Keedy and Alice had bought. Ellen began upstairs, tackling the sash windows. To clean the outside of them, she had to lean backwards out of the windows and feel the force of the biting wind. She ignored the gibes from passers-by who found the sight of her amusing. Alice, meanwhile, was downstairs, working hard to finish a job that

Keedy had already started on. She was scraping off the last of the wallpaper in the living room, wetting it first to weaken its resistance. Though she had never done any decorating before, she was keen to accept the challenge. She and Keedy had already chosen the new wallpaper. Alice wanted to transform the room before he moved back into the house.

When her mother came back downstairs, Alice was still scraping away at a wall.

'You're doing a much safer job than I did,' said Ellen. 'When I leant out of the window to clean it, people laughed at me.' She peered at her daughter's handiwork. 'How are you getting on?'

'I should be able to finish this in half an hour or so.'

'You're doing a good job.'

'Thank you, Mummy.' Alice broke off and turned to her. 'I've been thinking about what you said earlier. Maybe we should get in touch with Joe's family, after all.'

'It's only right. I know you don't like Dennis, but he should be told.'

'I'm just afraid to make the phone call.'

'Then let me do it,' volunteered Ellen.

'No, no, it's my responsibility.'

'Contact the hospital first to find out the latest news.'

'I will,' said Alice.

'What changed your mind?'

'I tried to put myself in their position. It's wrong of me to hide the truth from them.'

'Yet you said you thought it was what Joe would want you to do.'

'He's not here to make the decision,' said Alice. 'I have to make it for him.' She turned to her mother. 'Thank you for bringing me here, Mummy. It's stopped me brooding. In a strange way, it's cheered me up. Somehow, I know for certain that Joe will survive now. That's all that matters.'

'I agree.'

'It means we'll escape the thing I feared most.'

'What was that?'

'Losing Joe and being forced to attend a funeral organised by his brother. I'm not sure that I'd have been able to cope with that.'

Hector Garland always kept a close watch on patients on whom he had operated. When he had a free moment, he went to check up on Joe Keedy. Nurse Bell was in the room when Garland arrived.

'How is he?' he asked.

'Stable,' she replied.

'Let me see.'

Garland picked up the board attached to the end of the bed and looked at the progress report. Everything he had specified had been ticked off at regular intervals. Glancing at the patient, he saw that Keedy was fast asleep and unaware that he had a visitor.

'Take good care of him, Nurse,' he said. 'This is no ordinary patient. Sergeant Keedy is a very brave man. We must do our utmost to keep him alive. He's a real hero.'

'I know,' she murmured.

* * *

Edwin Melrose was a middle-aged man who clearly dressed to make an impact. Tall, slender, and well-groomed, he stood behind the counter in a striking pin-striped suit that looked as if he was wearing it for the first time. It was so smart and beautifully cut that it made Clifford Burge blink when he first saw it. As soon as he explained the reason for his visit, he was led into an office at the rear of the premises. Melrose's place in the shop was taken by one of his assistants.

When they had both sat down, Burge was ready with his first question.

'I believe that you had a visit from an elderly lady who wanted a valuation for an opal necklace.' Melrose nodded. 'Do you happen to know the exact date of her visit?'

'I took the trouble to look it up,' said the jeweller. 'It was on 7th November last year.'

'And when was your shop burgled?'

'14th December.'

'But you saw no connection between her visit and the loss that you sustained.'

'Of course not,' said Melrose, loftily. 'Dozens of people come in and out of here. Many of them seek valuations of various items they wish to sell. This woman was one of many customers. Why should I even remember her?'

'What name was she using?'

'Mrs Mallow.'

'That's very different from Mrs Corkwell,' said Burge, writing the name down. 'I don't suppose you can recall how long she was actually here?'

'Less than five or six minutes, Sergeant Burge. I've been in this business for many years. It doesn't take me long to put a price on a piece of jewellery. I gave this woman a card with the valuation on it and off she went. I thought no more of it at the time.'

'And now?'

'Well, if she does turn out to be connected in some way to the burglars who descended on us not long before Christmas, I'll be embarrassed by my failure to notice anything suspicious about her.'

'You were not the only one, Mr Melrose.'

'Really?'

'Mr Winckler's shop in Limehouse was the target last night.'

'That will have upset Manny,' said Melrose with a smirk. 'How much did he lose?'

'He was lucky, sir. Before they could get anywhere near his safe, they were disturbed by policemen on patrol. One of the officers was shot dead.'

Melrose blenched. 'Heavens!'

'The other bravely pursued the burglars to their house and summoned help. During the siege, one of my colleagues, Detective Sergeant Keedy, was badly wounded.'

'Were the men arrested?'

'I'm afraid not, sir. They'd planned their escape in advance and got away. However,' said Burge, 'let's go back to the lady with the opal necklace. Mr Winckler described her as being in her sixties and rather shabbily dressed. She needed to sell the necklace. Is that how you remember her?'

'Not at all,' said the other. 'She was well dressed and clearly educated. The only reason she wanted a valuation was that she intended to leave the item to one of her nieces in her will. Yes, she was in her sixties, but she was clearly robust. I don't think that anyone is going to inherit that necklace from her just yet.'

'Oh, I see.'

'I'm sorry to disappoint you, Sergeant,' said Melrose, 'but I've got the feeling that the woman who came here was very different to the one who visited Manny Winckler's shop. Mrs Mallow was not being forced to sell the necklace at all. She was wearing a gold brooch on her fur coat and, when she took off her gloves, I noticed expensive rings on her fingers.'

'Ah, that's . . . disappointing.'

'We're talking about two entirely different women. I appreciate that you must follow various lines of enquiry but, in this case, you have been led woefully astray.'

Burge left deflated.

CHAPTER SEVEN

Having spent several hours at the house, they could see that they had made a noticeable difference. With time and effort, they could improve it even more and startle Keedy when he was able to return there. Alice had wanted to prove to him that he did not have to do absolutely everything at the property. She was more than ready to do her share.

When they'd locked up the house, they headed for the bus stop in the gathering gloom.

'What about furniture?' asked Ellen.

'Joe and I agreed to choose it together, Mummy.'

'He may not be fit enough to go shopping with you for some time. I think he'd be grateful if you made a few purchases to make the place feel more like a home. Also, you're going to need a bed in the spare room. I'm wondering if you'd like to have Paul's.'

'Oh,' said Alice, startled. 'Are you ready to get rid of it at last?'

'Yes, I am. We must face facts. Paul is never going to come back home. His bed and his chest of drawers might as well go. You need them and it will save you buying new ones.'

'That's very kind of you, Mummy.'

'It's not only kindness,' said Ellen. 'To tell you the truth, I'd be glad to see the back of them. We should take all the furniture out of that room. It gives me uncomfortable memories.'

'Then we'll certainly have the bed and the chest of drawers, please. Joe would agree, I'm sure. I just wish that I could tell him the good news.'

'You will in time, Alice.'

'Instead of ringing the hospital, I'm wondering if I should actually go there.'

'Well, don't rely on Mr Biddle to give you a lift. He's still serving in the shop.'

'I looked up the bus routes,' said Alice. 'It would mean travelling on three different buses, but I can actually get there that way.'

'Stay at home and use the telephone.'

'I want to be closer to Joe.'

'Of course, you do but you must be sensible. It's a long way to go to discover something that you can find out more easily. Besides,' said Ellen, 'you don't only want to know how Joe is for your own benefit – you want to pass on the latest news to his family.'

Alice sighed. 'That's true.'

'Will you speak to Joe's father?'

'No, I'll talk to his brother. Dennis will probably be at work. I'd much rather he passed on the news to his parents.' She grimaced. 'I know how they'll react.'

'Do you?'

'They'll wag a finger and say that this would never have happened if Joe had stayed working in the family business. In a sense, I suppose they're right. I'm just grateful that Joe did have the urge to join the Metropolitan Police Force. I wouldn't have met him otherwise. And one thing I do know,' said Alice, firmly, 'is that I could never have married an undertaker.'

When he returned to Scotland Yard, Burge had lost the surging optimism that had taken him to Bethnal Green. He chided himself for reaching a decision on insufficient information. The discussion with Edwin Melrose had been salutary. It had robbed him of the belief that he was on the point of solving the series of burglaries at jewellery shops. Burge felt that he had let himself down. Given the disappointment he had to report, he was not looking forward to a conversation with Marmion.

His fears were ill-founded. In fact, the inspector was very understanding. When he had listened to Burge's account, he felt sorry for him, even taking some of the blame.

'We were both at fault,' said Marmion. 'The idea that the same woman visited both shops raised our hopes far too high.'

'There were two different women, sir. The one who went to Bethnal Green was nothing like the woman who asked for a valuation from Mr Winckler.'

'While you were away, I rang the other jewellery shops that had been burgled during the recent spate. Not one of them could recall having served a female customer who wanted an opal necklace valued. We can at least eliminate one possibility,' decided Marmion. 'The burglars did not routinely use a woman as an accomplice. Unless . . .'

'Go on, sir,' encouraged Burge.

'Well, there is the fact that two valuations were given for the same opal necklace. Mr Winckler was shown the card on which the first valuation was recorded. We may be dealing with two different women but there is surely only one necklace.'

'That's what I keep thinking.'

'Then how do you explain it?'

'I'm still trying to work it out.'

'Let's take it in stages,' advised Marmion. 'Mrs Mallow takes the necklace to the shop in Bethnal Green. She explains why she needs a valuation. Jewellers usually have a sixth sense about customers, yet no warning bells rang for Mr Melrose. He felt that he was dealing with a legitimate request.'

'He still believes that. In fact, he was very impressed by Mrs Mallow. Many of the customers who come through his door are not as well off as she appeared to be. She was in a different class to them and spoke with such confidence.'

'Appearances can be deceptive.'

'How could that valuation from Melrose turn up at Mr Winckler's shop in the hands of a different woman? It's baffling.'

'There's only one possible explanation,' said Marmion,

thoughtfully, 'and we should cheer ourselves up by accepting it.'

'I don't follow, Inspector.'

'Mrs Mallow and Mrs Corkwell are one and the same person. After leaving Bethnal Green, the lady changed her name and her clothing before she went to the jewellery shop in Limehouse weeks later. She also changed her story about the necklace. Mr Winckler believed it.'

'Are you saying that this woman is working with the burglars?'

'I'd say that she was their greatest asset.'

'Then why did neither of the two jewellers realise they were being misled?'

'It's because she gave a convincing performance to each of them. While she was in their respective shops, she was quietly noting details to pass on to the burglars who sent her there. I reckon that we are on the right track, after all.'

'Thank goodness for that!' said Burge.

'The search widens,' declared Marmion. 'From now on, we are not only looking for three burglars. We are searching for three burglars and a very clever female accomplice.'

The room was small but deliciously cosy. As she lay on the sofa, the woman looked up at the array of cards and photographs on her mantelpiece, each one reviving a treasured memory. In pride of place on the wall above was a framed poster for a play in which she had starred many years earlier in the West End. Her name had been well known then. It had been long forgotten now. In her prime, she had been slim, shapely, and strikingly beautiful. What she saw in the mirror now was a fat, tired old woman whose best days were behind her. When she stood up to poke the fire, she felt a surge of heat from the coal. It reminded her of the exhilaration she used to receive during a curtain call from a grateful audience.

When she sat down again, her eye fell on the evening newspaper that lay beside her. Its headlines had given her a profound shock. A policeman had been shot dead during a daring robbery in Limehouse. A detective had been wounded in the house where the burglars had taken refuge. Had they escaped? Were any of them hurt? What had they managed to steal?

Why on earth didn't they get in touch?

Expecting too much, Alice was bound to be disappointed. When she rang the hospital, all that she was told was that Keedy was stable and under constant supervision. She had to fight back the urge to go there and demand more detail. Reading her face, Ellen saw what she was thinking.

'You're staying here, Alice,' she said. 'Now, please ring Joe's brother. Will he still be at the funeral home at this time of the evening?'

'He always works late, Mummy.'

'Then pick up the receiver again and dial his number. Go on,' she urged as Alice shook her head, 'it's on that piece of paper in front of you.'

'Don't bully me.'

'If you're afraid to do it, I'll ring him myself.'

'No, no, it's my job. Just give me a moment to . . . get myself ready.'

After taking some deep breaths, Alice rehearsed what she was going to say, then picked up the receiver. She dialled the number and waited to be put through. There was a swift response.

'Keedy Funeral Home,' said a familiar voice. 'Dennis Keedy speaking.'

'It's Alice,' she replied.

'Alice who?'

'Joe's fiancée.'

'Oh, hello, Alice,' he said, voice softening. 'How are you?'

'I'm fine, thank you, but I have some bad news about Joe.'

'What is it?'

'He was involved in a siege in the early hours of the night. Three burglars had been cornered in a house. When the door was battered open, Joe was the first to go in.'

'Was he injured?'

'I'm afraid so. He was shot – but he's still alive. The surgeon who operated on him believes that he'll recover. But it may take time.'

'How seriously was he hurt?' asked Dennis.

Alice was struck by his extraordinary calm. She had to remind herself that he heard every day about people dying or with little time to live. He showed no emotion. Dennis had cultivated a low, respectful voice that was oddly reassuring. There was no hint of alarm in it and no sense that he was talking about someone from his own family.

'Are you still there?' he asked.

'Yes, yes,' she told him. 'We went to the hospital and waited until the operation was over. Then we came home. I've just spoken to them again and they told me that Joe's condition is stable. He's . . . on the mend.'

'Where exactly is my brother?' asked Dennis.

'Mile End Military Hospital.'

'Why did they take him there?'

'It was the nearest.'

'Could you give me the telephone number, please?' he asked.

'Of course. I have it right here.' She read out the number on the paper. 'I was hoping that you could pass on the news to your parents.'

'I will, indeed. I'm very glad that you contacted me first. Father is not well, as you know, and has even stopped popping in to see how the business is going. Mother, I'm afraid, is frail and easily upset. I'll call on them when I've spoken to the hospital myself.'

'The surgeon's name was Hector Garland.'

'That's good to know. How are you and your mother?'

'We were fine until we had a phone call in the middle of the night.'

'I can imagine,' he said. 'Was your father involved in the siege?'

'He helped to bring Joe out of the house. An ambulance was called immediately.'

'When will you be able to see him?'

'Tomorrow morning, I hope.'

'Give him our love and tell him that we'll be praying for his recovery.'

'Yes, of course.'

'Thank you for calling. I know that it's not been an easy thing for you to do.'

'That's true,' she confessed. 'Goodbye, Dennis.'

'Goodbye . . .'

When she heard the line go dead, she put down the receiver. Ellen could see the relief in her daughter's face. The ordeal was over for Alice.

'What did he say?'

'It's not what Dennis said, it was the way he said it. You'd never have believed he was talking about his brother. He was so detached and . . . well, cold and professional. I know that he's a good man and devoted to his work, but I'd like him to sound more like a normal human being.'

'I'm sure that Dennis will grieve in his own way.'

'One good thing,' said Alice. 'He's taken the burden of telling his parents off my shoulders. I'd have had a very different phone call with either of them.'

Now off duty, Maisie Bell was due to leave the hospital. Before she did so, she went back to the room where Joe Keedy was being kept. The nurse who had replaced her gave an understanding smile.

'Don't worry,' she said. 'I'll keep him alive until you come back.'

Maisie took a last, fond look at the patient, then left the room.

To quell her fears, the woman was leafing through the large scrapbook that contained the history of her professional life.

Though she had read them many times before, the glowing reviews of her performances still had the power to lift her spirits. Photographs of her in younger days conjured up wonderful memories. She had kept the programmes of every play in which she had appeared even if she had only had a small role. There were also letters or notes from friends and lovers. Her life had been so rich and exciting in those days. Things were different now. It was three years since her agent had bothered to call her, five since he last sent her to an audition for a play. It was convenient for her to blame the war for the end of her career. The truth was too cruel to bear.

When she heard a key being inserted into the door of her flat, she sat up in alarm.

'Who is it?' she asked, rising to her feet. 'Oh, it's you, Dan!'

'Who else were you expecting?' he asked.

She put a hand to her heart. 'You gave me such a shock.'

'I was hoping for a better reception than that,' he complained. Taking off his hat, he stepped across to her and planted a kiss on her cheek. 'That's better.'

'You're not even supposed to be here. You know the rules.'

'Rules are there to be broken.'

'Male visitors are not allowed in this block of flats after six o'clock in the evening. They're very strict about it. This place is supposed to be a female haven.'

'Since when have you needed a haven?' he asked with a laugh. 'I'm surprised that there isn't a queue of men waiting to get in here.'

'Stop being so vulgar,' she said, sharply, 'and explain why you didn't send word earlier.' She pointed to the headlines on the front page of the newspaper. 'I had to learn what happened from this. It frightened the life out of me.'

'We've been on the run. This is the first chance I had of getting in touch.'

Haskins was a big, solid, square-shouldered man in his late fifties with a beard flecked with grey. Thrusting a hand into his pocket, he brought out a wad of notes and handed them over.

'This is what I found in the till,' he told her. 'You pulled the wool over Mr Winckler's eyes and left him thinking that you really were a dear, unfortunate old lady, forced to sell an opal necklace that your first husband bought you.'

'Are you safe?' she demanded. 'That's all I want to know.'

'I'm safe and the others are in the Midlands.'

'Every policeman in London will be searching for Dan Haskins,' she warned.

'Then it's just as well that it isn't my name any longer. There's nothing at all in that house to give anyone the slightest idea of who I really am. To make sure, we burnt the place to a cinder.'

'But you killed a policeman outside the jewellery shop first. There'll be a manhunt.'

'I shot another one in the house,' he boasted. 'With luck, he'll be dead as well.'

She winced. 'You have such a mean streak.'

'Stop worrying,' he said with a smile. 'They're looking for a man who doesn't exist any more.' He began to peel off his overcoat. 'It's so hot in here. That fire is like a furnace.'

'I like to keep warm.'

'Then there's one good way to do that,' he said, grinning.

'We've got something to celebrate, haven't we?' His voice became a whisper. 'Let me stay and I'll keep you warm all night.'

'No,' she said, eyes flashing. 'We work together, that's all. Thanks to you, we've got the whole of the Metropolitan Police Force searching for us. Now sit down and give me the full details of what happened. When you've done that, out you go. Do you understand?'

'Yes,' he said, trying to appease her with an apologetic smile. 'Of course . . .'

When Marmion delivered his report to the superintendent, Chatfield was unimpressed. They were in the latter's office and Marmion was made to feel like a naughty schoolboy hauled up in front of the headmaster. Chatfield sucked his teeth in disapproval.

'I hoped that you'd make more headway than this, Inspector,' he said, sharply.

'We believe that we have made progress, sir.'

'All you've done is to come up with a theory that has little foundation in known facts. I don't need to tell you that every editor of a national newspaper is breathing down my neck. A dead policeman, a detective sergeant's life also in peril – it's the kind of thing that gives everyone the jitters. The British public demands reassurance.'

'The fact that you are in charge of the case should provide that, sir,' said Marmion with a straight face. 'The British press is well aware of your record.'

'I want to keep that record untarnished. To do that, I

need to have men at my command who can act quickly and decisively in a murder investigation.'

'Clifford Burge acted very quickly, sir. His interviews with Constable Foley and Mr Winckler were masterly. Then there was his visit to Bethnal Green to speak to another jeweller. The information he gathered there gives us a base from which we can operate.'

'I beg to differ.'

'We've discovered how they planned their robberies, sir,' argued Marmion.

'Don't be ridiculous,' retorted Chatfield. 'You've simply dreamt up a possible way in which two jewellery shops were raided – that's two out of a total of seven altogether. If employing a woman worked in two cases, why didn't they use the same person each time? Yet they clearly didn't, as you discovered. In my view – and I've thought long and hard about this – I don't think a woman was used in either of the two cases on which you're basing your assumptions.'

'Then why did she visit the premises of jewellers in Bethnal Green, then Limehouse?'

'Might it not be that she simply wanted the highest price she could get for her opal necklace? If she was disappointed by the first estimate, she probably decided that she ought to make a different kind of impact the second time, so she gave the impression that she was in desperate need of money. In short,' said Chatfield, 'she was trying to deceive both men and was in no way connected with those burglars we failed to arrest. Talking of which,' he added, 'how is Sergeant Keedy?'

'When I rang the hospital earlier, they said that his condition was stable.'

'Is he out of danger?'

'We believe so, sir.'

'If only Keedy had conducted the interviews that Burge handled,' said Chatfield, ruefully, 'he would have got far more information out of them. And he certainly wouldn't have subscribed to this fanciful notion that you've produced. I told you that Burge was promoted beyond his competence.'

Marmion gritted his teeth. 'I still have the utmost confidence in him, sir.'

'I'm sorry that I'm unable to share it.' The telephone rang and he snatched up the receiver. 'Oh, hello Sir Edward,' he said, modifying his tone. 'No, I'm afraid that I don't have any news to report on the case just yet but, under my guidance, Inspector Marmion is working hard on the case. It should not be long before we start to gather hard evidence . . .'

Chatfield waved a hand to send his visitor on his way. Marmion was glad to escape, annoyed at the way the superintendent had so comprehensively dismissed his theory about a female associate in two of the burglaries, and more determined than ever to vindicate his reputation and that of Clifford Burge.

Time had no meaning for Joe Keedy. When his eyes opened, he saw that he was in a room with subdued lighting, but he had no idea where it was. While he was not in pain, he found it difficult to move. When he tried to sit up, the effort was too much for him and he moaned in disappointment. A nurse appeared quickly at the side of him.

'Are you in pain?' she asked, gently.

He peered at her. 'Where's Nurse Bell?'

'She doesn't come back on duty until morning.'

'I want to speak to her. Maisie is a friend.'

'I'm looking after you now,' she said, adjusting the bed sheet. 'I'm Nurse Donaldson. What you need most, Sergeant Keedy, is rest. Forget about everything else. We'll take care you.'

Before he could speak, he fell asleep again.

CHAPTER EIGHT

Iris Goodliffe had forced herself to go to work that morning even though she had two very good reasons for staying away. The first was that her best friend, Alice Marmion, would not be there to accompany her on her beat and turn a routine duty into a pleasurable event. Alice would instead be praying that her future husband would survive being shot and recover to lead the kind of life together that the couple had talked about so often. Married bliss was no longer a certainty. Indeed, marriage itself was now in the balance. Desperate to offer support, Iris had toyed with the idea of going to the Marmion house, knowing that Alice would be there with her mother. But she sensed that they would rather be left to suffer alone so she pulled back from the idea of a visit.

The other good reason for missing a day's work was that Iris was doomed to spend another day in the company of

Jessica Porter, a young woman so relentlessly enthusiastic that Iris felt she was under constant bombardment. Jessica could simply not stop talking and her sole topic of conversation had been herself. After they had finished their first day together, they had been told about what had happened to Joe Keedy and why Alice would be away for some time. Left alone for the first time with her beat partner, Jessica had confided in her.

'I always wanted to marry a policeman,' she said.

'Joe is not an ordinary policeman. He's a detective sergeant.'

'It comes to the same thing. They're all so brave and daring and . . . well, trustful.'

'That's not true,' muttered Iris.

'Also, they know what they want. The boyfriends I've had were too shy and inexperienced. Policemen are real grown-ups. They know how to take charge with a woman.'

Iris had remained silent. Having had a short and disastrous friendship with a male colleague, she had been careful to avoid any romantic entanglement with one of them. And while she had confided in Alice Marmion about the brutal way she had been treated, she would never dare to do that with Jessica. The latter was not a person who could be trusted to keep secrets.

'If I was Alice,' Jessica had said, 'I'd enjoy nursing Joe back to full health and telling him that he was a hero. That's what he was, after all. Let's be honest, Iris. We all want to marry a hero.'

Iris had made a polite excuse and gone home. But she was now back for another day of listening to the endless stream of banal incidents in her companion's life. Jessica had shown a token sympathy for Alice, but she had none of the real anxiety and fear that Iris felt for a dear friend. As she waited with the other women, Iris saw Inspector Gale coming towards her. Ordinarily, she would have stepped back. This time, however, she lurched forward.

'Is there any news?' she gabbled.

Inspector Gale shook her head. 'All I can tell you is what I told you yesterday. Sergeant Keedy's condition is serious.'

'Was the operation a success?'

'I sincerely hope that it was. I've heard nothing to the contrary.'

Iris was forlorn. 'I see – thank you . . .'

Thelma Gale marched past her and went off to speak to someone else. Iris was not alone for long. Jessica Porter, tall, skinny and with a toothy grin, came bounding up to her.

'Hello, Iris,' she said, excitedly, 'I'm so looking forward to another day together. I've got lots and lots to tell you . . .'

Ellen and Alice Marmion arrived at the hospital over an hour before visiting time. Not wishing to trouble the friendly grocer again, they used three different buses to get to Mile End. When they asked for the latest news about Keedy, they were told that he was stable but reminded that he would need a period of recovery before he was released. Mother and daughter sat side by side in the waiting room and speculated on how long it would be.

'Are you going to tell Joe what we've done at the house?' asked Ellen.

'No, Mummy,' replied Alice. 'I want it to be a complete surprise.'

'I hope his convalescence will be in a hospital nearer to our home.'

'Daddy promised to see if it could be arranged, but there's no guarantee that it will happen. Also, of course, most of his time will be taken up by the investigation. That comes first.'

'We'll just have to hope for the best, Alice. The tricky question is where Joe will go when he's discharged.'

'He'll come to our own house, of course – and I'll nurse him.'

'Is that wise? You're not married to him yet. Tongues will wag.'

'Let them,' said Alice, defiantly.

'And what about your work at the WPF? You can't just abandon that.'

'I can, if necessary.'

'Well, I think that Joe should come to our house, not yours. You can look after him there.'

'We can't impose on you, Mummy.'

'We're family, aren't we? If I'm going to be Joe's mother-in-law, then I'll do whatever I can for him. It does mean that you can't have that bed I offered you just yet. If he sleeps in Paul's room, Joe will need it.'

'We shouldn't try to make decisions for him,' said Alice. 'Joe has a mind of his own.'

Before she could continue, she saw something out of the corner of her eye that made her sit up and glance towards the open door. Ellen looked in the same direction.

'There's nobody there,' she said.

'There was a moment ago,' insisted Alice.

'Who was it?'

'I can't be certain, but it looked very much like Joe's brother. No,' she added with a flick of her wrist, 'it can't have been him. Dennis is far too busy to find the time to come to London. I made a mistake. It must have been someone else.'

A couple of minutes later, Dennis Keedy walked into the waiting room.

When she awoke the next morning, she was still angry with him. During the burglary, he and his accomplices had been caught in the act. Before they fled, their leader had shot a policeman. That changed everything. They would all have to lie low for a while. When she had given him a key to her flat, she had stressed that it could only be used in emergencies, and during visiting hours. Ignoring his instructions, he had given her a fright by turning up unexpectedly then insulted her by trying to spend the night with her. She was still seething at the memory of his unwanted approach.

Hearing a key being inserted in the lock of her door, she sat up in bed, afraid that he might have returned. In fact, however, it was the maid who came every morning to light a fire.

'Good morning!' called the newcomer.

'Thank goodness you're here,' she replied. 'It's so cold.'

Nobody who saw Dennis and Joe Keedy side by side would guess that they were brothers. There were simply no similarities between them. Dennis was much older, taller, and fleshier than his brother. Wearing a black overcoat and hat, he looked as if he had been born to be an undertaker. Since he had been in London for many years, Joe Keedy had lost many of the traces of his Nottinghamshire accent. Dennis, however, had deliberately shed them all, developing a voice that had no hint whatsoever of geographical location. Since he had become engaged to her daughter, Joe always greeted Ellen with a kiss on the cheek. Dennis preferred a token handshake with both women.

'We never expected to see you here,' said Alice.

'I had to come,' he explained. 'Joe is my only brother.'

'Did you manage to speak to the surgeon?'

'Yes, I did, Alice. My work brings me into constant contact with hospitals. I know how to talk my way past receptionists,' he said airily, 'and get to the person who really matters. When I rang here, the surgeon was frank but hopeful. He told me that an older man with Joe's injuries would certainly have died. My brother, however, has more than a fighting chance of a full recovery – in time, that is.'

'Oh, I see.'

'He gave me a detailed account of the surgery involved.'

Though she was grateful to hear the news, Alice was peeved that Dennis had managed to get far more out of Hector Garland than she and her mother had done. They had been palmed off with a few standard phrases. Dennis had somehow merited more detail.

'Did they say that you'd be allowed to see Joe?' she asked.

'Of course – that's why I'm here.'

'You might only be allowed to see him through a window,' said Ellen, sadly. 'Alice was hoping to sit beside him.'

'That's quite out of the question, I'm afraid. He's watched around the clock by a medical team. Nobody else is allowed to go into his room – not even me.'

Alice felt a stab of pain. She was hoping to spend the rest of her life with Keedy, but his brother felt that he took precedence over her. The two of them had an odd relationship. When she had first met her future brother-in-law, she had found him friendly and welcoming. Each time they met, however, Alice discovered something else about him that she found disagreeable. The assumption on Dennis's part that he was more important in his brother's life than her was galling. Alice retreated into silence, allowing her mother to step in.

'We've been discussing what happens when Joe is released from hospital,' said Ellen.

'That's all taken care of, Mrs Marmion.'

'He's most welcome to come to our house.'

'That's out of the question,' said Dennis with a brittle smile. 'He'll come to us, naturally. It means that our parents will be able to see Joe whenever they wish. It's the reassurance they need after the shock they've had. Oh, no,' he went on, blithely, 'we couldn't possibly impose on you, Mrs Marmion. Joe will come back home.'

Ellen and Alice were speechless with anger.

Harvey Marmion did not believe in hiding criticism from his colleague, so he therefore told Clifford Burge exactly what the superintendent had said about their evidence regarding two burglaries. Effectively, they had to start again. Claude Chatfield had dismissed their theory about a female accomplice. He had also expressed his lack of faith in the new detective sergeant.

'I knew that already,' said Burge with a grin, 'so it doesn't upset me.'

'He's issued a challenge, Cliff. Let's get out there and prove him wrong.'

They set off in the back of a police car to Kentish Town, the area where the first of the seven burglaries had occurred. Having read the initial report on the crime, Marmion passed it on to his companion. Burge studied it carefully and noted something.

'It's another burglary in one of the poorer parts of London. Why pick on them? If they raided a jewellery shop in Mayfair, they'd have had a much bigger haul.'

'They'd also come up against better security,' Marmion pointed out. 'Larger establishments sometimes have a nightwatchman on duty. They also have the very latest safes. The ones broken into by the people we're after were no match for them. The burglars were in and out in a flash, leaving the owner to wish that he'd spent more on safeguarding his stock.'

'At least this one will be different,' said Burge. 'There'll be no talk of a woman wanting a valuation of an opal necklace.'

'You never know.'

'There's no mention of it in the report.'

'That means nothing.'

When they reached the shop in question, they found that they were in a noisy, bustling, working-class district that seemed to be interlaced with railway lines. After introducing themselves to the owner, they were taken into a room at the rear of the shop. Clive Bewley was a stooping, twitchy man with a rather ugly face. The one redeeming feature was a neat moustache. He peered at them over his spectacles.

'Have you made an arrest yet?' he asked, hopefully.

'No, sir,' Marmion said, 'but you may be able to help us do so. Yours was the first of seven jewellery shops to be targeted. We're looking at factors that link them together.'

Bewley gave a mirthless laugh. 'All seven of us have got red faces and empty safes. That's what links us, Inspector.'

'In the weeks before the burglary, can you recall a woman coming in here alone for a valuation of an opal necklace?'

'No,' said the other, firmly.

'Are you quite sure, sir?'

'Nobody around here owns an opal necklace. If they do, they stole it. And we rarely have a female customer on her own. As for valuations, we get a handful of requests but that's all. The only item in the last few months that was worth anything was a diamond engagement ring. An elderly couple came in to see how much it would fetch.'

'Was it valuable?'

'Oh, yes, the ring had real quality. The woman had inherited it when her mother died, but she never wore it for some reason. They wanted a valuation so that they could sell it and buy an eternity ring with the proceeds.' Bewley chuckled. 'You should have seen the look on their faces when I pointed out that I could very easily convert the engagement ring into an eternity ring with any design that appealed to them. The woman was delighted.'

'Did they agree to your suggestion?'

'Mr and Mrs West were interested, no question of that. I

showed them designs of the sort of ring they might like, and I even loaned them a catalogue. When they left, I had a feeling that they'd be back in due course.'

'And did they?'

'No, Inspector. Days later we were burgled and had to shut up shop for repairs. We never saw them again. It's a pity. I rather liked them.'

'How would you describe the woman?' asked Burge, taking out his notebook.

'Well,' said Bewley, choosing his words with care, 'she had been a handsome woman in her day but was showing distinct signs of age. She had a walking stick and hunched shoulders. When they moved, she had to use her husband's arm for support.'

'What about him, sir?'

'He was a few years younger at a guess, but they clearly doted on each other. Mr West had a dark beard salted with grey. He was about my height, Sergeant, and spoke very quietly. In fact, he left most of the talking to his wife. He told me that he wanted to buy her an eternity ring to celebrate their forthcoming wedding anniversary. His wife glowed with joy when he said that.'

'Did they tell you where they lived?' asked Marmion.

'Yes,' said the other. 'They had a house in Tufnell Park. The husband had recently retired as manager of a works there. He described himself as a gentleman of leisure, though I don't think he had much time for leisure. When they went out, he had to support Mrs West on his arm, and she was heavily built. It must have been an effort for him.'

'How were they dressed?'

'He wore a hat and a smart overcoat. Mrs West was even smarter and had a lovely silver brooch in the shape of a dragon on her lapel. Oh, and there was an ostrich feather in her hat. They were a lovely couple – and I can't say that about some of the customers who come in here.' Bewley rolled his eyes. 'I wish that they were all as pleasant as Mr and Mrs West.'

Marmion and Burge plied him with more questions, and he answered them obligingly. By the time they left, the detectives had a detailed picture of the two customers, and the home address they had given. After thanking the jeweller, they took their leave and climbed into the waiting car.

'What do you think, sir?' asked Burge.

'I think that we should call on Mr and Mrs West immediately.'

'Mr Bewley seemed to think that they were exactly who they said they were, and he must be a good judge of people. It's something he does every day.'

'Mr Winckler and Mr Melrose are also sharp-eyed jewellers,' said Marmion, 'yet they were both taken in by a woman in search of a valuation. I'm not saying that Mr Bewley is another victim of the same person and her associate, but . . . that couple interest me.'

'The shop was burgled days after their visit,' observed Burge.

'That might be significant. Then again, it might be a complete red herring.' He winked at Burge. 'Let's find out, shall we?'

* * *

Rain began to fall in earnest, so the two policewomen stepped into a shop doorway for shelter. Until that point, Iris Goodliffe had been spared her companion's incessant chatter. For some reason, Jessica Porter had been remarkably restrained that morning. It was as if she realised that she had irritated her companion and wished to make amends. Once out of the rain, however, she found her voice.

'I used to be so jealous of you,' she admitted.

'Jealous of me?' said Iris with a laugh of disbelief. 'Why?'

'Well, you spend every day with Alice Marmion, and everyone knows that she's the best policewoman we have. It must be wonderful to be on duty with her. You can learn so much.'

'It's true. Without realising it, Alice has taught me everything I know.'

'That's why you're so confident when you walk the streets.'

'We have to be confident,' said Iris. 'Gale Force has told us a hundred times that we're on duty to make an impression. The very sight of us reassures people.'

'What will Alice do if . . . Sergeant Keedy dies?'

Iris rounded on her. 'He's not going to die,' she declared, 'so please don't you dare say that again. People like Joe Keedy have got nine lives. He went into a war zone in France last year and came out alive. And he's been in lots of dangerous situations before that. He'll recover from being shot as well. I know it.'

'But he might be disabled in some way.'

'He'll still be the same Joe Keedy to Alice. They're so happy together.'

'My cousin was invalided out of the army with shrapnel in his leg. He's twenty-one and walks with a limp. Derek's not the happy person he was before. Being shot changed him, Iris. It's made him angry and spiteful. He uses foul language all the time.'

'That won't happen to Joe. There's always a smile on his face. He'll never change.'

'Has Alice been allowed to see him yet?'

'That's a question I've been asking myself since I woke up. It's what he needs most.'

'Not if his injuries are really bad.'

'He survived. That's all that matters to Alice.'

'What if he's forced to leave the police force? How will they manage?'

'That's their business.'

'I feel so sorry for Alice. She might be marrying a cripple.'

'Let's move on,' said Iris, sharply. 'And please talk about something else. You don't know Alice and Joe – I do. So don't you dare say another word about either of them.'

When he first saw her, Joe Keedy thought that he was dreaming. At one time, he and Maisie Bell had been close, but she had been offered a promotion in a hospital in Manchester, so they had drifted apart. Clearly, she was back in London now. She did not seem to have aged in any way. He could see that she was the same pert, pretty, curly-haired young woman he had known years earlier. For her part, she had taken an interest in his career.

'I'm always thrilled to see your photo in the newspapers,

Joe,' she said, admiringly. 'I'm so proud to have known you. It's just a pity that we meet again like this.'

'Seeing you again is the best medicine I could have,' he said.

She tittered. 'Thank you.'

They were in his room at the hospital, and she had just emptied his bedpan, making light of the task. She was now adjusting his pillows to make him feel more comfortable.

'I'm going to move the bed now,' she warned.

'Why?'

'You've got visitors, Joe. They can't come in here yet, but they'll be able to see you through the window. I'll put you in the best position to look at them.' She took hold of the bed. 'Hold on.'

Taking care to move it slowly, she eased the bed around on its wheels so that he was almost facing the window. Keedy was in two minds, delighted to hear that he had visitors but embarrassed that they should see him in that condition. Maisie slipped out of the room, then returned almost immediately.

'They've just arrived, Joe,' she said, moving to the window. 'Are you ready?'

'Yes, I am.'

She took hold of the cord on the blind and pulled it slowly. The blind went up to reveal his two visitors. Alice was staring lovingly at him and trying to control her emotions. Dennis, by contrast, wore his usual impassive expression. Keedy was confused. Delighted to see Alice, he managed to blow her a kiss and mouth a few silent words to her. He was less pleased to see his brother, wondering why he was there as well. There was, however, no chance of conversation with his visitors. Before he could ask for the bed to be pushed nearer to the window, he closed his eyes and fell asleep.

Outside in the corridor, Alice was distressed by what had happened. She'd hoped for much more than a brief glimpse. Dennis was sombre.

'Joe is bad, isn't he?' he said.

CHAPTER NINE

A summons from the commissioner always worried Claude Chatfield. It usually meant a rebuke of some kind, albeit delivered with exemplary politeness. As he walked along the corridor in Scotland Yard, therefore, he rehearsed his excuses for the slow progress made in the case involving the murder of a police constable and the wounding of a detective sergeant. When he reached the office, he took a couple of deep breaths before tapping on the door and opening it.

'Ah,' said the commissioner, 'come on in, come on in. Close the door and sit down.'

Chatfield obeyed his orders. Seated behind his desk, the commissioner lowered his voice.

'What I'm about to tell you is for your ears only,' he warned. 'I've just taken a call from the War Office. They passed on the latest intelligence.'

'I'll be interested to hear it, Sir Edward.'

'It will be no surprise to you to learn that the Germans are planning a spring offensive on the Western Front. They're being forced into it. General Ludendorff toyed with the idea of a concerted attack last year because he knew that the Americans were amassing a huge army on the other side of the Atlantic. He needs to strike before they come here to bolster our forces.'

'When is the attack likely?' asked Chatfield.

'Some time towards the end of March.'

'Do we know what their strategy will be?'

'I believe so. Our information is that the selected battlefield is likely to be an eighty-kilometre front from La Fère to Arras. It's being defended at present by the British army, and Ludendorff believes that it is weaker than its French ally.'

'I don't agree with that,' said Chatfield, stung by the insult.

'He'll come to regret his mistake,' said the commissioner. 'What it means to us is that we're going to have an invasion of American soldiers before they go on to France. Much as we need them, there may well be unfortunate consequences.'

'You don't need to tell me that, sir. Since they first came to London, we've had to double patrols to deal with fights and drunkenness and general mayhem. Americans don't seem to realise that they are guests here and should behave accordingly.'

'You'll need to devise a plan to deal with the problem. If they are let loose on the capital, they head for the pubs, then go in search of women. It's understandable, I suppose. They are young men being sent off to a theatre of war from which they may never return or – if they do – they may have hideous wounds, not to mention mental scars. Facing that possibility,' suggested Sir Edward, 'they're desperate for some pleasure before they cross the Channel.'

'Such behaviour is inexcusable,' said Chatfield, clicking his tongue. 'I speak as the father of daughters. Not every parent is as watchful as my wife and I.'

'You are an example to everyone, Superintendent. However, I sent for you to sound an early warning. In little over a month, the war is set to rage again on French soil. There'll be huge numbers of casualties among the Allies. The survivors will be sent back here to put our military hospitals under even greater strain. There'll also be deserters, of course, detestable cowards who come sneaking back here because they refuse to fight for their country. I want them hunted down.'

'They will be, Sir Edward.'

'The German spring offensive will take place in France, but its effects will be felt here. That's why forward planning is needed. Be warned. London will be inundated.'

'All the necessary steps will be taken,' said Chatfield.

'Good. I knew that I could rely on you.' He remembered something. 'Do we have any news of Sergeant Keedy?'

'The operation was a success, Sir Edward. It's now a question of rest and recuperation.'

'Quite so. Detectives like Keedy are irreplaceable.'

Chatfield scowled. 'I'm finding that out.'

* * *

Alice Marmion was inconsolable. Having made such an effort to get to the hospital, she had banked on getting the reward of time alone with the man she loved. Even if it had simply been a case of gazing at each other through a window, she would have been satisfied. In the event, she had been forced to visit Keedy in the company of his brother, whose presence was intrusive if not downright embarrassing. There had been worse to come. Before she could have any meaningful contact with Keedy, he had fallen asleep and did not come awake until after visiting time was over.

Alice was now being comforted by her mother in the hospital waiting room.

'It was agony, Mummy,' she said, holding back tears. 'Joe was only yards away, but I wasn't allowed to reach out and touch him. Having his brother there made it worse. Dennis was behaving as if he meant a lot more to Joe than I did.'

'That's nonsense,' said Ellen, supportively. 'Joe adores you. In any case, he and Dennis have never really got on together. It's one of the reasons he moved to London to join the police. He couldn't bear the thought of being at his brother's beck and call.'

'When they let him out of hospital, I want Joe to come to us.'

'He will do, Alice. I promise.'

'It was so disappointing when he couldn't even stay awake. That really hurt me.'

'Don't blame him,' said Ellen. 'It wasn't his fault. I daresay that Joe was trying desperately to keep his eyes open, but his strength has been sapped and he'll have been given something to make him sleep. Look,' she confided, 'I've never told you this before, but I had serious problems when you were born. Afterwards, I was completely exhausted. Once I held you in my arms, I was desperate for your father to come and see us and share my joy.'

'And did he?'

'Yes and no, Alice. I remember the smile on his face as he came through the door, then I passed out, apparently. What a welcome to give him! It wasn't just the fatigue. The doctor told me afterwards that I was so overcome with joy that it was too much for me.'

'Well, I don't think that Joe can make that excuse. There was no joy involved. He looked pale and weak. His eyelids were flickering away as if he was struggling to keep them open. The next minute, he dozed off. The nurse warned us that it had happened before.'

'And he never woke up again?'

'No, Mummy. Dennis and I stayed for the full hour, then the visit was over. We had to leave. Dennis is going back to Nottingham but I'm staying here until I can see Joe again this evening, when visitors can have another hour. He may be able to stay awake a little longer then.'

'I'm sure he will,' said Alice, 'but we can't just stay here.'

'Why not?'

'Because there are six or seven hours before visitors are allowed in again. We both need food and rest. That means going back home.'

'But I feel that my place is here.'

'You'd only be a hindrance.' Ellen got up. 'Come on. You're as hungry and tired as I am. For your own sake, I'm taking you back home. Think about seeing Joe this evening. It will be different the second time. Dennis won't be there. You'll have Joe all to yourself.'

Alice nodded and her resistance crumbled. They went out of the room together.

When they left the second jewellery shop, Marmion and Burge went to the address given them for Mr and Mrs West, only to find that it no longer existed. They therefore climbed into the police car and began the long ride back to Scotland Yard. After checking his notebook, Burge looked up.

'Are you quite sure that the burglaries were all the work of the same gang?' he asked.

'I'm certain of it,' said Marmion.

'There are big differences in some cases.'

'That's only to be expected. What I pay more attention to is the similarities. The three men we trapped in that house were clever, ruthless and systematic. If you mark their targets on a map of London, you'll see that they've been moving in a circle.'

'What will they have done with their hauls?'

'They'll have exchanged them for money. There are plenty of fences available. I've got officers putting pressure on them in turn. Haskins and his friends knew exactly where to get the best deal for that jewellery. It's hard cash they wanted, and they wanted it quickly.'

'Even if it involved murder,' said Burge, grimly. 'What happens now? Has their spree come to an end, or will they be planning more burglaries?'

'Oh, they'll be back,' replied Marmion. 'They'll keep quiet

for a while, then start up again. It may not be in London next time. They may shift to another city – Birmingham, for instance. There's a Jewellery Quarter there – and lots of small shops like the ones they've raided here. If we're going to catch them,' he added, 'we need to do so quickly, or they might decide to scarper.'

'What do we do next?'

'What you can do is to visit another jeweller on our list. I, meanwhile, will go into battle with the superintendent. We need to convince him that our theory holds water. Until we do that, solving these crimes will be an uphill struggle.'

'Should we take special precautions?'

'What do you mean?'

'Well, we know that one of them has a gun,' said Burge, 'and is more than willing to use it. If we pick up his trail, I'd feel safer if I had a firearm of my own. I've been trained to use one.'

Marmion nodded. 'I'll mention it to Superintendent Chatfield.'

Keedy was horrified to learn that he had slept through the whole of the visiting time that morning. Having had a mere glimpse of Alice and of his brother, he had lapsed into a deep sleep. As Maisie Bell was about to go off duty, he beckoned her over.

'Do you think they'll come back?' he asked. 'My visitors, that is.'

'They may do.'

'How can I stay awake next time?'

'That's up to you, Joe.'

'I keep nodding off all the time. Am I on some sort of sedative?'

'You endured a long and complex operation. Rest is important.'

'I can't sleep indefinitely, Maisie.'

'Then you'll have to rely on your willpower.' She smiled as she leant in close to him. 'I seem to remember that you had a lot of that.'

'Is that a complaint?' he murmured.

'No, Joe – far from it.'

Before she could say another word, she heard the door open to admit the nurse who was replacing her. Straightening up, she exchanged greetings with her colleague, gave her a verbal report of the patient's behaviour throughout the day, then said farewell to Keedy. After she had left the room, he crooked a finger to call the other nurse over.

'Is there anything I can get you?' she asked.

'I just want you to promise me something, Nurse Donaldson.'

'What is it?'

'If I get any visitors this evening, please keep me awake.'

'Why do you ask that?'

'Because, when I had two visitors this morning,' he told her, 'I fell asleep. It was cruel. I felt robbed and so did they, I expect.'

'If your body is telling you that you need rest, so be it. I'm not allowed to give you anything to keep you awake. What I can do,' she volunteered, 'is to check that your eyes are open just before visiting time. If you're asleep, I'll wake you up gently.'

He gave her a tired smile. 'That's all I ask, Nurse.'

* * *

Alice was quick to acknowledge that her mother had been right. Staying at the hospital for a long period would have been depressing. New cases were coming in all the time. Through the window in the waiting room, they had watched ambulances delivering the latest victims of the war, some of whom might well die there. What was upsetting for Alice to witness was even more dispiriting for her mother. Every time a new casualty was lifted out on a stretcher, she thought of her son, Paul, temporarily blinded at the Somme and brought back to a military hospital in Britain before being discharged. He had been a problem ever since.

When they had left the building, mother and daughter felt a sense of relief. They did not mope. There was still much more to do at the house that Alice and Keedy had rented. They made their way there. Hours slipped past as they laboured away in different parts of the property. They were too preoccupied with work to think about the disappointment at the hospital that morning. When they had a rest, Alice went out to the grocer's shop nearby to buy something they could have for lunch. They felt that they had earned it.

'What are we going to do about Dennis?' asked Ellen.

'He can't make decisions that affect us, Mummy. It's as if we don't matter at all. Dennis was so high-handed, insisting that Joe would go home to be looked after by the family.'

'How do you think Joe will react to that?'

'He'll be livid. He won't let his brother dictate what happens to him. Joe would much rather let us take care of him. He hates the way that Dennis always wants to be in charge.'

'Dennis did make the effort to come to London,' said Ellen. 'I'll say that for him.'

'Yes, I agree – but I was so glad when he went home again.'

When they'd finished their lunch, they started work at once. Alice made a stipulation.

'We must leave here in plenty of time to get to the hospital before visiting begins,' she said. 'I want to be at the front of the queue.'

'What if Joe falls asleep again?' asked Ellen.

'He wouldn't dare, Mummy,' said Alice, bunching her fists. 'If he does, I'll bang on the window until he wakes up again.'

Although he still didn't accept Marmion's theory, Chatfield listened patiently to him. While his superior sat behind his desk, Marmion felt the need to remain on his feet to present his argument and support it with gestures.

'Don't you see, sir?' he said, arms widening. 'It must have been the same woman. At two of the places, she was the owner of an opal necklace. When she visited Mr Bewley's shop, she claimed to be a married woman in search of an eternity ring to celebrate a wedding anniversary. Her husband – if that's what he really was – accompanied her. She was very convincing. Bewley admitted that the pair of them seemed so genuine.'

'Perhaps that's exactly what they were.'

'Then why did they lie about their home?' asked Marmion. 'We took the trouble to visit the address they'd given, but the house no longer existed. In its place was a patch of waste ground. A neighbour told us that a German bomb had scored a direct hit on the property.'

'What exactly is your point, Inspector?'

'The burglars were using a woman to gain access to the shops. She came alone on two occasions, and with someone else when she visited the other five. Sergeant Burge and I called in on another of the jewellers this morning. He, too,' stressed Marmion, 'had been visited by a couple who sounded surprisingly like Mr and Mrs West. They wanted a diamond engagement ring valued. I'll bet anything it was the one they showed Mr Bewley.'

'You've no proof of that.'

'It's an obvious deduction, sir.'

'Then why can't I make it?'

'I fancy that you may have difficulty believing that a woman would lend herself to such criminal deception. The answer, I suspect, is that she's well rewarded for her contribution. She may also have an attachment to one of the burglars and may even be his wife. At all events,' said Marmion, 'she needs to be caught and convicted. Her role in those burglaries is vital.'

Chatfield stroked his chin and pondered. Eventually, he snapped his fingers.

'How will you find this woman?' he demanded.

'I'll have to find the burglars first, sir. They will lead me to her. I did say that she was their greatest asset,' he reminded Chatfield. 'It's clear to me that she was directly involved in all seven burglaries. Catch the three men – and we catch her as well.'

* * *

Whenever she ventured out of the flat, she always dressed in her finest clothes. Even at her age, she could turn heads. A ten-minute walk took her into Baker Street. As she sailed along, she recalled the fright she'd had the previous night. Her friend's unscheduled arrival had shaken her and made her enforce her authority. Walking past a newsagent's shop, she made a mental note to buy some of the morning papers later so that she could read fuller details of the failed burglary.

As she strode along Baker Street, her legs eventually began to feel the strain. Even when she slowed her pace, the twinges remained before increasing in intensity. It was time to adjust to the weaknesses of age. By the time she reached Oxford Street, she had reached a decision. Pausing at the kerb, she hailed a taxi and climbed into the rear seat.

'Where to?' asked the driver.

'Shaftesbury Avenue!' she announced.

'Are you going to one of the theatres there?'

'Mind your own business.'

It was ironic. Until a couple of days earlier, Clifford Burge had never been inside a jewellery shop. He had simply never had cause to do so. There had been one or two women friends along the way who had tried to nudge him in the direction of buying an engagement ring, but he had always retreated politely from those involvements. He was still too fond of his freedom to make such a commitment. Yet he was now entering his fifth jewellery shop in two days and was rather enjoying it. This one belonged to a man named Charles Ormond, a rotund individual with a centre parting in his hair, watery eyes and a double chin.

When he was conducted into Ormond's office, Burge thought he detected a faint whiff of perfume coming from the older man.

'I was hoping that someone would tell me what progress you've made,' he said. 'As a result of that burglary, I lost my most precious stock.'

'I'm just here to check the facts, Mr Ormond. Having read the initial report of the crime, I've detected a few things that need clarifying.'

'Well, don't keep me long. I'm needed in the shop.'

'I understand, sir.'

Responding to a gesture from the other man, Burge took a seat and reached out his notebook. He flipped to a blank page, then looked up.

'I'm less interested in the actual raid than in events that led up to it. I'm sorry that you sustained such a loss. It looks as if the burglars had done their homework. When they struck, they did so with speed. In short,' said Burge, 'they knew exactly where to look.'

'Don't rub it in, Sergeant.'

'In the week or so leading up to the crime, did you have any customers who aroused your suspicion?'

'No, I did not,' said Ormond. 'And I am well-versed in spotting danger.'

'That's what the other jewellers told me, sir – yet they were still burgled.'

'With respect, I don't give two hoots about my rivals in the trade. All that concerns me is getting back what was stolen. The men who broke in here were animals. One of them – I shudder to mention it – relieved himself on my chair.'

'Sadly, that's not unusual. It is not always done with malicious intent, I may say. Some burglars are so tense and nervous that they . . . feel the need. However,' said Burge, 'that's irrelevant. Can you remember serving an imposing older woman who might either have wanted a valuation for an opal necklace or come in search of an eternity ring? She would not have been alone,' he went on. 'The woman in question would have had a middle-aged male companion.'

'You are wrong on both counts,' said Ormond, fussily. 'The woman was a real lady, and she was being pushed by a man in his early twenties.'

'Pushed?'

'She was in a wheelchair,' explained the other. 'Unlike most of my customers, she showed consideration. Before she came here, she put a note through my door the previous evening. It said that she'd arrive before our usual opening time next day so that her wheelchair didn't get in the way of other customers.'

'It's an unusual request, Mr Ormond.'

'But a very practical one. Our premises are rather cramped, as you saw, so a wheelchair would take up far too much room.'

'What name did this lady give?'

'Mrs Bandon.'

'And the young man?'

'He was her nephew and seemed to be devoted to her.' Ormond's face flushed with sudden shock. 'You're not telling me that Mrs Bandon was somehow involved in the raid on my shop, are you? No, I refuse to believe it. There was an abiding honesty about the lady. It shone out of her.'

* * *

When she alighted from the taxi, she paid the driver, then gazed fondly up Shaftesbury Avenue at the array of theatres there. She had appeared onstage in some of them. Walking slowly past them, she rekindled memories from happier days when she was in demand. She then turned into Frith Street and went into her favourite café. He was waiting for her. Wearing a long, black cloak, an elderly man rose to his feet and swept off his hat by way of welcome. He then kissed her on both cheeks before holding a chair for her so that she could sit at his table. There was no need to place an order. The café owner knew exactly what they wanted.

'You look as divine as ever, my dear,' he said.

'Thank you.'

'While I was waiting, I was thinking of the first time we came here.'

'I remember it well, Giles. We had both been to the Royalty Theatre for a matinee performance of *The Man Who Stayed at Home*. When we fell into conversation, I knew that you were a kindred spirit. Your wicked comments about the play made me laugh out loud.'

'It did not really deserve to be called a play, my dear,' he said. 'It was a silly diversion for people who are terrified that Britain is awash with German spies. The man in question was presumed by everyone to be a coward because he hadn't joined the army. His fiancée sent him a white feather out of sheer disgust. And what did he do?'

'He put it in his pipe and smoked it.'

'The audience hated him for that.'

'Some of them actually booed him.'

'They changed their minds when they realised that he was, in fact, employed by the War Office to keep an eye on German agents who'd sneaked into this country. In other words, he stayed at home to save us from being infiltrated by scheming Huns. Instead of being a coward, he was a brilliant spy-catcher.' He gave a dry laugh. 'Audiences are so easily pleased now. In our day, we gave them real drama.'

'Will it ever come back again?'

'We can but live in hope.' He appraised her for a moment. 'May I say that you look younger than ever, my dear.'

'Thank you,' she said, smiling, 'but I am a realist. Whenever I receive such compliments, I always remember what Ellen Terry once told me.'

'And what was that?'

'No amount of skill on the part of the actress can make up for the loss of youth.'

'You are proof that there are exceptions to the rule,' he said, gallantly.

'The mirror tells me otherwise,' she said. 'Now, what are we going to talk about today?'

'It's your turn to choose.'

'Then tell me again about your performance as Hamlet.'

He smiled. 'If you insist . . .'

CHAPTER TEN

Joe Keedy was taking no chances. Whenever he felt drowsy, he immediately pinched himself so that he came fully awake again. He was sorry to lose Maisie Bell as his nurse but realised that, in the circumstances, it was better if she were not there. Pleasant as their reunion had been, Maisie belonged to his past and he needed to focus on his future. He would feel inhibited if the nurse was beside him when he was responding warmly to Alice, albeit only with gestures.

Nurse Donaldson was as keen as he was to keep him awake that evening. Five minutes before visiting time began, she checked to see that he was wide awake, then moved the bed to a different angle. She also lifted the blind to give him a clear view of the corridor outside. When the bell went off to signal the start of visiting, he only had to wait a short time before Alice appeared breathlessly at the window. She blew him a kiss and he replied by raising a thumb to indicate that he was feeling better. After conversing in silence for a while, they were joined by Ellen, who had clearly taken longer to climb all the steps up to his floor. Evidently, Alice had raced all the way so that she got there first. Ellen's presence changed the mood altogether, but she did not stay long. She had simply wanted to see him with her own eyes and be reassured. She soon slipped quietly away.

The nurse also disappeared for a short while. Keedy and Alice were alone at last.

Marmion was used to working late. He never complained. If extra hours were needed, he was happy to stay at Scotland Yard and carry on. He was still in his office when Clifford Burge returned.

'I expected you a bit earlier,' he said.

'Sorry about that, sir. I realised that I hadn't eaten anything for several hours, so I popped into the canteen.'

Marmion grinned. 'That's allowed.'

'It gave me time to think. I do that best on a full stomach.' He took out his notepad. 'My visit to that last jewellery shop was very interesting.'

'Did you learn anything that surprised you?'

'I learnt a lot of things, sir. The first one is that I fancy Mr Ormond wears perfume of some kind – and he's very fussy about his appearance.'

'That's his business,' said Marmion, briskly. 'Give me facts relevant to the investigation.'

'That woman cropped up again. Mr Ormond called her a

lady, but my guess is that she behaves in a very unladylike way. She turned up with a much younger man this time. He was there to push her wheelchair.'

'Wheelchair? That's a novelty.'

Burge gave him a full account of his visit to the shop and how he believed that the owner had been taken in by the female customer. Ormond had been duly shocked when Burge had told him that the same woman may have featured in the raids on other shops. While the jeweller had been showing her a series of rings, Burge had suggested, she and her companion had been taking a close look at the interior of the building.

'I've read the reports on all seven burglaries,' said Burge, 'and this woman isn't mentioned in any of them. Yet she probably went to each of the shops in the interests of research. Somehow, she never triggered a single moment of anxiety. Mr Ormond described her as a picture of innocence. He insisted that ladies with her breeding simply don't do such things.'

Marmion laughed. 'Oh, yes, they do.'

'In a way, you have to admire her.'

'I never admire criminals,' said Marmion, 'male or female. Think of the damage they cause. In this case, we've had seven burglaries, a murdered policeman and a detective sergeant who will be unable to work again for some time.'

'Is there any word about Sergeant Keedy?'

'My wife rang me from the hospital. Joe was looking much better and managed to stay awake. Seeing my wife and daughter will have raised his spirits no end. However,' he went on, 'let's concentrate on the burglaries. One of the three men involved in them tried to put the sergeant into an early grave. We need to catch him as soon as possible.'

Dan Haskins, as he had called himself, was now unrecognisable as the man who had rented a house in the East End. A change of clothing and a wide-brimmed hat had transformed him into an anonymous figure who didn't merit a second glance. Having bought two of the morning newspapers, he was sitting in the refreshment room at the railway station and reading the reports of the burglary in which he had been involved. He was soon joined by a stocky man in his thirties who was also far too nondescript to attract attention. Sitting beside his friend, he looked around to make sure that they were not being overheard.

'What do the papers say?' he asked.

'According to them, we're monsters,' replied the other with a grin. 'I've been called worse.'

'So have I.'

'Where's Pierce?'

'He's in a safe house in Birmingham. I've just come from there to get my orders.'

'We're going into retirement for a while,' said the older man.

'Why?' asked the other. 'There are such easy pickings here.'

'There were, Tom. Things have changed. You should read the papers. They say that the police have launched a manhunt for us. The worst news is that Inspector Marmion is involved in the case. I've read about him before. He never gives up. More to the point, he has a special reason for hunting us down.'

'What is it?'

'The man I shot at the house was Detective Sergeant Keedy, his close friend,' he snorted. 'I've had trouble with Keedy once before. He deserved that bullet.'

'It was his own fault for charging into the house.'

'Marmion won't see it that way. He'll want revenge. He won't rest until he sees us dangling from the gallows.'

'All of us?' asked Tom. 'Does that include her?'

'They'll never track her down. She knows that.'

'What happens now?'

'I'll stay in London and wait for orders. I'll also do my best to get rid of Keedy altogether because I have a score to settle with him. I know the hospital where he is. I'll finish him off this time. You can go back to Birmingham and wait for me to contact you. Just stay out of trouble.'

'What about our haul from the burglary?'

'I'll pay a visit to the usual place and get the best price I can squeeze out of him. That's what we need. Every penny counts. Always remember it, Tom.'

'I will,' promised the other, seriously.

'We're not doing it for our benefit – and neither is she, come to that.'

'I know.'

'Have you had any breakfast?'

'Not really. I caught an early train.'

'See what you fancy on the menu. Get some grub inside you. Then you can read the newspaper reports of what terrible monsters we are – especially that older man with the gun.' He winked at his friend. 'They say I'm the worst.'

On the long journey home from the hospital next morning, Alice was able to reflect on her visit there. It had been at once cheering and worrying. There was far more colour in Keedy's cheeks and that lifted her spirits immediately. At the same time, however, he was clearly still a patient who had undergone extensive surgery and needed close attention. A full recovery would take weeks, even months. She had been able to understand some of the words that he mouthed at her, replying to him in the same way and supplementing them with gestures. But there was no chance of touching him or of having a proper conversation.

It was rare for the commissioner to take a close interest in an individual case, but he did so this time. The fact that the murder of a police officer was involved brought him to Marmion's office that morning. After enquiring about Keedy's condition, he explained the reason for his visit.

'I'm sorry to disturb you, Inspector,' he said, 'but I wanted a progress report.'

'Yes, Sir Edward. Do sit down and you can have it gladly.' He watched his visitor settling into a chair. 'I assumed that Superintendent Chatfield was keeping you well informed.'

'He was but his report was rather lowering. It had no indication of forward movement.'

'Then he misunderstood what I told him because we certainly have moved forward.'

'I'm relieved to hear it.'

'The basic facts are these . . .'

After clearing his throat, Marmion gave the commissioner a

full account of all the evidence that had been gathered, together with his interpretation of it. He made a point of praising the work of Clifford Burge, stressing that Burge had been both tireless and astute.

'That's good news,' said the other, 'and contradicts what the superintendent told me.'

'Having worked alongside him, I have a higher opinion of Burge. This case has helped him to blossom as a detective.'

'He's certainly gathered valuable evidence.'

'He has indeed, Sir Edward – even though he has been working in foreign territory, so to speak.' The commissioner's eyebrows arched. 'Burge is a bachelor, sir. He has never had any cause to go into a jewellery shop. It's an alien environment to him.'

The commissioner gave a polite laugh. 'Well, he's adjusted to it very quickly.'

'The person who interested me first of all,' confessed Marmion, 'was the burglar using the name of Dan Haskins. Apart from anything else, he came close to depriving me of my best detective, who also happens to be my future son-in-law. Now, however,' he went on, 'my focus is on this woman. She appears to have visited each of the seven shops in a different guise.'

'Did she use a different name each time?'

'It appears so. During one visit, she called herself Mrs Corkwell, then Mrs Mallow, then Mrs West, then Mrs Bandon, then . . .'

'Stop there,' said the commissioner raising a hand.

'Why?'

'Three of those names jumped out at me – Corkwell, Mallow and Bandon.'

'What is so special about them, Sir Edward?'

'They remind me of a holiday we once had in Ireland,' explained the other. 'We stayed in Cork, but we visited both Mallow and Bandon during our stay. Neither is very far from Cork.' He laughed. 'What a curious coincidence!'

'It's more than that,' said Marmion, seizing on the information. 'Why would a woman choose three names like that unless they had significance for her? I'm most grateful to you, Sir Edward,' he went on, mind racing. 'If you hadn't had that holiday, I would never have realised that there may be a political element to this crime.'

The commissioner sat up. 'I see what you mean.'

'It clarifies something that's been puzzling me. Why should a woman of that age allow herself to get involved with violent criminals? Their contempt for the law would shock most people, yet she accepted it – willingly, it appears.'

'It does seem uncharacteristic of the fairer sex, I grant you.'

'What if the burglaries were not crimes motivated by personal gain?' asked Marmion thinking it through. 'Dan Haskins and his accomplices might have been driven by something much stronger. It would explain why that woman was so ready to lend her skills to them.'

'Are you saying that they are . . . Irish republicans?'

'I think that there's a strong possibility of that. Ireland has provided many volunteers during the war, especially from Ulster, but there's been no compulsion to enlist. Ireland was deliberately excluded from the two conscription acts of 1916.

I fancy that the mere threat of it would cause a national outcry on the island. One of those burglars, we know, was young and, in theory, eligible for conscription – but only if he was living over here.'

'Patently, he is not a resident. He's only in London for one purpose.'

'Their female accomplice gave them valuable help,' decided Marmion, 'but she let them down when she chose the names that she used. At least, that's how it seems to me. It never occurred to her that a police investigation would discover that she was instrumental in all seven burglaries, each time using a different name.' He took a deep breath. 'Forgive my excitement, Sir Edward. I know I'm being unduly emotional, but one of these men almost killed Sergeant Keedy.'

'There's no need to apologise.'

'We must be careful, however. It could just be a strange coincidence, so we mustn't get carried away. On the other hand,' Marmion reminded him, 'it's almost two years since the Easter Rising in Dublin. The passions that led to it have not disappeared at all. Irish republicans are still very active and committed. They are probably in desperate need of money to fund their activities. Yes,' he went on, 'it might just be the explanation we need. Burge had wondered why the youngest of the burglars was not in the army. The answer is simple.'

'Yes, it is.'

'The young man could be in an army, after all – but it's not the British army.'

* * *

Giles Underhill was a striking man in his early seventies, tall, stately and with definite presence. Everyone who came into the café blinked when they first saw him. His voice was melodious, his gestures theatrical. Though she had heard it many times, his companion never tired of listening to his account of playing Shakespeare's most famous character. Her only disappointment was that he did not quote some of the soliloquies, but she accepted that they would be out of place in a café.

'Also,' he confessed to her, 'my memory is no longer as reliable as it once was.'

'I've trained mine,' she told him. 'I spend time every morning reciting speeches from plays in which I once appeared. That way, they remain locked into my brain.'

Meeting him had been an absolute joy to her. They were fellow thespians, washed up on the shore of neglect and unemployment. Talking about their careers helped them to believe that they were still viable actors, resting temporarily from the exercise of their craft.

'The wonder is,' he said, 'that our paths have never crossed before. We worked for the same managements and played in the same theatres, yet we never actually met.'

'Well, we have now, Giles,' she said, 'so let's make the most of it.'

'I do envy the time you spent at the Lyceum Theatre with Sir Henry Irving.'

'I had eight magical years there. The real thrill was acting beside Ellen Terry. I flatter myself that I have talent but hers was quite overwhelming. She was so kind to me. I'm eternally grateful.'

'What about Sir Henry?'

'He was a remarkable actor – handsome, magnetic, and able to speak verse as if it had been written especially for him. Sir Henry Irving's name will live forever in the annals of theatre.'

'He was actually christened John Henry Brodribb,' he told her. 'You can see why he felt compelled to change his name. That's not a criticism, mind you. I, too, was saddled with a name that was totally unsuitable for a life in the public eye.'

'May I know what your original name was?'

He chuckled. 'You'll have to wait until we are much better acquainted . . .'

All Saints' Church was within walking distance of their house and the vicarage was nearby. On the way there, Alice was able to explain to her mother what happened during the morning visit to the hospital. She was still bubbling with excitement.

'It was wonderful to see him looking better,' said Alice. 'He gave me a wonderful smile when he saw me through the window.'

'When will you be able to speak to him?' asked Ellen.

'Very soon, I hope. I've never known an hour fly past so quickly. We just gazed at each other and blew kisses.'

'I thought you were going to let him know about changing the date of the marriage.'

'That was the first thing I did, Mummy. It was all in mime. I tapped the finger that Joe will put the wedding ring on, then waved my arms about. He seemed to understand,' said Alice. 'He nodded and grinned. Joe is as keen as me to get married soon.'

'Then we must hope that the vicar will be able to offer us an earlier date.'

'If he can't, we may have to look elsewhere.'

'Don't even suggest it,' said Ellen, angrily. 'All Saints is our parish church. Your father and I were married there, and you and Paul were christened there. You can't even think about a wedding anywhere else.'

'No, of course not,' said Alice, surprised by her mother's outburst. 'You're right, Mummy.'

They walked on in silence until they reached the vicarage. When they rang the bell, the door was opened by the vicar himself.

'Come in, come in,' he said, standing back so that they could enter the hall. 'You've saved me a journey. I was planning to come and see you, Mrs Marmion, to find out if there was any news about Sergeant Keedy.'

'Alice was at the hospital earlier on,' said Ellen. 'In fact, that's why we're here.'

The vicar closed the front door and led them into the spacious living room. A fire crackled in the grate. When they had sat down, he looked at each of his visitors in turn. The Reverend Harold Sanders was a big, tubby man in his fifties with bushy eyebrows and a shock of frizzy hair. When Alice described her visit to Mile End, he listened carefully and nodded throughout.

'That's very reassuring to hear,' he said when she had finished. 'Joe has been in my prayers since I first read about his being shot during a siege. Thank heaven that he survived! It must have come like a bolt from the blue.'

'It did,' replied Alice. 'When I first heard the news, I was horrified. Joe and I have waited so long to get married, and it looked as if he might be snatched away from me before the wedding could take place. It made me reach a decision,' she told him. 'If Joe survives – and I'm confident now that he will – I wanted the date to be brought forward. Even though we didn't speak, Joe agreed.'

'Ah,' he said, 'so you want a spring wedding.'

'If it's possible . . .'

'I'll have to warn you that Saturdays are fully booked, I'm afraid. There's been quite a demand. The war is responsible for that. We have couples who wish to marry before the man goes abroad with his regiment, then there are those who are less fortunate – wounded soldiers who come home, desperate to forget the horrors of war in the joys of married life. Some have hideous injuries, as you can imagine, but their future brides nevertheless stand by them.'

'Quite right,' said Ellen.

He turned to Alice. 'Those who wed while they are on leave often wear their army uniforms at the ceremony,' he told her. 'I take it that you have no intention of wearing your policewoman's uniform at the altar.'

'I certainly don't!' she protested.

'Alice will be wearing a beautiful wedding dress,' explained Ellen. 'It's being made for her.'

'That's as it should be,' he said, rising to his feet. 'If you'll excuse me, I'll get my diary and check all the bookings.' His eyebrows lifted to expose his eyes in full. 'I might even see if I can persuade someone to make us a pot of tea . . .'

* * *

Clifford Burge was astonished by the latest turn of events. It took him a few moments to absorb the information. He was forced to look at their evidence from a different angle now.

'They were Irish?' he asked.

'It's a strong possibility,' said Marmion. 'We owe the discovery to the commissioner. If he hadn't recognised the names of places in Ireland, we'd still be looking for London burglars.'

'Have you discussed this with the superintendent?'

'I tried, Cliff, but he wasn't persuaded. Chat still thinks that these are men who know the capital inside out. According to him, their choice of targets proves that. How could three Irishmen devise such a plan when none of them is familiar with London?'

'They may not be, but that woman probably is. Maybe she was the one who selected the jewellery shops.'

'We know that she visited them, each time in a different guise. Sometimes she was on her own, but she had a man with her on other occasions.'

Burge raised a warning hand. 'Wait a moment, sir. There's something we're forgetting.'

'Is there?'

'Yes. The man using the name of Dan Haskins went with her twice. I got a good description of him from both jewellers. Neither of them mentioned that he was Irish. He'd surely have heard that lilt in his voice.'

'You don't need to have an Irish accent to be Irish. When I talked to Haskin's neighbours in Limehouse, they told me that he sounded as if he came from somewhere in the

Midlands. That house was only rented to give the three of them somewhere to hide.'

'I see.'

'The commissioner may have given us the breakthrough we need,' said Marmion, hopefully. 'It will help to focus our minds. Meanwhile, Sir Edward will ask Special Branch to provide us with details of Irish republican activity in London. While Britain is fighting in one war, Irish extremists are fighting in another, albeit in secret.'

'I'm amazed that the superintendent doesn't accept the facts.'

'What he can't stomach is the idea that the burglaries have been organised by a woman. He still thinks that a member of the female sex would never sink to that level. Strange, really,' said Marmion. 'Chat is a devout Roman Catholic. In fact, he keeps a Bible in his office. Perhaps I should remind him of Salome's request.'

'Salome?'

'When she danced before the king, he was so delighted that he said he'd reward her with whatever she wanted. Salome asked for the head of John the Baptist on a plate.'

Burge gulped. 'What happened?'

'She got it.'

The woman was very sorry that they had to part. Giles Underhill paid the bill, then escorted her into Shaftesbury Avenue. After a few affectionate words, he flagged down a taxi, then gave her a kiss on the cheek before helping her into the vehicle. He had made her feel important and respected. She waved to him as the taxi pulled away and reflected on the pleasant hour they had spent together. It had transported her back into a world she had loved and now missed dreadfully. The pleasure was reciprocal. He had been her audience and she had been his. They had talked in a language that was incomprehensible to anyone else in the café.

The fond memories soon faded, and she confronted reality once more. She played a very different role now. It involved danger and daring. Instead of receiving a round of applause, she enjoyed a far deeper satisfaction. It was the joy of helping a cause in which she fervently believed.

She had been given the chance of helping to rescue a country from its hated overlord. That was now far more important than anything else in her life. She wondered how Giles Underhill would react if he knew about her activities and concluded that he might have to be cast ruthlessly aside one day. Country came before friendship. No exceptions were made.

CHAPTER ELEVEN

While she missed being on duty with her best friend, Iris Goodliffe was finding her new partner less maddening than before. There was a noticeable improvement in Jessica Porter's behaviour. She seemed to sense that she should talk less and listen more. Also, she had begun to take a genuine interest in Alice Marmion. They were walking side by side on their beat when Jessica's curiosity prompted her.

'What makes her such a wonderful policewoman?' she asked.

'Instinct.'

'Don't we have that as well, Iris?'

'Yes, but ours can't compare with what Alice has. Think of her background. When she was young, she saw her father go to work every day in a police uniform. Alice told me that her brother, Paul, was always asking for lurid details of any crimes he was involved in. The family talked about law and order all the time. It was bound to rub off on Alice.'

'What about her brother? Didn't he want to be a policeman?'

'No,' said Iris. 'He'd have lost too many of his friends if he did that. They came first. He enjoyed their company at work and at play. When Paul joined up, the rest of his football team did the same.'

'That was brave of them,' said Jessica. 'Oh, I know what I meant to ask you. Why is there such an age gap between Alice and Sergeant Keedy?'

'There's no such thing as an age gap when you're in love.'

'I suppose that's true. But it is noticeable. I mean, he's in his thirties. Couldn't Alice find a boyfriend of the same age?'

'According to her,' said Iris, 'she had a whole string of them, but they never lasted. Alice always found them a bit childish. She'd been very fond of Joe Keedy but did nothing about it because she thought he was beyond her reach.'

'What changed her mind?'

'He did, Jessica. Joe made the first move.'

'If only a handsome man like him could do that to me!' sighed Jessica. 'I wouldn't care how old he was. I'd jump into his arms.' She brought them to a halt. 'Alice can't have been the first woman in his life. He must have been very popular.'

'He was, but he's put that life behind him now. Joe is ready to settle down at last.'

'That must have caused a lot of upset.'

'In what way?'

'The obvious way.'

'It's not obvious to me,' said Iris.

'Open your eyes,' suggested Jessica. 'I mean, you only need to look at Sergeant Keedy. When he proposed to Alice, he must have left a trail of disappointed women in his wake.'

Nurse Bell attended to his needs with more than her usual efficiency. Spending long periods of time with Keedy, she was both attentive and indefatigable. Now that he depended on her completely, she was drawn to him again. Propping him up, she helped him to take his medication.

'You're so kind to me, Maisie,' he said after he'd swallowed the last pill.

'You don't deserve it.'

'Why not?'

'You know only too well.'

He shrugged. 'That was a long time ago.'

'It seems like yesterday to me.'

'I thought you'd be married by now,' he said, 'and have three children.'

'I wish that was true, Joe, but you never proposed to me.' She lowered her voice. 'At least, you never proposed marriage to me. You certainly proposed everything else.'

He felt a stab of pain and gritted his teeth. After a few moments, the pain eased.

'Are you all right?' she asked with concern.

'I get these twinges from time to time.'

'So do I, Joe. But, in my case, they're twinges of regret.'

'Oh, I've had those as well,' he confessed. 'When we split up, I had them every day.'

'So why didn't you do anything about it?'

'I did for a while. I even came to see you in Manchester. But I didn't think you'd really want me back, Maisie.'

She smiled at him and kissed him gently on the forehead. 'Well, I did,' she said, drawing back. 'Alice is very pretty.'

He was startled. 'How do you know her name?'

'You told it to me.'

'I don't remember that.'

'I'm not surprised,' she explained. 'You were fast asleep at the time. I could hear you trying to whisper something, but it wasn't clear. When I put my ear close to you, I picked up what you were saying. It was Alice's name.'

'Oh, I see . . .'

'Don't apologise. Obviously, she can give you what I failed to do.'

'That's not true at all, Maisie.'

'But I did enjoy our times together. I wondered what happened to you, then saw a photo of you in a newspaper. You and Inspector Marmion were praised for catching a killer.'

'I carried on chasing killers and got too close to one of them this time.'

'You always liked danger. It's in your blood.'

'That's why I had to get out of the family business. I didn't want to end up like my brother, Dennis. He never smiles. Dennis says that it's unbecoming. Nice word.' He looked at her seriously. 'Can I ask you something?'

'Of course, Joe. That's why I'm here.'

'I am going to come through this, aren't I?' he said, momentarily uncertain.

'Yes, you will,' she replied with confidence. 'You'll get better and better each day until it's time to get out of hospital altogether. And the best thing of all is that you'll find Alice waiting patiently for you.'

He could sense the sadness behind her smile.

Alice Marmion felt a profound sense of relief. A date for her wedding had been set early in April. She and her mother were still in the vicarage, enjoying a cup of tea and a biscuit. Harold Sanders was beaming at them, glad that he had been able to respond to Alice's request.

'Nearer the time,' he said, 'we'll need to have a few meetings.'

'What sort of meetings?' asked Alice.

'You and your future husband need to be prepared for holy matrimony. It's not something you embark on without understanding its full implications.'

'Your father and I did the same,' said Ellen. 'We had two or three meetings beforehand with our previous vicar, the Reverend Stacey. They were very helpful discussions.'

'There's no compulsion,' explained the vicar. 'In fact, I once had a couple who refused point-blank to have any private sessions with me. They regarded them as irrelevant.'

Ellen was curious. 'What happened to them?'

'I'm sad to report that the marriage was not a happy one. The husband never came near the church afterwards, but his wife did. She admitted to me that they had got married too quickly and with their eyes closed. She wished that they'd given me the opportunity to discuss the full nature of their commitments to each other.'

'Joe and I will certainly come,' said Alice, 'though you will have to wait until he is well enough.' She smiled. 'Oh, I can't say how grateful I am to you for agreeing to an earlier date.'

'I was happy to do so, Alice.'

'Thank you.'

'Do you have any idea of numbers for the ceremony?'

'We're still working on the list,' she said.

'Am I to assume that . . . ?'

'Yes,' said Ellen, firmly. 'My son will not be among the guests. Paul has chosen . . . his own path in life. We've come to accept that.'

'That's very sensible of you.' He rubbed his palms together. 'Now, is there anything else that I can do for you?'

'Yes,' said Alice. 'I wonder if you would say a prayer for Joe's recovery.'

'I'll do more than that,' he replied with a smile. 'We'll go into the church itself and kneel in prayer together. God's house is the proper place for something of this importance – even if it may be a trifle colder in there.'

Joe Keedy was getting increasingly restive. While he accepted the importance of complete rest, he was annoyed that he was unable to take part in the investigation. He still felt that he could contribute from his hospital bed. Maisie Bell had come to the end of her shift, so he crooked a finger to call Nurse Donaldson across to him.

'Do you need anything?' she asked, coming over.

'Yes, I do. I need to speak to Inspector Marmion as a matter of urgency.'

'His daughter will soon be coming to visit you, Sergeant Keedy. Surely, she will be able to take a message to her father.'

'I simply must speak to him in person,' he insisted. 'Is there some way I can do that?'

'Well . . .'

'Then please find me someone who can help me. It's important. I don't simply wish to chat to him. I have information about the crime that put me here.'

'I'll see what I can do,' she said. 'Excuse me . . .'

Marmion was working alone in his office when the telephone rang. He picked up the receiver.

'Inspector Marmion speaking . . .'

'This is Dr Warrender from Mile End Military Hospital,' said a man's voice.

Marmion's stomach tightened. Was it bad news about Keedy?

'Go on,' he said, nervously.

'Sergeant Keedy is anxious to speak to you. To be honest, he's not well enough to do so but he's adamant, so we've bowed to his wishes. I'll hand the receiver to him.'

After a momentary pause, Keedy's voice came on the line.

'Harv?' he croaked.

'How are you, Joe?'

'I'll survive, thank God! But I had to tell you something.'

'Go on.'

'When I woke up earlier, I had a clear image of the man

who fired that shot at me. I know it happened in a split second, but I did get a clear look at him. I'd recognise that face anywhere.'

'That's good to know, Joe, but you must forget about us until your recovery is properly under way. We can handle the investigation. You're off duty.'

'Listen to me, please!' implored Keedy.

'Don't get so upset. It's bad for you.'

'I've seen him before, Harv. I've seen those mean eyes staring me in the face once before. It can only mean that I've either met him, or seen his mugshot. Can you hear what I'm trying to tell you?' he went on. 'A photo of the man who shot me may well be tucked away in police files. Is there some way you can find it?'

He was still burning with resentment. After six burglaries that netted them a substantial amount of money, they had been caught raiding their seventh jewellery shop. He had been forced to shoot dead a policeman, then run away with his accomplices. After retreating to their hideaway, they had been besieged. To keep the police at bay, he'd been compelled to shoot one of them before leading the way through the escape route he had planned in case of an emergency. All three of them were still free but they were being hunted. It meant that they had had to postpone any additional burglaries for a while.

Having called himself Dan Haskins, their leader was now using another alias and living in a small hotel not far from Euston Station. He had just haggled for a long time with the man who bought the jewellery stolen from the shop owned by

Manny Winckler. Had the burglars been uninterrupted, they would have had a more worthwhile haul. As it was, they only had cheaper items that yielded a low price. When he read the evening paper, he saw that he was named and described. He also learnt that the man he'd shot during the siege – Detective Sergeant Joseph Keedy – had survived and been taken to Mile End Military Hospital. It was possible that Keedy had had a glimpse of his face before the bullet hit him. He could take no chances.

Crossing to the washbasin in his room, he stared in the mirror at his beard. It was mentioned in the description of him in the newspaper, so it had to go. He used a pair of scissors to cut some of the hair away. After a close shave with a razor, the whole beard had soon disappeared, making his face look very different. The hotelier would be bound to notice the change and wonder what had prompted him to remove the beard. Deciding that it was time to find somewhere else to live, he slipped out of the building with his belongings and vanished into the gloom.

When they got to the hospital for the evening visit, the two women found a surprise awaiting them. Standing outside the waiting room was Marmion. He embraced them in turn, then explained why he was there. Alice was astounded.

'You actually spoke to Joe?' she asked.

'They let me into his room for a short period. Joe rang me earlier to say that he felt certain he'd recognise the man who shot him because he'd seen him before. I came to get more details. I can't burrow through police files until I have information that will help me to narrow down the search. Besides, I leapt at the chance of seeing him.'

Alice was hopeful. 'Does that mean we'll be allowed into the room, Daddy?'

'I'm afraid not.'

'That's unfair.'

'Yes,' said Ellen. 'We've got so much to tell him. The main thing is that we've seen the vicar and he's agreed to bring forward the date for the wedding.'

'That's good news,' said Marmion. 'It will cheer him up.'

'I wish that we had something to cheer us up,' complained Alice. 'We get so frustrated, trying to talk to Joe through a plate glass window.'

'There is some good news for you,' he told them. 'I've got a police car waiting outside for me. When you've finished here, it will take all three of us back home.'

He put an arm around each of them and pulled them close.

Clifford Burge was proud of being promoted, if only for a limited period. Determined to show his gratitude, he had stayed at Scotland Yard well beyond his allotted hours. He pored over a map of London that evening, trying to decide why the burglars had chosen their targets. They seemed to have been moving in a circle, making sure that there was a substantial gap between each of the shops. Where would their next projected burglary have taken place? He used a finger to trace the circle, then continued roughly the same distance from Limehouse to what he guessed might well be the next district chosen.

Beside him on a shelf were business directories for various

districts of the capital. He selected the one that covered Shadwell and thumbed through it until he found a list of jewellery shops. Burge was working on the assumption that some homework might already have been done on the next target in line. Since the burglars had used the same woman on seven consecutive occasions, it was likely that she might have been employed once more to inspect a property for them. Which jewellery shop might it have been?

Reaching for the telephone, he dialled a number and waited.

When the bell rang to summon the visitors, Alice was near the front of the pack. As she hurried up the stairs, she tried to fight off any sense of jealousy. Why had her father been allowed to see the patient face to face when she and her mother were kept outside the room? The answer was that a murder investigation took priority. Only an urgent summons from Keedy would have brought her father to the hospital. The two men had to be able to converse face to face. Alice could simply hope that the information given by Keedy would turn out to be of value. Meanwhile, he was hers.

She had come prepared. Instead of having a mimed conversation with him, she had brought a notepad and a black crayon. When Keedy first saw her through the window, therefore, he read the message she held up for him – WILL YOU MARRY ME IN APRIL? His eyes lit up and he nodded with enthusiasm. Alice had other questions for him. She flicked from page to page and earned a nod of agreement each time in response. Keedy was delighted with their new form of conversation but frustrated that he could not reply in the same way. Knowing that she would have met her father there, he tapped his head to indicate that his brain was helping to solve the attempted murder that had put him in hospital. Alice used the crayon to write another message – GET WELL FIRST.

He shook his head defiantly. Keedy had to be involved.

Ringing a series of jewellery shops had tested Burge's patience and good manners. Two of the owners refused to believe that he was a detective while another three were angry at being disturbed during their evening meal with the family. One irate owner even threatened to report him to the police. At least that gave him a laugh. Burge was relieved when he finally found someone who accepted that he was involved in the investigation of a string of burglaries.

'I'm grateful that the police are trying to solve these crimes,' said the man. 'I've read about them in the papers. I'd hate it if anything like that happened here.'

'I hope that it doesn't, Mr Quentin,' he said. 'These men are dangerous and need to be caught. I'm afraid that there's a possibility your shop might have been on their list.'

'Dear me!' exclaimed the other. 'I sincerely hope not. At my age, a shock of that kind could do me real harm. I have a dicky heart, you see. We've been so lucky in the past. I suppose that I've taken it for granted.' He heaved a sigh. 'Are we really in danger?'

'Let me tell you how they work.'

Burge went on to explain how instrumental an older

woman had been in visiting every place that was on the list of targets. He talked about the various guises she'd used and the different excuses she'd given to win the confidence of the successive owners of jewellery shops. When he stopped, there was a prolonged silence. Burge was worried.

'Are you still there, Mr Quentin?' he asked.

'Yes,' said the other, uneasily. 'I am.'

'Has a woman like that visited your premises recently?'

'She may have, Sergeant Burge – and it was only a matter of days ago.'

'Please describe her to me.'

'The woman was old and shabbily dressed, but she had an obvious respectability about her. I was impressed by her voice. It was so pleasant to listen to. Voices like that don't often come into my shop in an area like this. She was polite and well educated.'

'Was she alone?'

'Oh, yes. She told me that she'd been recently widowed. I felt sorry for her.'

'What had brought her to Shadwell?'

'She wanted an item valued for the purposes of insurance.'

'And what was the item – an opal necklace or a diamond engagement ring?'

'It was a string of pearls,' said the other.

'Did she intend to sell it?'

'Oh, no. She'd inherited them recently from her late sister and intended to leave them to her daughter in due course. I could see from the way that she looked at the pearls that she had a deep affection for them.'

Burge made an instant decision. 'Are you in the middle of dinner, Mr Quentin?'

'No, Sergeant – we've just finished it.'

'Then I'd like to drive across to Shadwell and speak to you in person, if I may.'

'By all means,' said Quentin. 'To be honest, you've got me rather worried. In my business, judgement of character is essential. I prided myself that I had it. Yet I didn't have the slightest qualms about this customer. It was a pleasure to meet her.'

Burge rose to his feet. 'I'm on my way, sir . . .'

CHAPTER TWELVE

During the ride home, Marmion was able to tell his wife and daughter about the progress of the investigation. They were pleased that it had been given priority and that additional detectives had now been assigned to it. When they reached the house, however, Ellen and Alice were disappointed that he was unable to go inside with them. His work had by no means ended for the day. Marmion therefore asked the driver to take him back to Scotland Yard. The car sped away through the darkness.

He used the journey to reflect on what he had been told. Keedy was certain that he recognised the man who shot him. They had, literally, come face to face. It meant that the burglar calling himself Dan Haskins had crossed paths with Keedy before. Ordinarily, he and Marmion rarely investigated burglaries. They specialised in murder cases. It just happened that this murder involved a series of burglaries. Concentrating hard, Marmion went back through a list of cases in his mind, trying to find one that might conceivably have involved Haskins. He realised that the man would probably have been using a different name at the time.

The one thing they did know about him was that he was dangerous. Having shot one policeman dead, he had tried to add a detective sergeant to his tally. Evidently, Haskins knew how to handle a gun. He was also clever enough to devise an emergency escape route from the place where he and his accomplices were hiding. All three of them had fled from a blazing house and clambered across a series of roofs before descending on a rope. They were brave and skilful. Marmion wondered if they had had military training of some kind. Then there was their record of success. During the six previous burglaries, they had entered premises soundlessly, opened and rifled a safe and escaped with a sizeable haul in each case. No real evidence had been left behind. They were professionals.

Where, then, had Keedy encountered their leader? Marmion had no idea. When he got back to his office, he resolved, he would go through their recent cases with great care, searching for a face that had lodged itself firmly in Keedy's memory. It didn't matter how long it took him. Marmion was determined to stare into the man's eyes himself.

David Quentin was a slim, stooping man in his sixties with a pallid face and a blue-veined nose. A few last wisps of hair remained but he had a habit of sweeping the flat of his hand over his bald head as if pushing back a luxuriant mop of curls.

Detective Sergeant Burge met him in the shop itself, a sizeable room filled with display cabinets. It was impossible not to notice the array of mirrors, carefully placed so that customers were under surveillance wherever they went.

When he showed his visitor in, the proprietor made a point of standing behind the counter.

'This is where I was when the woman came into the shop,' he explained.

'What was your first impression of her?'

'I felt sorry for her. She looked so weary when she trudged in here. The first thing I did was to suggest that she sat down on that chair beside you.'

'That was kind of you, Mr Quentin.'

'She needed a few moments to get her breath back.'

'What name did she give you?'

'Mrs Bennet.'

'On the telephone you told me that she was of medium height, full-bodied and in her late sixties. Also, that she had a sort of dignity about her.'

'It's true.'

'Yet she seemed to be struggling.'

'I had the feeling that she was short of money.'

'Did she have an accent of any kind?'

'No, Sergeant, she did not. She had a lovely voice. I wish that all my customers could speak English so precisely. Cockney slang always grates on my ear.'

'How much of what she said could you remember?' asked Burge, taking out his notebook. 'Take your time. There's no hurry.'

'I can remember almost everything. She had a strange charm. In a way, it was captivating. As for her actual words . . .'

Quentin quoted whole sentences that had stuck in his mind. As he jotted them down, Burge could see nothing unusual about them. The customer was making a simple request. The jeweller went on to describe everything that happened during her visit.

'And then,' he added, 'just before she left, she made a request.'

'What was it?'

'Well, she asked if she might speak to my female assistant. Mrs Calder was behind the other counter. She listened to the woman.'

'I think that I can guess what she asked,' said Burge.

'Knowing that I would agree, Mrs Calder was happy to oblige her. Indeed, she showed Mrs Bennet to the toilet at the rear of the shop.'

'May I see it myself, sir?'

'Yes, of course. I take it that—'

'No, no,' said Burge. 'I've no need to make use of it myself. I just want to see where it was and how deep into the shop it took your customer.'

'It's at the very back, Sergeant Burge.'

'Lead the way, please . . .' As he followed the proprietor, he had another question. 'How valuable was that string of pearls she showed you?'

Quentin turned to him. 'Extremely valuable . . .'

* * *

Alone in her bedroom, she sat in front of a mirror surrounded by light bulbs. Around her neck was a string of pearls that she fondled affectionately. It had been a present from an admirer who had died almost two years ago. Wearing the pearls from time to time brought him alive again in her mind. She glanced up at his framed photograph on the wall. He had a craggy face, a broken nose, and a sense of quiet authority. It didn't matter to her that the pearls had been stolen during a burglary. If anything, that fact only added to their value because he had taken great risks on her behalf to get them.

Without warning, another memory intruded. She recalled the moment when she saw a different photograph of him altogether. It had appeared in a newspaper. Her friend lay dead on the ground at the feet of British soldiers. The image was burnt forever into her brain.

Marmion was eager to get back to Scotland Yard. When he arrived there, he found a request from Claude Chatfield awaiting him. He went straight to the superintendent's office and found him seated behind his desk. Chatfield rose to his feet and picked up a file.

'The commissioner was as good as his word,' he said. 'He made contact with Special Branch, and they have provided us with information that may be of value.' He handed the file over. 'It's classified material so must be kept under lock and key.'

'Yes, of course, sir.'

'Did you get to see Sergeant Keedy?'

'I did and I was both shocked and heartened – shocked to see him in such a state but heartened by his iron determination to help the investigation. He believes that he recognised the man who shot him. I promised to search through details of recent cases in the hope that I can unearth Dan Haskins, as he called himself.'

'You might also look at the photographs in that file,' said Chatfield, indicating it. 'They are men who are – or have been – under surveillance by Special Branch.'

'Then I'll be interested to see who they are.'

'Do that.' His tone changed. 'Is Burge still here?'

'No, sir. He isn't.'

'He's sneaked off early, has he?' said Chatfield, sourly. 'Haven't you told him that he is supposed to work all hours on a case as serious as this?'

'Detective Sergeant Burge is not here because he has gone to interview a jeweller in Shadwell. He left a note on my desk to say that he believes the shop might have been the next on the list for the burglars.'

'Oh, I see.'

'Far from sneaking off,' said Marmion, pointedly, 'he is using his initiative. I'll be most interested to learn what he found out.'

'Be sure to pass on the details to me.'

'That goes without saying, sir.'

'No, it doesn't,' retorted Chatfield. 'There has been more than one occasion when you somehow "forgot" to keep me informed of a development in an investigation.'

'It won't happen again, Superintendent.'

'I should hope not.'

'If you'll excuse me, I'll get back to my office and go through this file.'

'One more thing . . .'

'Yes, sir?'

'Don't you dare try to get the commissioner on your side again,' snarled the other. 'I stand by my judgement. Burge was wrongly appointed. Sooner or later, he'll let us down. According to Sir Edward, you told him that Burge would come through with flying colours. In other words,' said Chatfield, 'you tried to undermine my authority.'

'I was merely putting an alternative view to the commissioner,' said Marmion.

'He accepted your opinion over mine. I won't stand for it. There is a chain of command in this building,' Chatfield emphasised. 'Remain aware of it.'

'I do, sir. I never forget that you are senior to me. However,' added Marmion, waspishly, 'I also remember that the commissioner is senior to you.'

He went quickly out of the office and left Chatfield spluttering.

Alice Marmion and her mother were enjoying a light supper at home, looking back at their visit to the hospital, then discussing what other improvements they could make to the house where Mr and Mrs Keedy would begin their married life. As she added another task to the list, Ellen looked up.

'It's time we discussed the wedding as well,' she said.

'Yes, of course, Mummy. We'll have to send out invitations

straight away. Now that we've changed the date, people need to be told.'

'Have you decided to invite Iris?'

'I'd like to, but Joe is not so keen. Iris always annoys him somehow.'

'But she's your closest friend at work. Leaving her out would be a real snub.'

'I agree,' said Alice. 'She's already decided that she's on the list so I can't let her down. Iris even offered to come here ahead of the wedding to help me get into my dress.'

Ellen was firm. 'That's my job and I don't need an assistant.'

'That's what I told her, Mummy. Oh,' she went on, sighing with exasperation, 'we have so many decisions to make at short notice. There's the house to work on, the catering for the wedding to arrange, the wedding itself, our brief honeymoon somewhere, Joe to look after, and his brother to fight off.'

'You said he'd refuse to go anywhere near Dennis's house.'

'His brother won't give up without a fight,' warned Alice. 'Dennis is very persistent. I'm not looking forward to the moment when I come down the aisle on Joe's arm and see Dennis glowering at me.'

'Doesn't he ever show any sign of pleasure?'

'He must do, Mummy – but I've never seen him doing it.'

They laughed. Ellen then got up from the table, opened a drawer in the little dresser and took out a list of the wedding guests. She ran a critical eye down the names.

'There are well over twice as many guests as your father and I had,' she complained. 'Do you really need all of them?'

'Yes,' said Alice, 'we do. Apart from Iris, there's nobody

Joe objected to. I just hope that he's fit and well enough to go through with the ceremony.'

'Don't forget those sessions beforehand with the vicar.'

'I won't say a word about those until nearer the time. Joe needs to get his strength back before I tell him.' She glanced up at the clock on the mantelpiece. 'What time will Daddy be home?'

Ellen sighed. 'Don't even ask.'

When he got back to his office, Marmion was grateful to find Clifford Burge waiting for him. He was impressed by the way that Keedy's deputy had deduced that the burglars would have already lined up the next in their catalogue of raids. As he listened to the latter's report, he was struck by its detail. When he came to the end of his recital, Burge closed his notepad.

'That's about it, sir,' he said.

'Well done, Cliff!'

'The burglars were very methodical. They chose their targets, then employed that woman to get inside the premises to size them up. She called herself Mrs Bennet this time. Mr Quentin, the proprietor of the shop, admitted that he was completely fooled by her.'

'As a result of your visit,' said Marmion, 'he'll have tightened his security. Not that they are likely to be active for a while. The burglars will have gone to ground.'

'What's our next step, sir?'

'Your next step is to write a report for the superintendent. When you deliver it, wait until he's finished reading it. Don't expect any gratitude for your good work. He's still not persuaded that you are the right man for the job – even though you've just proved that you are.'

'Thank you, sir.'

'I wonder how far ahead they were working,' said Marmion, thoughtfully. 'Was Mr Quentin's shop their latest target or had they planned another burglary after that?'

'It's possible that they had. That means they'll have sent that woman ahead on a scouting expedition. It was clever of her to visit the toilet like that. It was the one place where there was no mirror to keep an eye on the customers. Mr Quentin boasted about the way that he'd arranged them,' said Burge. 'When he glanced up at the mirrors from his position behind the counter, he could see everyone who was in the shop – except for a customer in the toilet.'

'Mrs Bennet only went there to see what was at the rear of the premises.'

'Why does she keep changing her name?'

'It's because she's a different person each time,' explained Marmion. 'She changes her voice, appearance, and manner completely. No ordinary woman would do that so effectively. In my opinion, it means that we're looking for a professional actress.'

'How can we find her?'

'I've been thinking about that, and Sergeant Keedy may have the answer.'

'Really?' said Burge, taken aback.

'Do you remember that case involving a surgeon from Edmonton Military Hospital?'

'Yes, he was hacked to death in his own home.'

'In the course of his enquiries,' said Marmion, 'the sergeant visited Pegasus Costumes Ltd, a company that hires out costumes to London theatres – and beyond the capital, I daresay. Sergeant Keedy told me that the woman who ran it was like a theatrical encyclopaedia. She might be a good person to start with. I'll find the address for you.'

'Thank you, sir.'

'Off you go to write that report. I've got this file to go through,' said Marmion, tapping it. 'It's just possible that it might contain the photograph of the man who shot Sergeant Keedy. Let's hope that we have some luck for a change.'

Keedy awoke early next morning to find that Maisie Bell was gazing fondly at him. When his eyes opened, she drew back. He blinked a few times.

'What were you doing, Maisie?' he asked.

'I did all sorts of things while you were still asleep. I took your temperature, checked your blood pressure, then went on from there.'

'You were staring at me.'

'There's no law against that, is there?' she teased.

He clicked his tongue. 'You were taking advantage of me, Nurse Bell.'

'I'm entitled to get my own back, aren't I? You took advantage of me lots of times.'

'Yes, but you weren't in a hospital bed with tubes stuck in you,' he said. 'Besides, I don't recall that you ever complained.' He winked at her. 'We had good times together, Maisie.'

'We did, Joe. But let's forget about those. You're not

supposed to become excited. It's bad for you. Just relax and let your body get slowly better.'

'To be honest,' he confessed, 'it's my mind that's causing me problems. I keep getting flashbacks of being shot by that burglar. They're quite frightening sometimes. I wake up sweating.'

'I'll mention that to the doctor. Meanwhile,' she said, 'I have a message to pass on from Inspector Marmion. He rang earlier.'

'What did he say?'

'I didn't speak to him, Joe, but it seems that he's coming to see you this morning.'

'Do I have to wait until visiting hours?'

'No, you don't. This is urgent. He needs to see you as soon as possible. That means he's probably on his way right now.'

Having rung the hospital from his house, Marmion was picked up by a police car and taken in the direction of Mile End. Beside him on the seat was a briefcase containing the file from Special Branch. For someone who had managed less than five hours of sleep, Marmion was feeling surprisingly alert. There had been a distinct sign of progress in the investigation. Burge had made an important discovery, the intelligence from Special Branch had been invaluable and there was an outside chance that he was travelling with a photograph of the man they most needed to catch.

Now that her partner had stopped irking her so much, Iris Goodliffe had warmed to Jessica Porter. While the latter would never be her ideal companion, she had now become pleasant company. When they set off into the cold together, Iris had news for her.

'I spoke to Alice yesterday,' she said. 'My father let me use the telephone at the pharmacy. I knew that Alice was most likely to be with her mother, so I rang their home number.'

'What did she say?' asked Jessica.

'First of all, she told me that she'd been to the hospital several times to see Joe. Alice was not allowed to go into his room and could only look at him through a window, but she soon got used to that. He looks better every time she goes there.'

'That's good.'

'But he's still likely to stay there for some time. However,' said Iris, brightening, 'the big news is that Alice has managed to get the date of the wedding moved forward to April. She's thrilled about it – and so is Joe, of course. I can't wait.'

'Are you going to be involved, Iris?'

'Of course I will. When the service is over, I'll be outside the church door with a big bag of confetti ready. They won't know what hit them.'

'I thought you told me you'd help Alice get into her wedding dress.'

Iris's face clouded. 'I'm afraid not. Mrs Marmion will do that. It's only fair, really.' She grinned broadly. 'But I'll be in some of the wedding photos. Alice wants one taken with her closest women friends and that includes me.'

'Oh,' sighed Jessica, 'I wish that I could have something as exciting to look forward to.'

'You could always come to the church and watch.'

'I'll be on duty – and so should you be, Iris.'

'Gale Force understands. She knows how close I am to Alice and said that I could have the time off as and when necessary. Oh, isn't it wonderful?' she went on. 'Joe and Alice have had a rotten time since he was shot. They deserve something to cheer them up – and I'll be there to see it happening.'

'What about our beloved inspector?'

'I don't follow.'

'Well,' said Jessica, 'has Gale Force been invited to the wedding?'

Iris exploded into wild laughter.

When he was shown into the room at the hospital, Marmion sat on the chair beside the bed. He shook Keedy's hand gently.

'How are you, Joe?' he asked.

'Oh, I'm as right as rain. In fact, they may be letting me out this afternoon. At least,' said Keedy with a grin, 'that's what I'd like them to do. Unfortunately, I'll be here for quite some time.'

'That's right,' said Maisie Bell, hovering nearby. 'If you'll excuse me, I'll leave you alone.'

After distributing a smile between them, she left the room.

Marmion frowned. 'That young woman looks vaguely familiar.'

'You're mistaken, Harv,' said Keedy. 'Nurses all look the same in uniform. Now, what's brought you here so early? It's good news, hopefully.'

'It is, Joe. The good news is that Cliff Burge is turning out to be a good replacement for you. He's got a true copper's instinct.'

He told Keedy about Burge's discovery of another jewellery shop visited by the woman who worked with the burglars. It had had a lucky escape. Forewarned by Burge, the owner had been able to safeguard his premises even more.

'That woman sounds interesting,' said Keedy. 'If she can trick all those jewellers, she must be a brilliant actress.'

'I believe that she is, Joe. That's why Cliff Burge will be going to Pegasus Costumes Ltd this morning. Do you remember it?'

'I do. The woman there gave me a lot of help. She lives and breathes theatre. I got the feeling that she might have been an actress herself in her younger days.'

'I'm hoping that she might have some idea who might be helping those burglars. Actresses of a certain age tend to fall out of favour. Work usually dries up. Apart from anything else, they have difficulty learning lines.'

'That doesn't mean that they turn to crime, Harv.'

'Agreed – but I fancy that this one might have done just that.'

'If anyone can help Cliff, the woman at Pegasus Costumes can. She's an interesting woman. I enjoyed meeting her.'

'It's Cliff's turn now,' said Marmion, opening the briefcase to extract the file. 'Sir Edward managed to get this from Special Branch. I'm supposed to keep it locked up, but I couldn't resist the urge to bring it here. It's a revelation, Joe. I had no idea that we had so many Irish dissidents active in this country.'

Keedy became animated. 'Did they send any photographs?'

'They did, Joe, and one of them jumped out at me.'

'Is it him? Is it Dan Haskins?'

'It could be. All I know is that, when I looked into this man's eyes, I saw the glint of madness there.' He opened the file. 'Before I show you, I need your promise that you won't get agitated. You're supposed to stay calm and untroubled.'

'Let me see him,' begged Keedy.

'If you wish . . .' Extracting a photograph, he held it up for Keedy to look at. 'Well, do you recognise him?'

'Yes,' said Keedy, snatching it from him and studying it. 'That's him. That's Dan Haskins. That's the black-hearted devil who shot me!'

CHAPTER THIRTEEN

Clifford Burge had been told how difficult it was to find Pegasus Costumes. Keedy admitted to walking straight past it on his first visit. Burge therefore took the precaution of asking a policeman for directions. As a result, he turned off a side street behind Shaftesbury Avenue and into a mews. The place was an optical illusion. From the outside, the building looked small and neglected, but it soon opened out into a four-storeyed Victorian structure with real character. When he entered through the main door, he was confronted by a large foyer, decorated with framed posters of famous productions in West End theatres. Seated at the desk in front of him was a plump, middle-aged woman with abundant red hair, and wearing the sort of colourful attire that almost dazzled the eye.

'Can I help you, sir?' she asked, beaming at him.

'I hope so,' he told her. 'My name is Detective Sergeant Burge, and we need some help with a murder investigation.'

She gave a shrug. 'I can't see how I may be of assistance.'

'You were highly recommended by a colleague of mine, Detective Sergeant Keedy.'

'Ah, yes,' she said, fondly, 'I remember him well. He was such a handsome man. I was happy to provide the information he needed.'

'Perhaps you can do the same for me.'

Burge gave her a shortened version of the facts, stressing that his interest was in the woman who had visited eight jewellery shops in different guises. She listened with interest. He mentioned the names that the woman had used during her visits, including that of Mrs Bennet. After she had jotted them down on a pad, she ran an eye over them.

'Nobody comes to mind immediately,' she admitted, 'but the woman's age is the important factor. The various men she deceived all put her in her sixties. What that means to me is that she was probably well into her seventies. Clever make-up can take years off a woman.'

'She was obviously a very talented actress.'

'Then she probably had a career that stretches back to the 1870s – even further, perhaps. Well, Sergeant Burge, you've given me a problem. What actress would exchange the delight of performing before large audiences in a West End theatre with deceiving a lone jeweller in his shop?' She tossed her head. 'It's so demeaning.'

'Perhaps this woman is desperate for money?' said Burge, careful not to mention her links with Irish extremists.

'All that a true thespian wants is applause and she certainly won't get that from a man she's helping to rob.'

'Can you suggest any names?'

'There's Grace Whittington, of course,' she said, cudgelling her brains. 'If she's still alive, that is. Audiences used to love her, then she suddenly went out of fashion. I'm not quite sure why. It just happens to some actresses.'

'How good was she as an actress?'

'Grace was one of the best – in her prime. That was twenty years ago, mind you. After that, she went into decline and resorted to playing small roles that made no impact on an audience. Grace then dropped out of sight.'

'Could you imagine her turning to crime?'

'No, I can't,' said the woman, firmly. 'Grace would regard it as beneath her. She had standards. Being a successful actress is an achievement. Ending up as a confidence trickster is a betrayal of one's talent.'

'Do any other names come to mind?' he asked.

'I'll need time to think it over. The one big advantage of working here is that theatres who hire our costumes often give us free tickets for opening night. It means that I've seen every actress of real quality in the last thirty odd years.' She cackled. 'I've also had to sit through performances so dire that I wanted to reach for a hunting rifle to put some of the actresses out of their misery.'

'I'll leave it with you, then, Mrs . . . ?'

'Beatrice Naylor,' she said, 'and it's Miss Naylor. My wedding ring is just for show.'

'Here's the number where you can reach me at Scotland

Yard,' he said, handing her a card. 'If I'm not available, ask for Inspector Marmion.'

She smiled. 'What about that lovely Sergeant Keedy?'

'I'm afraid that he's in hospital, recovering from being shot by one of that woman's accomplices. It's another reason why we're so anxious to track her down.'

Conscious that Keedy needed complete rest, Marmion did his best to calm his friend down. It took several minutes. Discovering the name of the man who shot him had roused Keedy to a pitch of anger. It had also made him wince several times.

'Take it easy, Joe,' advised Marmion. 'You've got a lot of stitches in that wound. Do you want them to start popping out?'

'No, of course not.'

'Then take a deep breath and relax. We've got what we wanted. Dan Haskin's real name is Eamonn Corrigan. We even have a photo of him without that beard of his. He was arrested once but escaped from police custody.'

'He won't escape if I get my hands on him,' vowed Keedy.

'Let's forget him for a moment and concentrate on you. Alice was so keen to change the date of the wedding, but will you really be fit enough to go through with it?'

'I'll make sure that I am. The major damage was to the abdominal wall. That's where the bullet lodged. If I take care, I should get slowly better day by day.'

'Only if you avoid any excitement. Rest, rest, rest – do you understand?'

Keedy grinned. 'Yes, Doctor Marmion.'

The inspector rose to his feet. 'I'll be on my way. Oh,' he added, pausing, 'are you quite sure that I haven't seen your nurse before? That face of hers is so familiar.'

'It can't be. She's only just moved to London. You must be confusing her with someone else.'

'Maybe . . .'

Marmion gave him a long, shrewd look.

When he got back to Scotland Yard, the first person that Burge met was Claude Chatfield. The superintendent was coming along a corridor towards him. He glared at Burge.

'Where is Inspector Marmion?' he asked.

'He went to the hospital to see Sergeant Keedy.'

'Why wasn't I told?'

'I suppose he assumed you'd realise he'd be going to Mile End to visit the sergeant from time to time. Among other things, he'd want to keep him up to date with the latest developments.'

'It's a pity that he doesn't keep me up to date with them as well.'

'I'm sure that the inspector will be back very soon, sir, and will report to you immediately.'

'He'd better,' growled Chatfield. 'What have you been doing?'

'I'm just returning from the West End, sir. I visited Pegasus Costumes.'

'Now where have I heard that name before?'

'It was during the investigation into the murder of a surgeon from the Edmonton Military Hospital. Sergeant

Keedy got some valuable information there. I was hoping to do the same.'

'And did you?'

'That remains to be seen, sir.'

'Be more specific.'

'We believe that the woman involved in the burglaries must once have been a professional actress. Miss Naylor, the person I met earlier, has been involved with the theatre for many years and has extensive knowledge of the acting profession.'

'Ha!' snapped Chatfield. 'It's not a profession to me. It's a hiding place for people too lazy to do a proper job.'

'That's very harsh, sir,' said Burge. 'Did you never take your children to a Christmas pantomime?'

'Well, yes, but that's different . . .'

'I don't think so. You and your children were enjoying the work of actors.'

'They were entertainers,' argued Chatfield. 'Singers, dancers, speciality acts . . .'

'Whatever you call them, they were basically performers, doing what most people would recognise as a proper job. As for Miss Naylor,' Burge went on, 'she is going to search for the woman we believe is involved in the burglaries. When I told her what had happened to Sergeant Keedy, she was even more eager to help us.'

Beatrice Naylor was seated at her desk, working her way through a pile of theatrical magazines. Since they were lavishly illustrated, she saw the best actresses of their day, sometimes photographed in productions that she had seen. She marvelled at the way that the women always managed to look at their best the moment the camera clicked. It was an art that she had never quite mastered. When she had finished studying the last magazine, she was glad to see her assistant coming down the stairs with another pile in her arms.

'Ah,' she said, 'put them here, please, Eve.'

'Very well,' replied the young woman, setting them down on the desk. 'How many more will I have to bring from the storeroom?'

'That depends.'

'These are from the 1890s.'

'We may have to go back further than that,' said the other. 'Take a deep breath and bring me another load in half an hour.' She heard Eve's sigh of regret. 'We're helping to solve a murder and a string of burglaries so let's have a little enthusiasm, shall we?'

Alice Marmion arrived at the hospital mid-morning. She had spurned the offer of a lift from her father because it would have meant hours in a cold waiting room, feeling resentful that he had complete access to Keedy while she was limited to a specific hour and kept on the outside of a window. Having timed her arrival carefully, she had less than fifteen minutes to wait before she joined the general rush. Once again, Alice shot up the steps as fast as she could. When she arrived at Keedy's room, she was rewarded with the sight of him propped up in bed. His welcome smile helped to disperse her resentment.

Out came her notepad and she held up her first message –

I LOVE YOU. Keedy blew her a kiss in response. Flipping from page to page, Alice showed him a series of questions and he answered them as best he could. She tried to convince herself that there was a visible improvement in his condition, but it was obvious that recovery was still a long way off. All that Keedy wanted to do was to gaze quietly at her. She joined him in a prolonged silent communion until eventually jerked out of it by the sudden clang of the bell signalling the end of the visit. After a last wave and exchange of blown kisses, she drifted out.

'Thank you for trying to protect me, Cliff,' said Marmion. 'I'm sorry that the superintendent collared you this morning. I was hoping to be back before he finished his meeting with the commissioner and other senior officers.'

'I tried to divert him by telling him about my visit to that costume hire company.'

'Did he approve of it?'

'He was glad that I went but took the opportunity to take a swipe at actors in general.'

Marmion was back at Scotland Yard, talking to Clifford Burge. When the latter told him about the response he'd received from Beatrice Naylor, he was very pleased. She would be doing research on their behalf that might well prove fruitful.

'We've identified Dan Haskins,' he said. 'Let's unmask Mrs Bennet now.'

'They must be close if they worked together so effectively. Which one of them gives the orders?' asked Burge. 'Eamonn Corrigan or the actress?'

'You pick first.'

'Oh, I'm sure that it's him. Corrigan is the obvious leader. All that the woman has done is to reconnoitre the jewellery shops.'

'You undervalue her, Cliff. Before she even enters a shop, I bet she has a good look through the window to size up the owner. She needs to decide which performance she must give him. Corrigan does his work in the dark, but she has the more dangerous task of performing in broad daylight. That takes nerve. One slip – and she arouses suspicion.'

'Yet she never did.'

'That's why I think that she's the leader of the gang. All four of them are fully committed to the same cause, but the woman controls how they best serve it.'

'You could be right.'

'I look forward to finding out. We've only identified one of them, so we need to concentrate on flushing Eamonn Corrigan out of his hiding place. Once we've done that, we can go after the other two burglars. But the real prize will be that actress,' said Marmion. 'Where the hell can she be?'

When she arrived at Euston Station, she saw him at once. He was sitting alone on a bench and reading a newspaper. As she walked slowly towards him, he lifted his head enough for her to see that he had shaved off his beard. She was glad. It was a wise precaution. Reaching the bench, she sat at the opposite end to him, taking out a compact from her bag and pretending to powder her nose.

'Are you still in that hotel?' she asked.

'I shaved off my beard and moved out,' he grunted.

'That's two good decisions you've made. You're improving.'

'When I get up to go, I'll leave this paper behind me. My new address is written on the back page. I'm using the name of Ronald Morgan there.'

'And the others are still safe in Birmingham?'

'They won't stir until I give them the order.'

'And you won't stir,' she said, forcefully, 'until you get orders from me. Do you understand?'

'Yes, I do.'

She extended her hand. 'Give me the key.'

'Why?' he asked, stung by the command.

'You know quite well why.'

'That was a mistake. I apologised for it.'

'You had that key for an emergency but thought that it opened more than the door to my flat. You'll never be allowed to get in again.' She opened her palm. 'I want it now.' He hesitated. 'You treated me like some drunken tart you could take advantage of. It won't ever happen again.'

'I was excited. The drink had got to me.'

'Do I have to ask for that key again?' He handed it over. 'That's better.'

'Have you reported it?'

'No,' she replied, 'but I will if you step out of line again. There'd be repercussions.'

'I know,' he muttered, shamefacedly. 'Won't happen again.'

After shooting him a look, she stood up and walked briskly away.

* * *

The one virtue of hard work was that it kept the pair of them warm on a cold afternoon. Having finished removing the wallpaper in one room, Alice had moved on to another. In both cases, the original wallpaper had been a dull cream with a country scene printed on it. Neither Alice nor Keedy could have tolerated the colour or the design. They'd vowed to brighten every room in the house. Ellen was scraping away on one wall while her daughter was working on the one opposite. Neither of them broke off as they chatted.

'How will Joe react when he sees what we've done?' asked Ellen.

'He'll be delighted. Wouldn't anyone be thrilled in his situation? We'll have done something that Joe isn't able to do. It will be a huge load off his mind,' said Alice. 'He'll feel so guilty, being forced to take a complete rest.'

'When will you let him see it?'

'As soon as he's fit enough to leave hospital.'

'But he won't be moving in here, will he? He'll be staying at our house first. Don't you want to save the surprise until after the wedding?'

'I could do that, I suppose,' said Alice, considering the idea. 'In some ways, I suppose it will be even more of a surprise. On the other hand,' she added, 'it would mean that – on the big day itself – we'd leave for church from the same house. That doesn't seem proper, Mummy.'

'It isn't, I agree – but it's a lot better than setting off for his wedding from Dennis's house.'

Alice groaned. 'Joe would hate that.'

'How did Dennis react when Joe first told him you were going to get married?'

'I think he was pleased that his brother was settling down at last. The trouble was that Dennis assumed that he'd be the best man. They had a big argument about it.'

'Thank goodness Joe picked someone else,' said Ellen. 'No disrespect to Dennis but . . . well, can you imagine him making a speech that makes everyone laugh?'

'He's not that bad, Mummy. Dennis is just old-fashioned, that's all. When we got engaged, he and his wife gave us a lovely present. And I'm very fond of Lena. She's sweet. Joe says that his brother doesn't deserve her.'

Ellen stood back from the wall. 'What's the decision, Alice?'

'Decision?'

'Does Joe get to see the house before or after the wedding?'

'Before,' said Alice, firmly. 'It's cruel to make him wait. Besides, it isn't all our doing. Joe did a lot of work here on his own before we stepped in. He painted all the ceilings, for instance. That's a job I could never do.' She turned to her mother. 'The moment they let him out of hospital, I want to bring him straight here.'

Unaware that he was being discussed by the two women, Joe Keedy was watching Maisie Bell as she went through her routine before coming to the end of her shift. She was careful and methodical, checking that everything was in the right place for the nurse who replaced her. Absorbed in her work, she was unaware that she was being watched, or that she had stirred fond memories in her patient. Keedy was thinking of times they'd spent together and of how close they'd eventually become. There had been a moment, albeit brief, when he had considered proposing to Maisie, but she put her career first and secured a promotion that pushed them apart. Keedy had met her again with the tables turned. Instead of making all the decisions, he now had to do what Maisie told him. The strange thing was that he was getting used to it.

Eamonn Corrigan walked around the perimeter of Mile End Military Hospital before pausing at a gate at the rear of the building. As he peered through the bars, he saw armed soldiers on guard. Getting past them would be difficult. Inside the hospital was a detective he had tried to kill, a man who would recover in due course and want his revenge. Keedy had a reputation. Along with Marmion, his pursuit of killers was relentless. Corrigan was a marked man. Unless Keedy was put out of action for good, he would be on the Irishman's tail for ever.

But there was a risk involved. Getting in and out of the hospital safely was difficult. Even for someone as resourceful as Corrigan, it was a daunting task. He swung round, intending to walk away but found himself facing two armed soldiers. They eyed him suspiciously.

'What are you doing?' demanded one of them.

'I was hoping to visit a friend,' said Corrigan.

'Then why didn't you come to the front gate? This one is kept locked.'

'What's the name of your friend?' asked the other soldier.

'Joe Keedy,' said Corrigan. 'He's the detective sergeant who was shot during a siege. I used to know Joe when I was in the police myself. We were pals.'

'If you're that keen to see him,' said the second soldier, 'why didn't you check the visiting times first? And how do you know they'll let you in? If he was seriously wounded, they'll restrict visiting to family.'

'I never thought about that,' sighed Corrigan. 'Thanks for the warning.'

'You're wasting your time.'

'It looks as if I am. What a pity! I was hoping to cheer him up.'

'What's your name?' asked the first soldier.

'Ronnie Morgan,' said Corrigan. 'Is there any way I can get a message to Joe?'

'Do you have any form of identification on you?'

'Yes, yes, of course. I'll show you.' Taking out a wallet, Corrigan flipped it open to show them a licence with the name of Ronald Morgan on it. 'Satisfied?'

The first soldier nodded. 'You'd best be on your way, sir,' he said. 'My advice is to wait a week or so before trying to visit your friend. He may be well enough to see people outside the family by then.'

'You're right. I'll give it ten days.'

There was an exchange of farewells, then the soldiers parted to let him go on his way.

'What do you think?' asked the first soldier.

'Seemed genuine to me,' replied the other. 'He's just not very bright.'

'There was something odd about him. Can't put my finger on it but . . . I'm not happy. Might be worth checking if he really is a friend of Detective Sergeant Keedy.'

'Good idea,' agreed his companion. 'It'll put our minds at rest.'

Beatrice Naylor worked her way through the piles of theatrical magazines whenever she had a spare moment. She was reminded time and again how cruel a profession acting was. It was brutally hard, endlessly competitive and a test of physical endurance. Talent was not enough. Luck and good contacts were essential. The more careers that flashed before her eyes, the more lives she saw that had been doomed by failure. Only a small number of actresses were able to end their lives in honourable retirement, still revered by their admirers. The person she sought was not among them. The actress wanted by the police was a woman – perhaps soured by the failure of her career – who was using the talents she possessed for the purpose of crime. Beatrice felt that it was a betrayal.

Having started with one suspect, she now had almost a dozen, actresses she had seen in their prime on the boards and who had now faded from sight. Were they dead, declining, struggling through life on a walking stick? Which of them would sink to the level of burglary? Each of the people she had selected posed individual problems. Miranda Darnell was a prime suspect, an amazingly versatile actress who had once been a favourite on the West End theatrical scene. She had also become the mistress of a man who owned three London theatres. When she fell out with him, he banished her to the provinces where she dwindled into anonymity. For financial security, she married a much older man. There was certainly enough passion in Miranda

Darnell to drive her to perform somewhere, if only in front of a small audience. The more she learnt about the woman, the more Beatrice became convinced that she might have chanced upon the burglars' assistant.

Flipping over a page, she saw a photograph of her that had been taken almost thirty years earlier. Miranda Darnell was starring in the West End at the time. When Beatrice realised which role she was playing, she felt certain that she had identified the woman being sought by the police. Reaching for the telephone, she dialled a number and waited. When the receiver was picked up, she gave a number and was put through. A man's voice came on the line.

'Detective Sergeant Burge here . . .'

'Hello,' she said, breathlessly. 'This is Bea Naylor from Pegasus Costumes . . .'

'It's good to hear from you, Miss Naylor. How are you getting on?'

'I may have some good news for you.'

'What is it?'

There was a note of triumph in her voice. 'I think I've found her!'

CHAPTER FOURTEEN

After their encounter with a stranger at the rear gate of the hospital, the two soldiers reported the incident to a lieutenant. The officer's face clouded immediately. He glared at them.

'And you let this man go?' he asked, incredulously.

'We thought he was harmless,' replied one of the soldiers. 'He was polite and friendly and seemed to be telling the truth. Also, he showed us proof of his identity.'

'His name was Ronald Morgan,' added the other soldier.

'I beg leave to doubt it,' said the lieutenant, crisply. 'Didn't you think to ask him why he was loitering at the rear gate?'

'Yes, sir, of course,' said first soldier. 'The man told us he was looking for a way in. To be honest, I thought he was lurking there to watch the nurses going to and fro. They're very pretty. We've caught men doing that before. We tell them they should be ashamed of themselves and send them off with their tails between their legs.'

'Not only their tails,' added the other soldier. 'I hate perverts.'

'Let me get this straight,' said the officer, eyes flashing. 'You caught a man trespassing on hospital grounds and you let him go?'

'He seemed genuine, sir. He wanted to visit a friend by the name of . . .'

'Detective Sergeant Keedy,' said his companion.

'Didn't that name give the game away?' yelled the lieutenant.

'No, sir, it didn't.'

'Well, it should have. Don't you read the newspapers?'

'Well, I read the bits that interest me, sir.'

'That obviously excludes the front pages then, because Detective Sergeant Keedy was mentioned on them two days running. He was shot during a siege in Limehouse. It was only because he was rushed here that his life was saved.'

'I vaguely remember the name now, sir.'

'What use is that?' said the lieutenant, sarcastically. 'Detective Sergeant Keedy is under our protection. Don't you understand that?'

'Well, yes, sir . . .'

'If that man was a legitimate visitor with a good reason to visit Keedy, why was he looking for a way to climb into the hospital and miss the sentries at the main gate?'

'We don't know that he was going to climb in, sir.'

'He seemed quite harmless,' added the other soldier. 'He was no trouble, honestly.'

'That's more than I can say for you two,' rasped the officer. 'Trust nobody – that's the rule. You may not read the newspapers properly, but I bet Ronald Morgan did. He found out where Detective Sergeant Keedy was being held – and he came here on the prowl.'

'I'm sorry, sir.'

'We both are,' admitted the other soldier.

The lieutenant was fuming. 'You'll be even sorrier if that man turns out to have had designs on Keedy. What else would bring him here? Right,' he snapped. 'Get back on duty. And try to do it properly this time.'

After trading a rueful glance with each other, the soldiers slunk away.

Clifford Burge was so anxious to get to the premises of Pegasus Costumes that he kept urging his driver to go faster. The police car eventually squealed to a halt at the entrance to the mews. Burge leapt out and ran to the building he wanted. When he went in, however, Beatrice Naylor was busy with a customer, discussing the cost of some costumes the man wished to hire. There was a long, irritating wait for him to depart. It tested Burge's patience to the limit. The man eventually paid the money and left the building. Burge moved in at once, waving away Beatrice's profuse apologies and asking what the woman had discovered.

'Here she is,' said Beatrice, putting the magazine on the table with a theatrical flourish. 'It's the actress I may have mentioned before – Miranda Darnell. That's her stage name, anyway.'

Burge was mystified. 'But this woman is relatively young,' he complained.

'You're looking at a magazine printed in 1880.'

'Ah, I see.'

'Add thirty years or so and that would put her in her seventies now.'

'What do you know about her?'

'I know that she had a successful career in her younger days. Her gift was for comedy. I remember seeing her in one of Shaw's plays. She had the audience in hysterics. She was still going strong until seven or eight years ago,' explained Beatrice, 'then she was taken ill and forced to retire. I remember the tributes paid to her.'

'She's been in retirement, then?'

'I believe so. Miranda just faded away.'

'What makes you think that she may have turned to crime?'

'It was a memory that popped into my mind,' said Beatrice. 'I saw her onstage at The Haymarket in a dramatised version of *Pride and Prejudice*. It was brilliant.'

'But how does that connect her with the burglaries we're trying to solve?'

'She gave a quite stunning performance as the mother.'

'That may well be, Miss Naylor, but my sole interest is in finding someone who deceived eight jewellers in a row.'

'I believe that her name is Miranda Darnell.'

'What evidence have you found?'

'It's just a feeling I have in the pit of my stomach. When I saw her in *Pride and Prejudice*, she was brilliant as Mrs Bennet.'

'Bennet?' echoed Burge. 'But that's the name the burglars' accomplice used in a jewellery shop in Shadwell.'

'It may not be a coincidence.'

Burge stared at the photograph for a few moments and tried to imagine how the actress would look now. What began as a distant hope swiftly became something nearer to certainty. A slow smile spread across his face.

Joe Keedy was chatting to his nurse when he had an unexpected visitor. The door of his room opened, and Lieutenant Avenell was led in by the matron. After introducing the visitor, the matron went out with Nurse Donaldson, leaving the two men alone together.

'I'm sorry to disturb you, Sergeant Keedy,' said Avenell, 'but it's important that I speak to you in private.'

Keedy shrugged. 'Do I have any choice, Lieutenant . . . ?'

'The name is Avenell. I'm involved with maintaining security here. This hospital is filled with men who have fought bravely for their country. They need safeguarding – as do you.'

'I'm in no danger.'

'I believe that you are, sir. Allow me to explain.'

Lieutenant Avenell was a tall, lean man in his thirties with a straight back and a clipped delivery. He told Keedy what had brought him there and passed on the description of the man known as Ronald Morgan.

'I may be completely wrong, of course,' said Avenell, 'but I felt that you should be alerted.'

'I'm very grateful to you, Lieutenant,' said Keedy.

'Having heard what happened, I'd say that you drew the right conclusion. It seems that I could be in danger, after all. Unfortunately, I'm a sitting duck.'

'There'll be an armed soldier on duty outside this room at all times.'

'That's a relief. Any chance of getting me a gun as well?'

'Leave the security to us, sir,' said Avenell. 'What I came to ask was if you could put a name to the person who was caught by the rear gate.'

'Yes, I can. It's certainly not Ronald Morgan.'

'Then who is it?'

'It's a man by the name of Eamonn Corrigan. Your description of him was very good. I've seen a photograph of him. It was loaned to us by Special Branch. Corrigan has been active with Irish extremists.'

'Is there any reason why this man would wish to kill you, sir?'

'I can think of two reasons, Lieutenant. The first is that he wanted to do the job properly this time. During a siege in Limehouse, we battered down the front door. I was the first person into the house and Corrigan was waiting for me. He shot me in the stomach. Before I passed out,' said Keedy, 'I had a good look at his face and realised that we'd met before.' He took a deep breath. 'That brings me to the second reason why he'd wish to kill me . . .'

Marmion listened carefully to Burge's excitable account of his visit to Pegasus Costumes. When it came to an end, however, his face still had its serious expression. Burge was disappointed.

'I thought you'd be pleased,' he said.

'I am pleased, Cliff, and I'm very grateful to Miss Naylor. She sounds as if she's something of a detective herself. But there are too many unanswered questions.'

'Such as?'

'Is this woman, Miranda Darnell, still alive?'

'Yes, she's living in retirement under her real name of Jean Deale. Miss Naylor checked.'

'Did she tell you how old Jean Deale was?'

'She reckoned that the woman must be in her mid-seventies. That play in which she was Mrs Bennet ran for the best part of a year. She won awards for her performance. You can see why she was attached to the name of Bennet. She used it when she went to Mr Quentin's shop in Shadwell.'

'That's true,' conceded Marmion. 'What I don't hear about this woman is any connection with Ireland.'

'It's there,' insisted Burge. 'It must be.'

'Find it for me, Cliff. This woman is a credible suspect. I accept that, and I hope that she really is part of the gang. But I need more detail. Please thank Miss Naylor on my behalf, then ask her what she knows of Miranda Darnell's private life.'

'She really enjoyed doing the research for us, sir.'

'Then we must ask her to do a spot more,' said Marmion. 'The most important thing we need is this woman's address.'

Alone in her flat, she stood in front of the mirror and declaimed passages from Shakespeare as if she were onstage in front of a large audience. At the end of her performance, she gave an exaggerated curtsey, then retreated to her armchair and flopped into it. A full hour of ransacking her memory for quotations had tired her. She needed her rest. Her breathing was laboured, and her legs ached, but she was nevertheless thrilled by how much she had remembered. It was a tribute to her habit of regular sessions with the Bard of Avon.

As soon as she had recovered, she turned to a more serious task. Moving to the table, she picked up the letter she had received that morning. It was written in a code that would defeat most people. Having mastered the code years earlier, she sat down to write a reply. Though tempted to mention Corrigan's misbehaviour, she decided against doing so, feeling that it was better to keep it as a threat. He had been brought to heel and reminded that she gave the orders. Corrigan would never make the same mistake again.

When she arrived outside Keedy's room at the hospital, Alice was surprised and upset to see an armed soldier standing outside the door. He challenged her and demanded to know why she was there. When Alice explained who she was, the soldier nodded and stepped back.

'What are you doing here?' she asked.

'I'm obeying orders, Miss Marmion.'

'Are you going to stand there while I try to talk to Joe . . . to Sergeant Keedy?'

'I'll move if that's what you prefer,' he said, taking another couple of steps.

'Thank you.' Alice turned to the window and gave Keedy a gesture of despair.

He responded by trying to reassure her, but she was too

unnerved by the presence of the soldier. It was impossible to have a private conversation – albeit in silence – with the man only yards away. She resorted to her notebook, ready to hold up a series of questions she had written with the crayon. HOW ARE YOU? was the first one. Out of the corner of her eye, she saw the soldier snigger.

'Can't you go away?' she asked, rounding on him.

'I'm sorry, Miss Marmion. I need to stay. I'm afraid you'll have to get used to it.'

When she looked at Keedy, he was mouthing apologies to her. Alice felt cheated. Her plans for their conversation had suddenly gone awry. She had to hold back tears of disappointment.

Before he could contact Pegasus Costumes, Clifford Burge was pounced on by Claude Chatfield. The superintendent demanded to know where he had been and what he had discovered. Burge managed to convince him that progress of sorts had been achieved, but that much more needed to be done. Once he had escaped from Chatfield, he rushed to a telephone. He rang Beatrice Naylor's number and managed to catch her as she was about to leave the building and lock up for the night.

'I was hoping that you would still be there,' he said.

'This is quite early for me, Sergeant Burge,' she said. 'I often stay here until eight or nine. There's so much to do.'

'I just wondered if you'd found out anything else about that actress you mentioned.'

'Yes, I have, as it happens. I found a review of the

production of *Pride and Prejudice* in an old copy of *The Stage*. That's a weekly publication that's become the voice of British theatre. Hold on a moment and I'll get it.' The line went silent for the best part of thirty seconds, then she was back. 'Here it is,' she said, before clearing her throat. 'Everyone knows that the major protagonists in Jane Austen's most famous novel are Elizabeth Bennet and Mr Darcy. That was not the case in last night's performance. It was dominated by Elizabeth's mother, the redoubtable Mrs Bennet. Miranda Darnell gave such a brilliant portrayal of the character that she stole the show.' I agree wholeheartedly,' said Beatrice. 'In those days, Miranda was a gifted actress. Now, I'm afraid, she's just a poor, old woman, ignored by the profession she served so well.'

'She may also be a poor, old woman who drifted into crime,' he reminded her.

'That's true. You'll have to forgive me for being sentimental about her. If she really is the person whom you're after, I'll be shocked and disappointed. But I hope you catch her soon.'

'You may be able to help me to do that, Miss Naylor. We can try to track her down but you're likely to find her more quickly than we can because you know the world that she moved in.'

'I'll give you all the help I can, Sergeant Burge,' she said, 'but it may take time. London is a very large city with plenty of hiding places. It won't be easy to find the one that Miranda is in.' She clicked her tongue. 'What a shame! She made the part of Mrs Bennet her own. The only place she can play it now is in the shop of a gullible jeweller in Shadwell.'

* * *

It was excruciating. Trying to hold a silent conversation with Keedy through a window was impossible with an armed soldier standing nearby. There was no privacy. Alice felt that she was under suspicion, and she could see how distressed Keedy was by the situation. When the bell rang to end the visit, all that she could do was to blow him a farewell kiss. He responded with a smile of apology and a roll of his eyes.

Other visitors drifted past, and Alice joined the general exodus. As she descended the stairs, she wished that she had never even come to the hospital that evening. It had been more than a waste of time. It had been an ordeal. Seeing Keedy in a hospital bed was bad enough in itself. She had also endured the additional anxiety of a stranger watching everything that she tried to signal through the window of the room.

Tempted to slip into a toilet so that she could cry unseen, she decided that she must not give in to weakness. She had, after all, seen the man she loved, and he had looked slightly better. It was a crumb of comfort to hold on to on the long journey home. When she reached the bottom of the stairs, Alice was lost in thought. She was therefore startled when a man suddenly put his arms around her. Jerked out of her reverie, she realised that it was her father.

'Daddy!' she cried, eyes, moistening. 'I've had the most terrible visit.'

'I know,' said Marmion. 'As soon as I heard about it, I rang home but you'd already left. I'm so sorry I couldn't warn you. It must have been a nasty shock.'

'The worst thing is that I still have no idea what's going on.'

'Let's step in here and I'll explain.'

Detaching her from the crowd, Marmion took her into the empty waiting room and made her sit down. He took the chair beside her.

'I was contacted earlier,' he said, 'by a Lieutenant Avenell, who is involved with security here. Two of his men were patrolling the area when they found someone at the rear of the hospital. They were suspicious of him at first, but he had a reasonable explanation – or so they thought. They let him go but had the sense to report the incident to the lieutenant. To use his own phrase, he hit the roof and yelled at his men.'

'Who was this person they found?' she asked.

'It was Eamonn Corrigan, the man who shot Joe.'

Alice was shocked. 'What was he doing here?'

'My guess is that he was trying to get to Joe. He claimed that he was a friend of his. Luckily, the lieutenant had more sense than his men. He had an armed guard stationed outside Joe's room immediately. When he passed on the description of the man near the rear gate, Joe was certain that it was Corrigan. It must have scared him, Alice. He's so vulnerable in that hospital bed.'

'Thank goodness Joe had someone guarding him!'

'Lieutenant Avenell told me that he'd circulated a description of Corrigan to all his men. If he so much as puts his nose in here, he'll be arrested.'

'That's very reassuring, Daddy.'

'I'm coming off duty now,' he said, 'but I'd like a word with Joe before I leave.'

'Can you take me with you?' she pleaded.

'No, I'm afraid that I can't. You wait here until I've finished, then a police car will take both of us home. How does that sound?'

She smiled. 'It's a huge relief!'

Ellen Marmion was seated in the living room, trying to concentrate on the book she was reading. It was a novel about a young woman whose husband had gone to France with his regiment. A telegram had informed her that he was missing, presumed dead. She was devastated and grieved for over a year. The woman then found solace in the company of the organist at the church where she worshipped. Ten years older than her, he worked in a protected profession so did not have to join the army. Slowly, they were drawn together, and a romance developed.

Ellen had just reached the point where the missing husband was found alive when the telephone rang. Putting the book aside, she ran into the hallway to pick up the receiver, hoping that it would be Marmion. Instead, however, it was Keedy's brother.

'Good evening, Mrs Marmion. It's Dennis Keedy here.'

'I recognised your voice at once,' she said.

'Is your husband there, by any chance?'

'No, he isn't, I'm afraid. When he's in the middle of a murder investigation, he works very long hours. Did you want to speak to him in particular?'

'You'll do just as well,' he said, airily. 'I simply wanted to tell you that everything is in hand. We've got the spare bedroom ready for Joe when he's fit enough to be sent home.

Our parents are going to organise a welcome party for him.'

'But he'd prefer to come here,' she argued.

'That's out of the question, Mrs Marmion. It would be quite improper for my brother to be living under the same roof as the woman he is due to marry. That would be verging on scandal.'

'Alice doesn't live here. She has a flat much nearer the centre of the city.'

'That's immaterial. Besides, Nottingham is his true home.'

'Joe decided to leave the area,' she reminded him. 'London is his home now. He feels much happier here. Well,' she added, 'he did until the incident at the siege.'

'My brother needs to get well away from London and all its associations. Apart from anything else, he's in danger there.'

Ellen was shaken. 'What do you mean?'

'I'm in constant contact with the hospital,' he said, crisply. 'When I rang them earlier this evening, they told me that an armed guard is now standing outside his room. Joe is under threat, Mrs Marmion. He needs a place of safety.'

'Why?'

'Your husband will explain. And the two of you will surely realise that it's in my brother's interests to be well away from danger. That means he must be here in the bosom of his family.'

'I'm sorry,' said Ellen, 'but I don't agree.'

'The decision has been made, Mrs Marmion, and the family's wishes come first.'

'Joe simply won't accept that,' she insisted.

'He'll do whatever I tell him to do,' he said, confidently.

'I know my brother, believe me. Anyway, there's no point in discussing it any further. Give my regards to your husband. Goodbye . . .'

The telephone call was over. Ellen was left quivering with fury. She went back into the living room and picked up the book again, but she could simply not concentrate on the story. Setting the novel aside, she went off to make a pot of tea but was stopped by the sound of a car pulling up outside. She opened the front door and was relieved to see both Alice and her husband getting out of the vehicle. Ellen rushed out to greet each one of them with a hug.

'What's going on?' she asked.

'Let's go inside,' said Marmion, 'and I'll explain.'

The three of them were soon sitting down in the living room. Alice was on the sofa beside her mother. Marmion took the chair opposite them. He told his wife about the incident at the hospital and why Keedy was now under armed guard.

'When I first heard that,' Ellen told them, 'I was shocked.'

'How could you possibly know about it?' asked Alice.

'Joe's brother rang. He'd been in touch with the hospital.'

She went on to describe the telephone call with Dennis Keedy, admitting that it had left her feeling both angry and upset. Her opinion had been dismissed with contempt.

'I'll speak to him myself,' said Marmion, annoyed at the way his wife had been treated, 'and I won't mince my words. Dennis is far too high-handed. I know for certain that Joe would much rather be with this family than with his own.'

'I felt so helpless, talking to Dennis,' admitted Ellen. 'Not that I had much chance to speak. He just told me what had been decided and that we had to accept it.'

Alice clenched her fists. 'A family row is the last thing we need at a time like this.'

'I wouldn't like Dennis as a brother-in-law,' said her mother, 'I know that. I was very lucky in that respect. Your Uncle Raymond is a wonderful brother-in-law, Alice. He'd never speak to me the way that Dennis Keedy did.'

'Well, Dennis won't do it again,' promised Marmion, getting up. 'I'll ring him this minute.'

He went into the hallway and shut the door behind him. Alice turned to her mother.

'It's not often that Daddy gets this angry,' she said. 'I almost feel sorry for Dennis.'

Ellen was terse. 'Well, I don't. He deserves it.'

CHAPTER FIFTEEN

When she arrived at the café in Frith Street that morning, there was no sign of her friend. Their usual table was occupied by a couple of middle-aged women, conversing in low voices. For a moment, she feared that Giles Underhill was not coming, and she felt a pang of disappointment. Then she heard the rustle of a newspaper from a table in the corner and turned to see him looking at her over the copy of *The Times* that he'd just lowered. Underhill leapt to his feet at once and held the chair back for her. She sat down gratefully.

'I was afraid that you hadn't come,' she confessed.

'Nothing would keep me away,' he replied. 'I regard these occasional meetings of ours as sacred. I would never dare to let you down or forego the pleasure of seeing you.' After sitting down, he folded the newspaper. 'Have you had time to catch up with today's news?'

'No, I haven't.'

'I'm fascinated about this case involving a siege in Limehouse. Three burglars were trapped inside. The police had the place surrounded, yet somehow – when the house had been deliberately set alight – the three men escaped. How on earth did they do that?'

'I've no idea, Giles,' she said, dismissively. 'To be honest, I have little interest in reports of crime. They trouble me. I like to think that – apart from these beastly air raids, of course – we live in a city where danger is limited and where crime, for the most part, is largely under control. We have the Metropolitan Police Force to thank for that.'

'I couldn't agree more. Ah,' he said as the waitress approached with two cups of coffee on a tray. 'Here's our morning treat.' He put the newspaper aside. 'Let's forget all about burglars and turn to a more uplifting subject.' He waited until the coffee cups had been put on the table and the waitress had moved away. 'I've got some wonderful news to impart.'

'Do tell me what it is,' she said, excitedly. 'I need something to lift my spirits.'

'I've been offered a part in a new production of a play by Shaw.'

'Congratulations!' she said. 'I'll make a point of coming to see it.'

'I'll get you a ticket,' he told her. 'Then afterwards, I'll introduce you to the cast and the director. I'll have told them in advance what a seasoned professional you are.'

'No, no, please don't do that. My acting days are over. I'd feel out of place. What I'd value is an opportunity to speak to you after the performance so that I can shower you with praise.'

'I don't want praise – I want honesty. You're experienced enough to spot any mistakes that I make. I'm trusting you to point them out. I value your judgement.'

'That's very flattering,' she said. 'Which of Shaw's plays is it? *Misalliance.*'

'What role have you been offered?'

'I will play Lord Summerhays – not a large part but a telling one.'

She reached out to squeeze his arm. 'I couldn't be more delighted for you, Giles,' she said. 'The news has given me so much pleasure.'

Her broad smile concealed the awful realisation that she might soon lose him. Once he was in rehearsal with the company, he would be making new friends and having new commitments. There would be little room in his life for a morning cup of coffee and a long talk with her about their respective triumphs onstage. She was no longer an actress in demand whereas his career had just been revived. They would live in separate worlds from now on. Their friendship would be a misalliance.

'What are we going to talk about today?' he asked.

'We already have our subject – this wonderful news of yours!'

'I'd prefer you to have the limelight for a while. Tell me about your first appearance onstage with Ellen Terry. What an experience it must have been!'

'It was,' she said, basking in the memory. 'I felt invisible beside her, but she helped me so much and gave me some wonderful advice about acting.'

'Tell me what it was,' he said, eyes gleaming. 'Now that I've been given work at long last, I need any advice I can get . . .'

When the superintendent descended on Marmion in his office, it was usually to criticise the slowness of an investigation. That morning, however, he was in a more emollient mood.

'Thank you for that update you sent me,' said Chatfield, briskly. 'I applaud your deployment of officers.'

'It's kind of you to say so, sir.'

'There is one exception, of course – Detective Sergeant Burge.'

'He still has my full support, sir. With the help of someone well versed in theatre, he is on the trail of the woman involved in those burglaries.'

'Consorting with criminals is bad enough,' said Chatfield, 'but this woman is doing something far worse. She's doing it in the name of Irish nationalism.'

'Miranda Darnell was a leading actress in her day and that worried me at first. I felt that someone so well known would surely be recognised in a jewellery shop. It was Burge who pointed out that the premises burgled were in the poorer parts of London. The sort of people who live there are unlikely to be keen theatregoers. This woman would pass unnoticed.'

'I'm not persuaded by that argument.'

'Is that because it was put forward by Burge?'

'No, of course it isn't!' said Chatfield, irritably.

'How would you have reacted if I had been the person to make the same point?'

'I'd still be reluctant to accept it.'

'What if you are proved wrong, sir?'

'Then I'll be happy to lead the applause for Detective Sergeant Burge.'

'Don't expect to do so very soon,' warned Marmion. 'We still have a long way to go – in this country and in Ireland itself, probably.'

'Quite so.' Chatfield heaved a sigh. 'I must say that I was dismayed to hear that one of the burglars was caught lurking outside the hospital.'

'He was seen but not caught, sir. Lieutenant Avenell was very angry about that. When he realised that his men had let a suspect walk away, he decided to assign an armed guard to Sergeant Keedy.'

'Are you certain that this man was Eamonn Corrigan?'

'Joe Keedy recognised him from the description,' said Marmion. 'I'd already shown him a photograph of Corrigan that was in the file given to us by Special Branch.'

'That should never have left this building,' snapped Chatfield. 'You disobeyed me. You took classified information out of here.'

'I felt justified in doing so, sir – it gave us the name of the burglar who killed one man and wounded the sergeant.'

'How is Keedy, by the way?'

'He's chafing at the bit to return to duty.'

'No chance of that for some time,' said Chatfield. 'He must be patient.'

'Patience is not one of his attributes, sir.'

'You don't need to tell me that.'

'Whereas Burge has patience in abundance,' said Marmion, seeing an opportunity to speak up for him. 'He's also prepared to work around the clock on this case.'

'That's to his credit,' said Chatfield, before lowering his voice. 'Your daughter must be very distressed by the turn of events.'

'Alice is bearing up, sir. She knows that the worst is over. What worries her most is the armed guard outside Sergeant Keedy's room.'

'I would have thought that might reassure her.'

'Put yourself in her position,' suggested Marmion. 'Don't you remember a time before you were married when you and the future Mrs Chatfield wished to be alone together?'

'Yes, of course I do.'

'How would you have liked a third person to be present – a third person with a rifle?'

Chatfield glowered. 'I wouldn't have liked it at all.'

'That's the unfortunate position my daughter is in.'

'Then she has my profound sympathy. When you are young and getting to know someone very dear to you, privacy is essential.'

'Alice has none whatsoever.'

'That's a shame.'

'However,' added Marmion, 'the situation may well change. When she gets to the hospital this morning, she may be in for a surprise.'

For the first time since she had started visiting the hospital, Alice Marmion was not looking forward to it with any pleasure. Having a third person involved in her conversation with Keedy had blighted it. More to the point, it was a constant reminder that Keedy was still in danger, a target for a desperate criminal. Instead of being allowed to recover from his injuries, he was being stalked. When she got to the hospital, there was another cause for alarm. Arriving outside Keedy's room, she saw that the blind had been drawn down. She turned anxiously to the soldier on duty.

'Why can't I see through the window?' she asked.

'It's not for me to say,' he replied.

'Has something happened?'

'I've been told to take you to someone who will explain.'

Fearing the worst, Alice fell in beside him and walked down a long corridor. When they turned a corner, the soldier stopped outside an office and knocked on the door. It was opened by Hector Garland, the surgeon who had led the team operating on Keedy. He invited Alice into the room and closed the door. His face was expressionless. Her heart began to pound.

'Is Joe still alive?' she gasped.

'Why don't you sit down, Miss Marmion?' he suggested, indicating a chair. Alice obeyed but she remained tense. 'In answer to your question, Mr Keedy is still very much alive.' A surge of relief coursed through her. 'I spoke to your father yesterday. He pointed out that you are the best possible medicine I could prescribe for the patient. Mr Keedy counts the hours between your visits.'

'And so do I,' she confessed.

'The arrival of an armed guard must be a terrible imposition for you.'

'If it's necessary, we can put up with it.'

'You won't have to, Miss Marmion. Having examined the

patient today, I think that he has made sufficient progress for you to visit him in his room.' He saw the tears of joy in her eyes. 'I had a feeling that you'd be pleased by the news.'

'I'm thrilled,' she said.

'There is, however, a proviso. You mustn't expect any contact with him. You may sit beside the bed, but I don't want Mr Keedy to get unduly excited. Is that understood?'

'Yes, it is.'

'Then let's go and see him, shall we?'

She rose to her feet. 'Does Joe know I'll be in the room with him?'

'Yes, he does. He needed preparing. If you had walked in there without warning, it would have been something of a shock. Mr Keedy accepted the proviso I mentioned.'

'And so do I. Thank you very much,' she said.

'Don't thank me, Miss Marmion.'

'Why not?'

'I'm not the one who deserves gratitude,' he said.

'Then who is?'

'It's your father, Inspector Marmion. He realised how unsatisfactory your last visit had been when you had a soldier standing only feet away from you. This new arrangement will suit both you and, I suspect, Sergeant Keedy.' He opened the door. 'Let's go and see him, shall we?'

Alice stepped out into the corridor with alacrity.

During the ride back to her flat in a taxi, she reflected on the change in her situation. Until that morning, they had been equals, two talented actors exiled from the theatre they had served so well and for so long. At a stroke, there'd been a radical alteration. Giles had been plucked from the grave to live again in front of an audience. The effect on him had been visible. He had seemed years younger and filled with a new zeal. His good fortune had served to highlight her continuing obscurity. Yet she did not dwell on it. If anything, she was glad for him. She was realistic enough to accept that a parting would have had to come at some point. They might have similar histories, but their current lives and objectives were very different. In a month or so, when rehearsals began, they would move inexorably apart.

On reflection, it was not a cause for despair. When she considered the irony of it all, she burst into muffled laughter. The person who was ending their friendship was the celebrated playwright, Bernard Shaw. An Irishman.

Having waited so long to hear each other's voices, Alice and Keedy spent most of the time simply staring lovingly at each other in silence. Neither of them was aware of the presence of Maisie Bell, flitting around. All that concerned them was establishing proper contact at last.

'It was your father's idea,' he said.

'Then he was very naughty.'

'Why? Didn't you want to get close to me?'

'Of course, I did, Joe, but I'd like to have been warned about it beforehand. Daddy didn't say a single word to me. If I'd known that I could see you properly for once, I'd have run all the way here. Instead of that, I sat on three buses in succession, bracing myself for another experience like the one we had yesterday evening. That guard ruined my visit.'

'He was performing an important job, Alice – protecting me.'

'You're not in any danger now, are you?'

'Yes, I am,' he whispered. 'I'm in danger of giving into the urge to struggle out of bed to kiss you at last.' She laughed. 'Oh, it's such a tonic to see you.'

'Being so close means everything to me, Joe.' She looked up as she heard the door open and saw the nurse leaving the room. 'Is she looking after you properly?'

'Yes, and so are the other nurses assigned to me. I'm being spoilt.'

'Don't get to rely on it,' she said. 'I won't spoil you. I can tell you that.'

'What will you do?' he teased.

Alice grinned. 'Wait and see.'

Forgetting her promise, she reached out to grasp his hand.

Clifford Burge was relying heavily on Beatrice Naylor. When he called on her again, his hopes were high. Beatrice was seated behind the desk, but she leapt to her feet when she saw her visitor. She reached forward to touch the bell on her desk. Within seconds, her assistant, Eve, came into the foyer.

'Take over here for a while,' said Beatrice. 'I need to speak to Sergeant Burge.'

Eve was a slim, dark-haired woman in her twenties, wearing a plain dress. Beside the more ostentatiously clad Beatrice, she was almost invisible. Eve regarded Burge with eyes widening.

'Are you really from Scotland Yard?' she asked.

'That's right,' he replied.

'Bea tells me she's going to solve a murder with you.'

'I certainly hope that she is.'

'Come this way,' said Beatrice, indicating a door.

She led Burge into the adjoining room and picked up a magazine. Taking it from her, Burge found himself looking at a large photograph of Miranda Darnell. She looked even more striking than in the earlier photograph he'd seen of her. He was impressed.

'She's beautiful!' he said, admiringly.

'That photograph was taken well over thirty years ago,' she explained. 'That's why the quality is not very good. She was playing Lady Macbeth at the time. She could handle tragedy superbly as well as comedy. She was a complete actress.'

'Have you any idea where she is now?'

'No, Sergeant Burge, I don't. But I've spread the word. It won't be long before we find her.'

'That's wonderful!'

'Searching for a missing person is like being involved in a treasure hunt, isn't it?'

'I wouldn't put it that way,' he said. 'We're after a cold-blooded criminal, not treasure.'

'Instinct tells me that Miranda could never be a criminal.'

'Nevertheless, we'd like to find her.'

'Of course,' she said. 'By the way, is there any news of Sergeant Keedy?'

'Yes, there is. Inspector Marmion saw him last night and said that he is looking much better. That was good to hear.'

'Yes, it is. If you get to speak to him yourself, please give

Sergeant Keedy my warmest regards. It was kind of him to remember me.'

'Thank goodness he did. You've saved us a great deal of time, Miss Naylor.'

'I won't give up until I find Miranda for you – Jean Deale, I should say.'

'What I really want to know is if she had any connection with Ireland.'

'She was born in Scotland. That's why she loved to play Lady Macbeth.'

'Oh, I see,' he sighed. 'What a pity!'

'But she did have links with Ireland,' said Beatrice. 'I remember reading her husband's obituary. He was much older than her and died some years ago. Jack Deale was born and brought up in Dublin. You can't be more Irish than that.'

When she got back to her flat, she removed her hat and coat before settling into her chair. A fire was burning in the grate and turning the whole of the living room into a gentle furnace. As she recalled her time with Giles Underhill, she thanked God for providing her with such a congenial friend, even if only for a limited period. He had been one of many blessings. Unlike most friends of her age, she had retained all her faculties. Sight and hearing were still serviceable, and her brain still functioned well. Trained carefully over the years, her voice was still crystal clear. She read voraciously and was able to converse on a wide range of subjects. Though her strength was limited, she could still walk without the aid of a stick or the arm of a companion. On reflection, she decided that she was a true survivor. It gave her a sense of achievement and enabled her to fight on for her cause.

When something was slipped under her door, it made an almost imperceptible sound, yet she heard it. She knew that the postman had been because she'd collected the morning's mail from the vestibule of the building. Someone had now delivered a message by hand. As soon as she saw the envelope, she knew that her visitor had been Eamonn Corrigan. She was relieved that he had behaved himself this time, not daring to disturb her in any way. Opening the envelope, she read the words scrawled on a piece of paper – GOING TO B. YOU KNOW WHERE.

She tossed the paper on to the fire and sat down with a smile of satisfaction.

Ellen was delighted to hear about her daughter's visit to the hospital. Like Alice, she was unaware that permission had been obtained for access to Keedy's room. It had made all the difference. Alice was both thrilled and reassured by her visit. When she got back home around noon, she was positively glowing.

'Why didn't Daddy tell me in advance?' she complained.

'That's a good question,' said Ellen. 'He didn't tell me either.'

'I daresay that he wanted it to be a surprise.'

'You should still have been warned, Alice. If you'd known what was in store for you, it would have made that horrible journey to the hospital far less of a trial.'

'That's true. Oh, it was such a treat,' she recalled. 'We were completely unaware of the guard outside the door. It was wonderful. I could hear Joe's voice and see that sparkle in his eyes again. By the way,' she went on, 'he sends his love.'

'That was kind of him.'

'He also sent you an apology.'

'Why on earth should he apologise to me?'

'I told him about that unpleasant phone call you had with his brother.'

Ellen laughed. 'I'd almost forgotten it,' she said. 'Besides, your father rang Dennis and put him in his place. We won't be bothered by him again.'

'That's a relief. Joe warned me that Dennis could be bossy.' She lowered her voice. 'Oh, and there was something else that Joe confided in me as well.'

'What was it?'

'Do you remember those fears I had when I heard that he'd been shot in the stomach?'

'Yes, I do,' said her mother. 'You were afraid that there might have been extensive damage and that it might mean you and Joe were . . . well, unable to have children.'

'I was wrong, Mummy.'

'Are you sure?'

'Joe made a point of asking Mr Garland, the surgeon. He was told that there was no reason why we shouldn't have a perfectly normal married life.'

'Oh, that's so heartening,' said Ellen, hugging her. 'I was terribly worried that I might not have grandchildren. Paul is obviously not going to produce any,' she added, sadly, 'so you were my last hope. This news has really cheered me up.'

'Joe and I are both thrilled – though we're not planning to have a family straight away.'

'Don't leave it too long, Alice.'

'Why not?'

'It's because I want to be a granny,' said Ellen, forcefully. 'And I want it to happen soon, not when I'm too old to pick my grandchildren up or play with them for hours on end. This war can't go on for ever. I'm giving you a warning, Alice.'

'What is it?'

'When peace finally comes, I want to enjoy it to the full as a grandmother.'

'You will, Mummy. That's a promise.'

'I'll hold you to that,' said Ellen.

When he got to the jewellery shop in Shadwell, he found that it was quite busy. Burge had to wait several minutes before the proprietor was free to talk to him. Quentin took him into the room at the rear of the shop.

'Have you made an arrest?' he asked, hopefully.

'Not yet,' said Burge, 'but we expect to do so soon. I just wanted to show you a photograph of our prime suspect. Before I do so, I must warn you that it was taken decades ago, but it's such a distinctive face that the lady can't have changed all that much.'

'What's her name?'

'Jean Deale – but her stage name was Miranda Darnell. She was a famous actress.'

'That name means nothing to me. We don't go to the theatre.'

'I want you to take a long, hard look at her,' said Burge, taking out the magazine he had borrowed from Beatrice Naylor.

'This is a photograph of Miss Darnell onstage in a Shakespeare play.'

He handed the magazine to Quentin and saw him blink in surprise.

'Well?' he asked.

'She's a very striking woman, Sergeant Burge.'

'Imagine what she would be like in her sixties or seventies. I daresay that she would have put on quite a bit of weight. Forget that costume she's wearing. Concentrate on her face.'

Quentin scrutinised the photograph for several minutes, trying to work out if there was any resemblance to the woman who had come into his shop, posing as a customer. It was as if he were examining a piece of jewellery before giving an estimate of its value.

'It could be her, I suppose,' he said at length, 'then again . . .'

'I'd like you to be certain,' said Burge. 'Think of her wearing the clothing she had on when she came in here. Allow for her face to be much older and lined by age. You were very close to her, after all, so you had a good look at her.' He tapped the photograph. 'Now, then, is this Miranda Darnell – or is it not?'

'Well . . .'

'Are you looking at the woman who called herself Mrs Bennet?'

'I certainly might be.'

'She must have had distinguishing features of some kind.'

'Yes, she did. That chin of hers, for instance – and those high cheekbones. This woman's face does look vaguely familiar.'

'I don't want you to be vague, Mr Quentin,' said Burge,

patiently. 'I need you to be convinced that she came into your shop recently.

There was a protracted pause while Quentin studied the photograph again.

'It's those eyes that I remember,' he said. 'They were so bright.'

'Are you convinced that you may have seen this woman before?'

'I might well have done, Sergeant.'

'That won't do, sir. I need certainty. Can you give it to me?'

'Yes,' decided the proprietor, nodding his head. 'That's her, I'm sure of it. That's the Mrs Bennet who came here with a string of pearls.'

Burge felt a sense of sheer joy coursing through his body.

CHAPTER SIXTEEN

Aston was a busy suburb of Birmingham, filled with shops, churches, civic buildings, factories, workshops, a railway station and a veritable rabbit warren of streets. The first thing that Eamonn Corrigan noticed when he arrived there was the looming presence of Ansell's Brewery, standing next to the HP Sauce factory. Both places emitted a pungent smell. He walked past them and turned right into Upper Thomas Street, making his way along the terrace until he came to a house where he knew he would get a warm welcome. Putting his suitcase down, Corrigan banged on the front door with his fist. A curtain twitched and someone peered out. Seconds later, the door was flung open by Pierce Orr, the youngest of the burglars, who threw his arms around his friend.

'Wonderful to see you!' he exclaimed.

'Is there always this stink around here?' asked Corrigan.

'Sure, you soon get used to it, Eamonn.'

'I won't.'

Picking up his suitcase, he followed Orr into the house. Corrigan got another warm embrace from Tom Regan, the other member of the gang. Both men told him how different he looked now that he'd shaved off his beard. Orr, a short, scrawny young man, was surprised to see him.

'We thought you'd stay put in London,' he said.

'I planned to do that, Pierce.'

'What changed your mind?'

'I read something in a newspaper.'

'What was it?' asked Regan.

'I'll show you.'

Thrusting a hand into the pocket of his overcoat, he brought out a newspaper and opened it up for them. He pointed to an item at the bottom of the front page.

'That's why I'm here,' he explained.

'It's a piece about you,' said Regan in alarm. 'The police even know your real name.'

'I was careless,' admitted Corrigan. 'I went to that hospital to find out if I could get in there to kill Keedy. Thanks to him, my nephew, Niall, once spent a long time in prison. I wanted to get even with Keedy. But I was spotted by some soldiers on guard.'

'It's not like you to be caught,' said Orr.

'I wasn't caught. I talked my way out of the situation and got away. Somebody must have worked out who I was and what I was doing there. That's how my name got in the paper and why I came here. Birmingham's safer.'

'It is if you keep your head down.'

'Yes,' added Regan. 'Pierce and I are of an age when we should, by right, be in the army. But nothing on earth would ever make us wear a British uniform. We keep to the house by day and go outside when it's dark. Most of the neighbours don't even realise anyone is here.'

'What about food and drink?'

'We have it delivered from a grocery shop not far away. The owner is Irish, so he asks no questions. He even gets hold of Irish whiskey for us.'

Corrigan grinned. 'It sounds as if I've come to the right place.'

'What about that Sergeant Keedy?' asked Orr. 'Are you going to forget about him?'

'Oh, no,' said Corrigan, darkly. 'I'll catch up with him one day, believe me. Only next time, I'll put the bullet in his brain and not in his belly.'

Joe Keedy had dozed off that afternoon. Lost in sleep, he was unaware that Maisie Bell was standing beside the bed and studying him closely, remembering the happy times they had spent together and regretting that they had had to end. Now that he was engaged to marry someone else, her affection for Keedy was tinged with bitterness. Why had he chosen Alice Marmion instead of her? What was so special about the woman? During moments of intimacy, Keedy had made all sorts of promises to her. How had he forgotten them so easily? Her new job might have parted them, but they had kept in touch by letter for months. Keedy had even come to see her in Manchester once when she moved to a hospital there. Had he lost all interest in her?

Without warning, his eyelids began to twitch, then he woke up abruptly. When he saw her bending over him, he grinned.

'I've just been dreaming about you, Maisie,' he said.

'Then you should be ashamed of yourself,' she teased. 'You're spoken for.'

'Thought is free.'

'Be honest, Joe. You haven't thought about me for years.'

'That's not true.'

'Then why didn't you keep in touch with me?'

'I was always too busy.'

'Too busy finding someone else.'

'It wasn't like that,' said Keedy. 'Since I became a detective sergeant, I've had to work even harder. I simply never have the luxury of free time.'

'You found time to get engaged to Alice.'

'That's different.'

'It won't work, Joe,' she warned. 'I can tell you that now. You're not the marrying type. You're too fond of having the freedom to do what you want.'

'I've changed, Maisie.'

'Then why are you dreaming about me?' she challenged.

He squirmed. 'Well . . .'

'You're still the same old Joe Keedy, aren't you?'

'Look,' he said, taking a deep breath, 'why don't we change the conversation?'

'You started it by telling me that you dreamt about me. Or was that a lie?'

'No, it wasn't. It was the truth.'

She laughed. 'Male patients often have silly dreams about their nurses.'

'But I'm not any old patient. We were very close. I can't forget that.'

'Then why do you want to change the conversation?'

He was angry. 'Stop goading me, will you?'

'You haven't told Alice about me, have you?' she said with a taunting smile. 'I don't think you'd dare to do that. What would happen if she knew the truth?'

Before he could reply, the door opened, and Nurse Donaldson entered the room to begin her shift on duty. Maisie moved off to talk to her. Keedy was sobered. The exchange with Maisie had radically altered his view of her. When he first discovered that she would be looking after him part of the time, he was delighted. That pleasure had now ebbed away. Maisie could, in fact, turn out to be a problem. There was an additional fear. Marmion had sensed that he'd seen the nurse before. If he remembered that the woman had once been Keedy's girlfriend, it could be embarrassing. The thought jolted him. Keedy began to hope that he could soon be transferred to another hospital a good distance away from the one where Maisie Bell worked.

After a whole afternoon working at the new house, Alice and Ellen took a breather and admired what they had done. The living room had changed completely. It was now a bright, comfortable space into which the newly married couple could move. With a fire in the grate, and with some paintings on the walls, it would be the ideal place to relax with Keedy.

'When will you have your house-warming party?' asked Ellen.

'Give us a chance, Mummy! We haven't even moved in yet.'

'It's something to bear in mind.'

'Then I'll add it to a long list of other things that need to be done,' said Alice, wearily. 'We certainly won't be having a party until Joe is fully recovered. He needs a lot of rest.'

'Do you think that being shot will change his mind about being a detective?'

'If I know him, it will do the opposite. Joe will be dying to get back to work. Besides, he's had injuries before. He always bounces back with increased determination.'

'Your father was the same,' confided Ellen. 'Early in his career, he was attacked one night by a gang of drunken thugs. I've never seen so many bruises. It took him almost a fortnight to recover. Once he was back in uniform, he and his friends tracked down every member of that gang. They ended up in prison.'

'Why has Daddy never mentioned it to me?'

'It was out of consideration for your feelings, Alice. He didn't want you to know just how dangerous his job can be.'

'I only have to look at Joe to realise that.'

Ellen smiled. 'Just suppose that he did decide to leave the Metropolitan Police Force.'

'That would never happen, Mummy.'

'Imagine if he did. What would he choose to do for a living?'

'He'd want a job that involved action,' said Alice. 'Joe would become a fireman or something like that. He'd love the sense of danger.'

'Becoming an undertaker would be a safer job.'

'That's the last thing he'd choose.'

'But he'd be carrying on a family tradition.'

'Joe prefers to leave that task to his brother. Dennis was born to do it. Don't forget that Joe did work for the family firm at one time. He hated it. No,' said Alice, confidently, 'Joe's got the job he always wanted. The moment he's fit enough, off he'll go. And I'll be waiting here in our own home to welcome him back at the end of the day.'

Marmion had been pleased with the news that Clifford Burge had brought back from Shadwell. If the owner of a jewellery shop there had identified the woman they were after, it would be a major advance in the investigation. The two men were in Marmion's office, and he was studying the photograph of Miranda Darnell.

'She looks so fierce,' he said. 'Fierce but beautiful.'

'In Shakespeare's play, I'm told, Lady Macbeth is very fierce. In fact, she's a stronger character than her husband. When I showed the photo to Mr Quentin, I told him to ignore the expression on her face and the costume she was wearing. I made him look for something about her that reminded him of the woman who came into his shop.'

'And he found it.'

'It took him a long time, sir.'

'How certain was he?'

'Mr Quentin said that he'd swear he'd met our suspect before.'

'Then let's launch a search for her,' said Marmion. 'I don't want any newspaper publicity about it. If, by chance, we're accusing an innocent woman of a serious crime, there could be repercussions. Let's work by stealth.'

'That suits me, sir.'

'What about the woman at Pegasus Costumes?'

'She's started her own search,' said Burge. 'I can't wait to tell her that the photo has given us a positive line of enquiry. In fact, I plan to call on Miss Naylor as soon as I can to see if she's managed to find out where the woman lives.'

'It must be somewhere in London. This is where all the burglaries took place.'

'Yes, but they came to a dead halt when one of them killed a policeman, then shot Sergeant Keedy. If she is in league with the burglars, she might have decided to get far away from here for a while. Maybe she's gone to Ireland,' suggested Burge. 'Her husband was from Dublin so she must have family contacts over there.'

'That's a good point, Cliff.'

Burge rose to his feet. 'I'll get over to Pegasus Costumes and see if Miss Naylor has found out anything else.'

'Off you go, then,' said Marmion. 'No – wait! I've thought of another reason why she might want to leave London for a while. She's obviously an intelligent woman and is therefore likely to read the newspapers.'

'So?'

'She's going to be very upset by that mention of Eamonn Corrigan.'

The secret of remaining so alert at her age was that she paced herself. That, at least, was what she thought. By keeping to a regular routine, she sailed through each day with comparative ease. As a rule, she did not read a morning newspaper until late in the afternoon when she allowed herself a rest. One small item caught her eye at once. It was the announcement of a forthcoming production of Shaw's play, *Misalliance*. Actors playing the principal roles were named but there was no mention at all of Giles Underhill. She felt hurt on his behalf. His reputation should have earned him a place among the others.

When she turned the page, her friend disappeared completely from her thoughts. He was replaced by Eamonn Corrigan, who had reportedly been lurking around the hospital where Sergeant Keedy was recovering. He was named as the man who had shot the detective during the siege in Limehouse. Pulsing with anger, she threw the newspaper aside. At a time when he should be staying out of sight, Corrigan had drawn attention to himself in the most dangerous way. He was starting to become a liability.

The house was small, cluttered and rather ugly but Corrigan hardly noticed its defects. He was safe among friends and that was all that mattered. As the three of them sat in the living room, he began to think of the future.

'I might take a look around tomorrow,' he said.

'Where would you go?' asked Regan.

'I'll start off in the Jewellery Quarter.'

'Jesus!' exclaimed Orr. 'You're not thinking of trying our luck there, are you? It'd be madness, so it would. Every business there has got tight security.'

'It does no harm to look, Pierce.'

'I thought we'd been told to have a rest for a while.'

'You know me. I like to keep busy.'

'Has she told you to look around?' asked Regan.

'No,' said Corrigan, 'but we need to use our own initiative sometimes. I'll buy a map of Birmingham tomorrow. There must be dozens of jewellery shops in the suburbs. We can take our pick of the best ones.'

'What about her?'

'We don't need anyone's permission to do a spot of research.'

'Maybe not, but she won't let us burgle any premises until she's been inside them first. That's the method we stuck to – and it worked.'

'Yes,' said Corrigan, rancorously, 'until those coppers caught sight of us in Limehouse and tried to arrest us. That was sheer bad luck. We'll be more careful next time.'

'You know the rules. We need to tell her if we find a target.'

'That's right,' said Regan. 'She's in charge.'

'And she's the best cover we've got, Eamonn. If you and Tom go into a jewellery shop, then the owner gets wary. When one of us has a woman in tow – an older woman like her, who looks harmless and respectable – then we don't arouse suspicions.'

'Maybe it's time to work another way,' suggested Corrigan. 'Without her.'

'But she gives the orders.'

'She used to, Tom.'

'She's never let us down.'

'Do we have to be told what to do by a woman?' sneered Corrigan. 'Yes, she was helpful to us, I give her that, but she never took any risks. We're the ones who did that. Every time we burgled a shop, we faced danger. All she does is sit in that flat of hers and wait for the money to come in. Ask yourself this,' he went on, seriously, 'do we really need her?'

Clifford Burge jumped out of the car and ran to the door of Pegasus Costumes. When he let himself into the foyer, Beatrice Naylor looked up with a smile of pleasure.

'I was just about to ring you, Sergeant Burge,' she said.

'Then I've saved you the trouble, Miss Naylor.'

'Call me Bea – everyone else does.'

'That suits me, Bea. I've been back to that jeweller in Shadwell.'

'How did you get on?' she asked.

'He took a long look at the photo of Miranda Darnell – and said that he was fairly certain that she had come into his shop under the name of Mrs Bennet.'

'That's marvellous.'

'It's certainly a big step forward,' he said, handing her the borrowed magazine. 'Thank you for this. That photograph did the job. We now know the woman's real name – one of her real names, that is.'

'Miranda Darnell and Jean Deale. Actually,' she told him, 'Jean's maiden name was Judd. She obviously decided that

Darnell sounded better in the world of theatre.'

'At least we know for certain that she was involved in those burglaries.'

'Oh, we know something else about her as well.'

'Do we?'

'Yes, Sergeant. I told you that I put the word out.'

'Have you had any luck?'

'Yes and no,' she replied. 'I've got an address for her, but it's one that she moved out of a year or so ago. It's here in London.'

Burge was thrilled. 'That's wonderful!' he cried. 'Someone at the property may well know where she went. Well done, Bea! We've picked up her scent at last. Thank you so much.'

'Don't thank me. It's been exciting to help you – though I still have doubts about Miranda Darnell working with burglars.'

'She wouldn't call them that. To her, they'd be something else,' he said, concealing from her his belief that they were Irish nationalists. 'Now, then,' he went on, taking out his notebook. 'What was that address?'

Keedy's eyes never left the clock on the wall. He was waiting for visitors to be let in that evening. When the bell sounded, his gaze shifted to the window. The blind had been lifted so that, minutes later, he was able to see Alice flit past. After knocking on the door, she was let into the room by Nurse Donaldson.

'How is he?' asked Alice.

'He's behaving himself,' replied the other.

'Where are you?' said Keedy. 'You came to see me, remember.'

Nurse Donaldson gave an understanding smile and slipped out of the room. Alice moved quickly to the chair beside the bed and sat down. They had to resist the temptation to hold hands.

'How are you feeling, Joe?' she asked.

'As fit as a flea. I'm ready to discharge myself.'

'Stop teasing!'

'I miss you, Alice.'

'I should hope so,' she said. 'I see that you've still got that guard outside your room.'

'I feel completely safe now. The only visitor I fear is my brother. I hear that he was very rude to your mother.'

'Mummy got over it.'

'I'll give Dennis a piece of my mind when I see him.'

'That may not be until the wedding,' she said. 'At least, I hope so.'

'What have you been doing since this morning?'

'Waiting for the next chance to see you.'

'Have you given up work altogether?'

'No,' she said, 'but being available for you is far more important than pounding the streets with Iris Goodliffe. Your need is greater. If it was left to me, I'd move in and help to nurse you.'

'That wouldn't work,' he protested.

'Why not? Don't you want me here?'

'You're not properly qualified, Alice. Besides, you'd be a distraction for me.'

'I'd hope that I'd be able to keep your spirits up,' she said, 'but I daresay the nurses you've got already do that – especially that very pretty one. What's her name – Nurse Bell?'

'Yes – she's off duty now.'

'Daddy said something odd about her. He thought he knew Nurse Bell somehow.'

Keedy laughed to hide his embarrassment. 'Ignore him. Your father's getting senile.'

'He was certain he'd seen her before.'

'That's highly unlikely,' he said, briskly. 'She's only recently moved here. Nurse Bell was working at a hospital in Manchester before that.'

Alice stared at him. 'Why has your voice suddenly changed?'

'I didn't know that it had.'

'What's going on, Joe?' she pressed. 'You seem so . . . defensive.'

For once, he was lost for words. The look on his face made her laugh.

He was hurt. 'What's so funny?'

'You are, Joe Keedy. We both know that you're hiding something. There's only one way that Daddy could have recognised Nurse Bell and that's because he must have seen you with her at some point. Why deny it?'

'It was years ago, Alice. We were . . . just friends.'

'Then don't look so guilty about it. Before we got close, I had one or two boyfriends. Then you came along, and my life suddenly changed. Nobody else mattered.'

'It was the same for me, Alice. Suddenly, I knew that I'd

found the person I wanted to spend the rest of my life with. And that's you.' He pulled a face. 'It was a pity that Maisie – Nurse Bell, that is – suddenly reappeared.'

'There's no need to be embarrassed about it. I'm grateful that Nurse Bell has been looking after you so well.'

Keedy was relieved. 'I thought you'd be angry if you found out.'

'Do I look angry?' she asked, smiling at him.

'I love you, Alice Marmion,' he said, reaching out impulsively to grab her hand.

'Then don't hide anything from me again. Is that clear?' He nodded. 'And let go of my hand before Nurse Donaldson comes back in. I gave my word that I wouldn't touch you.'

He released his grip. 'And you didn't – I was the one who touched you.'

When he got to the address in Lisson Grove that Beatrice Naylor had provided, Burge saw that it was a sizeable Victorian house in a tree-lined avenue. The owner explained that, when he and his wife had seen it on the market, they were fortunate enough to make an offer that was accepted at once. They never got to meet Jean Deale because she had already moved out, but neighbours had all spoken fondly of her. Burge took the opportunity to speak to some of them himself and every one of them was sad to lose the friendly old lady. They said that the woman had moved into a flat in central London, leaving the address with a few close friends so that they could exchange Christmas cards with her.

When he got back into the car, Burge's optimism was

surging. He was certain that he was about to come face to face with the woman who had been instrumental in the series of burglaries. He expected no resistance from her. Although he carried handcuffs, he did not anticipate making use of them. Having seen two photographs of Jean Deale – alias Miranda Darnell – he had some idea of what to expect. Allowances had to be made for the passage of time, but he was certain that the woman would still have a resemblance to the actress in the photographs.

His driver pulled up outside what looked like a luxury apartment block. Burge entered the building to discover that Jean Deale occupied a flat on the ground floor. When he rang the bell, he heard feet scurrying towards him. The door was then opened by a thin, well-dressed, middle-aged woman with grey hair and a pair of searching eyes.

'Yes?' she said, eyeing him up and down.

'I'm looking for Mrs Jean Deale,' said Burge.

'Then you've come at the wrong time, I'm afraid. Mrs Deale always goes to bed at this hour of day. That's why I need to turn you away.'

'My name is Detective Sergeant Burge,' he said, producing his warrant card, 'and I've no intention of being turned away. May I know your name, please?'

'Miss Edna Pym.'

'Are you a relative of Mrs Deale?'

'No, but we are close friends. When she worked in the theatre, I was her dresser. Miranda, as she was then known, refused to part with me. I've been her companion ever since she retired.'

He was about to explain why he was there when a voice rang out from inside the flat.

'Who is it?' demanded Jean.

'It's a detective, Mrs Deale,' said Edna. 'He's obviously come here by mistake so I will send him on his way.'

'I'm afraid that you can't do that,' said Burge, firmly. 'I'm investigating a series of burglaries and I've reason to believe that Mrs Deale may have been involved in them.'

She was aghast. 'That's a ludicrous suggestion!'

'I must ask you to let me in, Miss Pym.'

'What's going on?' asked Jean in a voice that would have reached the back of any theatre. 'Come here, Edna. I need help.'

'You should be asleep,' said Edna.

'Do as I tell you, woman.'

Leaving Burge at the door, Edna went into the flat at once. When she returned, she was supporting an old woman who could barely walk unaided. In her dressing gown and slippers, Jean Deale needed time to focus on her visitor.

'Who are you?' she asked.

'I'm Detective Sergeant Burge from Scotland Yard,' he explained.

'Did I hear something about burglaries?'

'I'm sorry to disturb you, Mrs Deale. There's been a mistake.'

'That's what I tried to tell you,' Edna told him. 'We moved to this address so that we had accommodation on the ground floor. Mrs Deale is losing her sight. She had a couple of nasty falls on the staircase in Lisson Grove.'

'What did you wish to ask me?' said Jean.

'It doesn't matter,' said Burge, sagging with disappointment. 'I obviously came to the wrong address, and I do apologise. Goodbye.'

Turning on his heel, he left the building and got into the car.

'Any luck?' asked the driver.

'No,' grunted Burge. 'Drive me back to the Yard.'

CHAPTER SEVENTEEN

The visit to Mile End Military Hospital seemed to last only a matter of seconds. Keedy and Alice were so absorbed in each other that time flew past. They did not even hear the bell that brought the visit to an end. Nurse Donaldson had to point out that it was time for her to leave. Alice rose to go.

'Hold on,' said Keedy. 'There's something I need to tell you. It's good news that I've been saving up until the last moment.'

'What is it?' she asked.

'This is my last night here.'

Her face lit up. 'Are they letting you come home?'

'No, but they told me that it was safe to move me to another hospital. I'm grateful, really, because I feel a bit of a fraud taking up a bed in a military hospital. The other patients here risked death on the battlefield.'

'You risked your life as well,' she reminded him.

'I know, Alice, and I paid the penalty for it. Anyway, when I leave here, there'll be two advantages. The first is that I'll be completely safe. Corrigan, the man caught hanging about outside here, won't have any idea where I'll be so I won't need an armed guard outside my room. The second advantage is that the hospital is in Shepherd's Bush, much closer to your family home so you won't have to take three different buses to get to me.'

'That'll be a relief!'

Conscious that Nurse Donaldson could hear him, he lowered his voice to a whisper.

'There's a third advantage as well,' he said.

Alice understood. He would no longer be nursed by Maisie Bell.

When Burge came into his office, Marmion could see at once that his colleague had bad news to report. He offered his visitor a chair and Burge flopped down into it.

'What happened?' asked Marmion.

'I made a mistake,' admitted Burge. 'I got carried away. I was so certain that I'd found the right woman, I thought I was about to make a significant arrest. Instead of that, I'm cursing myself for counting my chickens before they were hatched.'

'We've all been in that position, Cliff.'

'I felt so stupid.'

'Stop blaming yourself and tell me what happened.'

Burge told him about his latest visit to Pegasus Costumes

and how he had left there with the certainty of being able to confront the retired actress, Miranda Darnell, and take her into custody. When he met her, however, he realised that she could not possibly be involved in the burglaries.

'She had difficulty standing and is virtually blind,' said Burge. 'I was stunned.'

'Look at it another way,' suggested Marmion. 'On the face of it, the woman was a legitimate suspect. You've just eliminated her from the list.'

'Yes – and I end up wanting to kick myself. It was that link with Ireland that fooled me. When I heard that her late husband had been born in Dublin, I thought it was conclusive proof of her involvement with Irish nationalists.'

'Irish citizens are not all demanding Home Rule, you know. Look at how many of them volunteered to fight in the British army. As for this woman – Miranda Darnell – she's not the only actress whose name came up. Didn't you tell me that there were others?'

'It's true. Miss Naylor said she'd found a dozen or more possibilities.'

'Then work your way through the list until you find the right woman.'

'I feel embarrassed to admit that I made a fool of myself with Miranda Darnell.'

'It wasn't your fault, Cliff. You were acting on information from that woman at Pegasus Costumes. I'd say that each of you should take some of the blame.'

'I suppose so,' agreed Burge. 'Miss Naylor raised my hopes when she told me that this actress had enjoyed great success playing the role of Mrs Bennet. That was the name chosen by the woman involved in the burglaries. We were both fooled by the coincidence. It seemed to be conclusive evidence to me.'

'Bennet is a common name. As it happens, I know two or three Mrs Bennets.'

'I was too blinkered.'

'Well,' said Marmion, sympathetically, 'the blinkers are off now, and you've got far better vision. Look at each suspect in much greater detail before you act. Miss Naylor will have gone home from work by now so you can't reach her. First thing in the morning, we'll both go to the place where she works. I want to see who else is on her list of suspects.'

'So do I.'

'Chat is starting to bark at my heels. He wants an arrest.'

'Well, he may have to wait,' said Burge. 'I need to gather evidence more carefully.'

'You don't have unlimited time,' warned Marmion.

'What do you mean?'

'I've heard that Joe Keedy is moving to another hospital. That means he's shown sufficient improvement to be able to leave Mile End. You've been doing his job, remember. Prove yourself worthy of it. Joe will soon be itching to get back to work.'

Before he left Scotland Yard that evening, the commissioner paid a visit to Claude Chatfield, knowing that the superintendent would still be there. Sir Edward gave him a friendly smile.

'Don't you ever go home?' he asked.

'Work always comes first, Sir Edward.'

'Your wife and family will forget what you look like.'

'They have plenty of photographs of me to remind them,' said Chatfield with a rare grin. 'I take it that you've come for a progress report on those Irish burglars.'

'Has the woman been identified yet?'

'No, but Marmion assures me that they have several suspects. He and Sergeant Burge are working their way through them.'

'What could possibly make a woman get involved in these crimes?'

'I'm beginning to wonder if she may be married to that fellow, Corrigan, the leader of the gang. It would explain the close contact between them. The woman was at the centre of all seven burglaries and would have gone on providing help if they had not been stopped in their tracks.'

'Does the inspector approve of your theory?'

'No, he doesn't,' admitted Chatfield. 'He's convinced the woman has been a professional actress at some point in her life. Marmion thinks that she's impelled by political motives – just like Corrigan and the others.'

'I'd hoped that the failure of the Easter Rising two years ago had quashed the demand for Home Rule. The ringleaders were all hanged.'

'That only served to increase nationalist activity. It's a huge problem. We're at full stretch fighting the Germans and their allies. Every soldier is needed to win the war. We simply don't have enough manpower to be able to police Ireland effectively.'

'I agree,' said the commissioner. 'When our Russian allies withdrew from the war, it meant that the Germans could move over a million soldiers from the Eastern to the Western Front. And these are no ordinary soldiers. They are battle-hardened men who will make the German offensive much more powerful.'

'We'll be ready for them,' said Chatfield with patriotic fervour.

'I applaud your faith in our army, but I wish that I could share it. Yes, we have American soldiers to call on but many of them have had no experience at all of conflict. They're raw recruits. Are they going to be a match for highly trained German soldiers?'

'I have complete faith in our generals, Sir Edward.'

'Unfortunately,' said the commissioner, 'we've lost the best of them. Kitchener was killed almost two years ago when the ship carrying him hit a mine near the Orkneys. It was a tragic loss. We have no general quite like him.'

'But we still have experienced leaders, making vital decisions.'

'The Germans have experienced leaders as well.'

Chatfield was upset. 'I hope that you are not anticipating a Germany victory.'

'We must consider every possibility,' said the commissioner.

'You've always been so confident of our ultimate victory.'

'That confidence is starting to wear thin, I'm afraid.'

'I'm shocked to hear you say it, Sir Edward.'

'We must be realistic. Of course, I hope and pray that we finally crush the enemy. But we're up against a deadly foe. That's why the War Office is so concerned about Ludendorff's plan for a spring offensive. There's going to be an almighty battle,' he warned. 'My heart tells me that we will prevail, but my head disagrees. We may well come off worst.'

As soon as she got back home, Alice told her mother about Keedy's move to another hospital. Ellen was as delighted as her daughter. She knew that her future son-in-law would not be transferred to an ordinary hospital unless it was safe to move him. It meant that his recovery was already under way. How long he'd spend in the next hospital was uncertain, but the move would be a tonic for him.

'He was uncomfortable where he was, Mummy,' said Alice.

'But he was getting the best possible care.'

'Yes, but Joe felt that he was taking the place of a wounded soldier, somebody in a far worse state than he was. He remembered what he saw when he was involved in that case at Edmonton Military Hospital. Joe watched ambulance after ambulance rolling up to unload patients who were in the most appalling condition. They really deserved to be there.'

'Joe deserved to be at Mile End Military Hospital,' argued Ellen. 'He was close to death when they carried him in there. The surgeons had to perform an emergency operation.'

'He's very grateful to them.'

'And someone from the nursing staff has been with him around the clock.'

'Yes,' said Alice, thinking of Maisie Bell, 'he owes a lot to them.'

'Do we have any idea when the new hospital will discharge him?'

'No, but he's going to be there for some time.'

'When he is finally released,' Ellen reminded her, 'you and Joe must make an appointment with the vicar. He needs to prepare you for marriage.'

'We've been prepared for months,' said Alice with a grin.

'No, you haven't – not properly, anyway. There are lots of things to discuss. If you plan to raise a family, for instance, the vicar will want a promise that the children will be brought up as members of the Anglican church.'

'Of course they will.'

'We made that promise about our children,' recalled Ellen. 'You both went to Sunday school every week.' She sighed. 'I always wanted Paul to be in the church choir, but he hated the idea. Singing hymns came a poor second to playing with his friends.'

Alice bit her lip. 'I do wonder where he is now.'

'There's no point in speculating. Paul will be surviving somehow. That was his choice. We must accept it. He's gone for good.'

'Paul is my brother. He should be at my wedding. I can't help feeling sad that he won't be there. I'll miss him.'

When they got to Pegasus Costumes next morning, it had only just opened. Marmion was introduced to Beatrice Naylor and made a point of thanking her for the help she had given to the investigation. Anxious to hear of the latest development, she was disappointed to learn what had happened when Burge had met Miranda Darnell.

'She's almost blind?' she said in horror. 'Poor woman! I'm so sorry for her. It must have been embarrassing for you, Sergeant Burge. Oh dear! I should have found out more details about Miranda before I sent you on a fool's errand.'

'You weren't to blame,' said Burge. 'I still believe that the woman we're after is a trained actress. We just happened to pick the wrong one.'

'That was my fault.'

'No, it wasn't,' said Marmion. 'You've given us invaluable help, Miss Naylor, and we're grateful. I have a particular reason for wanting to catch this woman. Sergeant Keedy is engaged to marry my daughter. He was almost killed by one of the burglars. You can understand why I'm so determined to catch all three of them as well as their female accomplice, of course.'

'As long as they're still at liberty,' added Burge, 'they're a danger to the public. We don't want them to add any more victims to their list.'

'Just tell me what I can do,' she said.

'We'd like you to name other possible suspects,' said Marmion. 'Sergeant Burge tells me that you picked out a dozen or more.'

'That's true, Inspector.'

'We need their names and anything you can tell us about them.'

'In fact, I managed to cross a few names off my list. I discovered that two of the actresses had died and that a third had emigrated to Canada years ago.'

'Who are the others?'

'I've got their names right here,' she said, opening a

drawer to take out a piece of paper. 'And I've managed to find photographs of most of them.'

'Let's have the names first, Bea,' said Burge, flipping open his notebook. 'As for the photographs, I'll be more careful how I use them next time. I pushed Mr Quentin into identifying one of Miranda Darnell taken decades ago. I didn't allow for the fact that she was wearing heavy make-up for the part of Lady Macbeth.'

Beatrice read out the names and he made a note of them. When he had finished, he ran his eye down the list and his brow furrowed.

'You've included Grace Whittington,' he observed.

'That's right, Sergeant.'

'When her name came up before, you told me that she'd never stoop to crime.'

'I was mistaken,' she confessed. 'I talked to an old friend of hers and she told me that Grace had fallen on hard times. She's moved back to London to live in a flat somewhere. A year or so ago, Grace was accused of stealing something from Swan & Edgar. In fact, the charges were dropped but only because she'd managed to persuade the store detective that she had made an innocent mistake.'

'In other words,' said Marmion, interest sparked, 'she talked her way out of trouble.'

'It may be that it was an innocent mistake, of course, but I doubt it somehow.'

'Why?'

'Grace was such a positive person. In my younger days, I queued outside the stage door of a theatre to get her autograph.

She had the leading role in a comedy there. I saw it three times. Years later, she came here for a costume fitting, and I was able to chat to her properly. To be honest,' said Beatrice, 'she was a bit overwhelming. I had the impression she was the sort of woman who always got what she wanted.'

'What was she caught stealing from Swan & Edgar?'

'It was a beautiful silk scarf.'

'Was it expensive?'

'Yes,' she replied, 'I believe it was. Grace had standards.'

'But her name is only second on your list,' said Burge, glancing at his notepad. 'You've put someone else at the top – Sarah Standish.'

'That's a name I've heard before,' recalled Marmion. 'She was famous.'

'Yes,' said Beatrice. 'Until five or six years ago, she was still working in the theatre. Sarah was only playing supporting roles then, but she still had all her faculties.'

'Why have you picked her out?'

'There was a rumour that she'd been in trouble with the police. I don't know the details, but she disappeared off the London stage. Her real name was Irene Peck, by the way.'

'If it was a serious offence, we should be able to find it in our records.'

'Oh,' said Beatrice, 'the crime wasn't committed in this country.'

'Then where was it committed?'

'In Ireland.'

* * *

Seated beside a warm fire in her flat, she studied a map of Ireland to remind herself of times spent there. Having lived most of her life in England, she regretted that she had not lived for any length of time in the place she had come to love. She consoled herself with the fact that she had helped in the fight for an independent Ireland. When the search for her and her associates had died down, she hoped to continue that work. Meanwhile, she would enjoy her limited social life and her visits to the theatre. Losing the friendship of Giles Underhill was a setback, but it meant that he would retain only fond memories of her and remain ignorant of her true character.

Meanwhile, she would await news from Corrigan and hope that he was obeying orders. Even though he was being sought for the murder of a policeman and the wounding of a detective, he had taken unnecessary chances in London. He was much better off in Birmingham, she reflected, hidden away, and keeping himself out of mischief.

On a cold, windy morning, Corrigan ambled around the Jewellery Quarter with the collar of his overcoat pulled up and his cap pulled down over his forehead. He missed nothing during his tour. Every time he glanced in a shop window, he was impressed by the value of the stock on show. The area had a good and well-deserved reputation. He could understand why. When he came to the end of a street, he paused to look in the window of a large shop. As he was studying the jewellery on display, he heard footsteps coming up behind him and turned to see two policemen.

'Looking for anything, sir?' asked one of them.

'Yes,' answered Corrigan with a grin, 'I'm after something that I can afford. My wife and I are celebrating our silver wedding next week so it must be something special.'

'How well do you know the Quarter?'

'This is my first visit. A friend told me I'd be bound to find what I wanted here.'

'Then don't look here. Prices here are very high. Turn left and walk on down to Mallory's. You'll find their merchandise is just as good but a lot cheaper.'

'Thank you. That's good advice.'

After waving farewell, Corrigan turned the corner and walked slowly away, conscious of the fact that the policemen were watching him carefully.

Since there was no possibility of visiting the hospital that morning, Alice and her mother went straight to the new house and started to work their way through the list of jobs they'd drawn up. Brisk activity meant they hardly noticed the absence of any form of heat. Alice kept checking to see if she had any paint on her hands and arms.

'I'd never forgive myself if I spoilt the surprise for Joe,' she said.

'He's going to have quite a shock when he finally gets here.'

'I'm hoping that he'll be delighted.'

'Don't let him think that this is your job from now on,' warned Ellen. 'As well as being a policewoman, you'll be a housewife as well, so you'll be kept busy with various chores. Make it clear to Joe that he'll have to do any painting and decorating in the future.'

'But I've loved sprucing the place up, Mummy.'

'It's a man's job, really.'

'There's no such thing,' said Alice, forcefully. 'Before the war, you'd have said that policing the city was essentially a man's job, yet the Women's Police Force has proved that we can do our share. You ask Gale Force.'

'I'd rather not, to be honest. Inspector Gale is rather frightening.'

'She's not too bad, really. In some ways, I miss her.'

'Well, you're not going back on duty until Joe is out of hospital,' insisted Ellen. 'His needs come first.'

'He's dying to get back to work.'

'There'll be a long wait yet before he can do that. He must learn to be patient. Meanwhile, there's your wedding dress to think about. It needs to be ready months earlier than planned.'

'Yes, I know.'

Ellen smiled at her. 'Joe will be thrilled when he sees you coming up the aisle on your father's arm.'

'I do hope he'll have recovered by then,' said Alice. 'Otherwise, it will be Joe who needs to come up the aisle on Daddy's arm.' They laughed. 'When we finish here, it will be time to tackle Paul's room so that it's ready for Joe to move into.'

'I'm not looking forward to that,' confessed Ellen.

Alice was hurt. 'I thought you wanted Joe to move in with you.'

'Oh, I do – and so does your father. It's just that we'll have to get rid of a lot of Paul's things from that room. There'll be painful memories.'

'Would you rather that Joe went back to his brother's house?'

'No,' exclaimed Ellen. 'We must save him from that fate at all costs.'

On the drive back to Scotland Yard, they were able to discuss their visit to Pegasus Costumes. It had given them an insight into the perils of the acting profession. Marmion had been impressed by Beatrice Naylor.

'She's an intelligent woman,' he said, 'and she's given us information we could never have found anywhere else.'

'More to the point,' noted Burge, 'she lent us photographs of those two actresses she picked out – Sarah Standish and Grace Whittington.'

'The one with the link to Ireland sounds the more promising.'

'I think we should take a close look at both of them, sir.'

'I agree.'

'That theft from Swan & Edgar interested me. I don't believe that it was an innocent mistake. In my opinion, Grace Whittington stole that scarf on purpose. Store detectives have good eyesight. They rarely arrest the wrong person.'

'I think that you should challenge her about her theft,' said Marmion, 'and see how she responds. Meanwhile, I'll be trying to find this other actress, Sarah Standish. I want to know exactly how she got into trouble in Ireland.'

'Unfortunately, we don't have an address for either of these women.'

'That's true, but we can't expect Miss Naylor to do all the work for us. We're the detectives, Cliff. We must unleash the bloodhounds and track the suspects down ourselves.'

'I agree. Soon after the war broke out,' Burge recalled, 'they put up a huge poster on the Piccadilly side of Swan & Edgar.'

'I remember it well.'

'It read "Make Victory Swift and Sure".'

'That's exactly what we must do as well,' said Marmion, determinedly. 'Except that we're not up against the might of the German army. Our enemies are three burglars and a very cunning woman. Let's make our victory against them swift and sure.'

Joe Keedy had been delighted when told that he would be moved to another hospital that morning. It was proof positive that he had begun his recovery during the short time he'd been there. He was no longer on the danger list. As he waited to be taken down to an ambulance, he was conscious that Maisie Bell was unhappy about his imminent disappearance. She had hardly spoken to him and, on the rare occasions when she did so, she was almost curt. Maisie was now sorting out the paperwork that had to go with him. He was anxious to part from her on good terms.

'I can't tell you how grateful I am to you, Maisie,' he said.

She turned to him. 'I was only doing my job.'

'That's not true. When they first wheeled me in here, you couldn't do enough to help me. Every time I opened my eyes, you gave me an encouraging smile.'

'I do that to all my patients, Joe.'

'It was so reassuring to see a friendly face. With the best will in the world, hospitals are rather impersonal places. The staff are all dressed in uniform, and they speak in a sort of private language.'

'That's necessary, I'm afraid.'

'You stood out from the others, Maisie.'

'Did I?'

'Yes – you looked like a real human being.'

She shook her head. 'I think you imagined that.'

'My body may be injured but my mind certainly isn't. I can recall every word you said to me, especially the ones when I first recovered from the anaesthetic. You asked me if—'

'Yes, yes, I know,' she said, holding up a palm to silence him. 'I don't need reminding. That was then, Joe. It's different now. We're moving apart.'

'Why do you sound as if you're glad to get rid of me?' he protested.

'Don't be ridiculous!'

'You've been the same all morning, Maisie. What have I done wrong?'

'Nothing,' she said with a shrug. 'I suppose that I'm sorry to see you go, that's all. The next patient I'll be looking after will have terrible wounds that need to be dressed regularly. And he may well be missing an arm or a leg. I've nursed soldiers who've had no legs at all, and I've seen facial wounds that horrified me. Can you hear what I'm saying, Joe?'

'Yes, I can. Working here is something of an ordeal. I take my hat off to you.'

'I'm not complaining. I took this job because I wanted to do my bit towards the war effort. Every time a new patient comes in here, I grit my teeth.' She lowered her voice. 'Then in comes someone I actually know, someone who was once a . . . close friend.'

He grinned. 'Did I make you grit your teeth as well?'

'No, of course not,' she said with a laugh. 'You just reminded me of . . . happy times we spent together. Except that you were no longer the free and easy Joe Keedy I used to know. You'd changed completely. You'd met someone else.'

'That doesn't mean that we're no longer friends, Maisie. Nurse Donaldson looked after me very well and so did Nurse Jellings during the night shift. But you're the only one I'll remember fondly. You're still very special to me.'

'I'm just not special enough,' she said, resignedly. 'I wish you well, Joe, I really do. But I think it might have been better if our paths hadn't crossed in this way.'

'I disagree.'

The door opened and two male nurses came in with a trolley.

'Time to go, I'm afraid,' she said.

'Are you kicking me out?'

'Good luck, Joe.'

'I won't forget you, Nurse Bell,' he said, touching her arm. 'Thank you for everything.'

CHAPTER EIGHTEEN

When they got back to Scotland Yard, they found the superintendent waiting to ambush them. Marmion told him where they had been and what they had found out, injecting a note of optimism into his voice. Burge supported him, arguing that the latest information marked a giant step forward in the investigation.

'I remain unconvinced,' said Chatfield, icily. 'The commissioner will agree with me.'

'We are confident of an early arrest, sir,' said Marmion.

'Then why can't I share that confidence? And why do the newspapers remain sceptical? You obviously haven't read this morning's editions. You are criticised by name, Inspector. A report in *The Times* suggests that you are far less effective without Sergeant Keedy at your side.' He glared at Burge. 'I'm bound to agree with that judgement.'

'It's both hasty and wrong,' said Marmion, defensively.

'Luckily, the press is unaware that we are relying heavily on the assistance of a woman who has no training whatsoever as a detective and who spends her life hiring out theatrical costumes. Imagine the mockery we'd receive if that were revealed.'

'Miss Naylor has been very helpful,' insisted Burge.

'I met the woman myself,' added Marmion, 'and found her eager to give us any information that she could. Having helped Sergeant Keedy in an earlier investigation, Miss Naylor was shocked to hear what had had happened to him. It spurred her on to help us.'

'Is she going to send you up another blind alley?'

'That's unfair, sir.'

'Is it? Relying on the judgement of this woman, Sergeant Burge went off to arrest a key figure in those burglaries and what happened? He found a frail old woman, almost blind, who could hardly stand up without the aid of her companion.'

'That's no reflection on Miss Naylor, sir,' said Burge, stoutly. 'Because of remarkable coincidences, the evidence pointed clearly to an actress by the name of Miranda Darnell. We were right to act on that information.'

'And we intend to act on the latest information she's given us,' said Marmion.

'In what way?' pressed Chatfield.

'We were about to weigh up the new evidence in my office, but you intercepted us out here in the corridor.'

'You needed interception. It's the only way to get results.'

'We work best when we have freedom of action, sir.'

Chatfield bridled. 'Are you daring to criticise me?'

'Of course not,' replied Marmion. 'I respect your seniority.'

'Quite right, too!'

'In essence, sir, our plan is this. Sergeant Burge will go in search of more information about this retired actress, Grace Whittington, and I will concentrate on this other woman, Sarah Standish.'

Chatfield sniffed. 'Grace Whittington, Sarah Standish, Miranda Darnell . . . where do they get such fanciful names?'

'They're stage names, sir,' explained Marmion.

'And I can tell you exactly how the first of them got her name,' said Burge. 'Her given name was Peggy Dark. She used it when she was in a pantomime about Dick Whittington. Because of its associations with London's history, she liked the name of Whittington, so she changed from Peggy Dark to Grace Whittington. It does have more of a ring to it, sir. You must agree.'

'Is this information at all relevant?' asked Chatfield, raising an eyebrow.

'We think so, sir,' said Burge. 'It was Miss Naylor who told us what the woman's real name is. She was a great admirer of the actress, you see. When I interview one of the store detectives at Swan & Edgar, I'll be interested to know which name Grace Whittington gave to the man when he arrested her.'

After poking the fire to release more heat, she settled down to read her newspaper. There was more encouraging news than on the previous day. Inspector Marmion, leading the investigation into the string of burglaries, was criticised for making no apparent progress. It was suggested that he missed the expertise of Sergeant Keedy, recovering in hospital after being wounded during the siege. Enraged by the earlier article, she was greatly soothed by the latest news. Evidently, the police were no longer closing in on them. She and her associates were safe.

Keedy had had to endure a bumpy ride in an ambulance before he reached the hospital in Shepherd's Bush. When the rear doors were opened, he was able to look at what would be his new home for a while. It was markedly different to the place he had just left. There were no armed guards at the gate and no other ambulances queueing up to discharge severely wounded patients. It was an ordinary civilian hospital built for public use. Male nurses were waiting to lift him gently on to a trolley and cover him quickly with blankets to keep him warm. They pushed him into the building and along a corridor until they came to a lift. Standing outside it was a shapely young nurse with what Keedy thought was a close resemblance to Maisie Bell. When she turned to look at him, however, he saw that he was mistaken. The woman had a narrow, puckered, unattractive face, lined by fatigue. She gave him no more than a glance.

The lift took him up to the second floor. Wheeled out, he was taken along a corridor to the ward at the far end. A senior nurse stepped out to intercept the trolley. After checking details of her new patient, she stood aside so that the trolley could pass. A shock awaited Keedy. At the military hospital in

Mile End, he had been given a room of his own and constant care. That situation had now changed. His new home was a ward full of other male patients. He was wheeled the full length of it to an empty bed in the far corner. The other patients looked at the new arrival with interest. Keedy's initial fear was that he and Alice would have no privacy at all during her visits. A subsidiary problem was that there would be no Maisie Bell to console him and to trigger happy memories of their friendship. He had to face a cold, hard, uncomfortable fact. The transfer to another hospital had robbed him of the privileges he'd enjoyed in Mile End. Keedy was just an ordinary patient now.

The store was busy when Burge arrived at Swan & Edgar. He had to pick his way through a crowd to reach the manager's office. It was clear that such large numbers favoured any potential thieves. When he introduced himself to the manager, he asked what proportion of the stock was stolen. The manager, a tall, striking, impeccably dressed man of middle years, was realistic.

'We have to expect a small amount of shoplifting,' he admitted, 'because it's impossible to have eyes everywhere. Repeat offenders are the easiest to spot. They just can't keep away from us. If they've served a sentence in prison, they head for Swan & Edgar the moment they're released.'

'Force of habit,' observed Burge.

'The most difficult ones to spot are the pickpockets. They love a crowd. Even if my store detectives catch one of them, he or she often can't be charged because they've already passed on stolen items to someone else.'

'I don't think that the person who interests me would do that, sir.'

When Burge explained why he was there, the manager opened a record book and flicked through it until he came to a page on which recent customers who had been challenged then released were listed. His finger jabbed at a name.

'Here she is,' he said. 'Miss Patricia Inigo.'

'I was expecting a different name. This must be a new alias. Which of your detectives accosted her?'

'Jonah Freeman,' said the manager. 'He's one of our best. You'll enjoy meeting him.'

'Why?'

'He used to be in the Metropolitan Police Force.'

Marmion's search was frustrating. Though he had spoken on the telephone to various members of the Royal Irish Constabulary, he got disappointing replies. It was almost as if he were up against a conspiracy of silence. He pressed on relentlessly, but his patience was wearing thin. The problem was that nobody recognised the names of either Sarah Standish or Irene Peck. He tried ringing Beatrice Naylor, but she could add little to what she conceded was simply a rumour. She promised to contact the person who had first mentioned the incident to her. Marmion could only keep his fingers crossed and hope that more detail would soon come to light.

Jonah Freeman turned out to be a sturdy man in his forties with a square jaw and a broken nose. Carrying a bag with the name of Swan & Edgar printed on it, he looked like a visitor to the store. The first thing that Burge asked him was why he had resigned from the police force.

'If I took my shirt off,' said Freeman, 'you'd have your answer because the scars are still there. When I tried to arrest a burglar, he pulled a knife out and stabbed me in the neck and chest. I had well over thirty stitches in all. That was far too many for my wife. Doris put her foot down. If I didn't leave the police, she'd leave me – and she really meant it.'

'But you're still in a job that involves arresting criminals,' Burge pointed out.

'Yes, but they rarely carry knives and many of them are women. When I put a hand on them, their first instinct is to run for the door. What they learn is that I have colleagues outside – male and female – who will intercept anyone who dashes out through an exit.'

'Tell me about a Miss Patricia Inigo.'

'Ah, yes,' said Freeman, grinning. 'I remember her well.'

They were in a rest room set aside for employees to take an occasional break. Burge was impressed by its size and relative comfort. It had a homely atmosphere.

'Miss Inigo was an unlikely thief,' recalled Freeman. 'To begin with, she was far too old. Also, she was extremely well dressed. Ordinarily, I wouldn't have given her a second look.'

'Then why did you do so?'

'It was that silk scarf peeping out of her bag. If she'd bought it here, it would have been wrapped up. When I confronted her, she was genuinely upset. She told me that she had no idea how the scarf had got into the bag. To begin with,' said

Freeman, 'I didn't believe her, but she seemed so honest. And we've had elderly people before who've been used as mules.'

'Mules?'

'Thieves steal a small item, pop into a bag carried by someone like Miss Inigo, then follow her out. When they're well clear of the store, they grab the stolen item from the bag and run off. That's what would have happened in this case.'

'Are you quite sure?' asked Burge.

'Yes – why should a woman who is clearly well off need to steal a silk scarf?'

'I can think of a lot of reasons. Perhaps she wanted it as a gift for a friend. Or maybe she wasn't as well off as you imagined.'

Freeman was insistent. 'It was an honest mistake. I know sincerity when I hear it.'

'This woman once made a living as an actress,' Burge told him. 'I daresay that she can turn on sincerity like a tap. She appeared in plays in the West End.' He opened the magazine he was carrying and flipped the pages until he came to a photograph of a handsome woman in her forties. 'This is Grace Whittington,' he said.

'So what?'

'I think she was the woman you arrested. Take a good look at her.'

Freeman stared at the photograph, then shook his head. 'No, that's nothing like her. Miss Inigo was much more full-bodied.'

'The photo was taken the best part of forty years ago,' said Burge, 'and she might have put on a lot of weight since then.

Take another look at that face. It's quite distinctive.'

Freeman stared hard at the photograph for a couple of minutes. 'I suppose there could be a vague resemblance, Sergeant,' he said, reluctantly. 'But I can't be certain. No, on balance, I'd say that this is not Miss Inigo.'

'Did you make a note of her address?'

'Of course, I did. I have her name, address and even the name of the vicar from the church she goes to. She insisted on giving me that. She said that the vicar would vouch for her.'

'And did he?'

'I didn't bother to get in touch. There was no point. The woman was clearly innocent. If she had been a shoplifter, she'd never have left the scarf visible.'

'What happened to it?'

Freeman was uneasy. 'I'm not quite sure.'

'But you wrote a report on the arrest,' said Burge. 'The manager told me that.'

'It's standard procedure, Sergeant.'

'So how did the incident end?'

Jonah Freeman looked shamefaced. Burge had his answer. Patricia Inigo had complained to the manager about her treatment, and he'd sought to make amends by letting her keep the silk scarf that she claimed she had not stolen.

'If you don't mind,' said Burge, 'I'd like that address she gave you – and the name of the church, please. I might just have a chat with the vicar.'

It was late afternoon when they got back home. There were still hours to go before visiting time at the hospital in Shepherd's

Bush, but Alice was keen to get rid of any evidence of the painting she'd spent hours doing at the new house. Ellen, meanwhile, made a start on clearing out some items from her son's bedroom. She broke off to share a cup of tea with Alice in the kitchen.

'There's no need to start on Paul's room yet, Mummy,' said Alice. 'It may be weeks before Joe will be released from hospital.'

'I want the room spick and span for our guest.'

Alice laughed. 'It was never like that when Paul was living here.'

'I know – the place was like a jungle sometimes. Mind you,' Ellen went on, 'he did improve. We have the army to thank for that. When he first came home from France, he kept his room almost tidy. They obviously taught him good habits.'

'Yes, he stopped keeping a muddy football and dirty football boots under the bed.'

'He lost interest in the game altogether, Alice. It was another pleasure that the war stole from him. Paul used to love playing every Saturday afternoon. Talking of which,' she added, 'have you any idea what happened to that photo of him with his football team?'

'It was always pinned up near the dartboard.'

'Well, it's not there any more.'

'It must be in the room somewhere, Mummy.'

'I couldn't find it. Then again,' admitted Ellen, 'I might have put it away somewhere when Paul left. Yes, that must be it. The photo is in that box of his belongings I put in the attic.'

'When the war broke out,' remembered Alice, 'every player in his team joined the army. How many of them are still alive, I wonder?'

'At least four of them died at the Somme. We know that for certain. In some ways, Paul was another victim of that dreadful battle. He certainly wasn't the person we sent off to war.'

'He's still a member of the family. We can never forget that.'

'I know,' said Ellen, sadly. She brightened immediately. 'Well, you'll be off to see Joe in his new hospital this evening. What are you going to wear?'

'I thought I'd give him a treat and put on my Sunday best.'

'Make sure you keep your gloves on to hide that paint on your hands.'

'What paint?' asked Alice, examining her hands. 'I got rid of it earlier with turps.'

'I was only joking,' said her mother, laughing. 'You should have seen the expression on your face. It was so funny.'

Marmion was annoyed. After a fruitless telephone call with an Inspector Doyle of the Royal Irish Constabulary, he put down the receiver and sat back in his chair. It was maddening. He still had no idea why a retired actress named Sarah Standish had got into trouble with the police. To get the information he needed, he toyed with the idea of going to Dublin in person. The telephone rang. Hoping that it might be Inspector Doyle again, he was disappointed to hear a female voice.

'Inspector Marmion?' she asked.

'Speaking . . .'

'This is Bea Naylor from Pegasus Costumes.'

'It's good to hear from you, Miss Naylor,' he said, brightening at once. 'As it happens, I've been following up that lead you gave us regarding Sarah Standish. Nobody in the Royal Irish Constabulary seems to have heard of her.'

'I may be able to explain why,' she said.

'I wish that somebody would.'

'The woman who told me that Sarah had been in trouble with the police went off to find out more details for me. Then she called in here this afternoon to tell me what she'd learnt. Sarah hadn't been questioned by the police at all. Her problem involved a property dispute, it seems. Having decided to retire to Ireland, Sarah put in an offer for a cottage not far from Cork. The offer was accepted,' Beatrice told her. 'Sarah expected to move in as soon as it was safe to do so.'

'What was the problem?'

'Somebody else stepped in with a much better offer.'

'Had contracts been exchanged?'

'Yes, Inspector. The estate agent simply refused to honour the agreement and tried to palm Sarah off with some rigmarole about having offered the property to the other party first. Since Sarah was living here in England and the other buyer was based in Ireland, the estate agent thought he could get away with it. That was a big mistake.'

'Why?'

'It seems that Sarah went over there to confront him. She turned up at his office with an Irish lawyer, who threatened to take legal action against the firm. They took a policeman along as well, just to give the estate agent a fright. It did the job. Sarah now owns the house near Cork.'

'Thank you, Miss Naylor,' said Marmion, 'and please pass on my thanks to your friend. It's made things much clearer.'

After bidding her farewell, he put down the receiver and smiled. He had not only established an Irish connection for Sarah Standish, he had discovered that she had bought a cottage near Cork. The burglars' female accomplice had called herself Mrs Corkwell on one occasion. She had also posed as Mrs Mallow and Mrs Bandon, two places within easy reach of Cork.

Marmion slapped his desk in triumph.

It did not take Burge long to establish that the address given to him by Jonah Freeman did not exist, so the woman calling herself Patricia Inigo could not possibly have lived there. St Luke's Church, however, did exist and so did the Reverend Edwin Lockhart, a sprightly old man with a mane of white hair and a white beard. As Burge had suspected, the name of Patricia Inigo meant nothing whatsoever to him.

Before Alice Marmion could leave the house, she had to withstand an inspection from her mother. Ellen looked her up and down with approval, the only change she made being a slight adjustment to the angle of her daughter's hat.

'You look wonderful,' she said. 'Seeing you like that is the best medicine Joe could have.'

'Thank you, Mummy.'

'If you leave now, you'll be horribly early.'

'That's exactly what I want to be.'

'They won't let you see him until visiting time begins.'

'I want to be ready and waiting for the bell.'

'Of course, you do. Give Joe my love.'

'I will.'

'And ask him if there's anything he needs – apart from the sight of you, that is.'

Alice left the house and walked to the bus stop. From now on, the vehicle would not be the first of three taking her to Mile End. All she needed was one bus and five stops before she'd reached the hospital in Shepherd's Bush. It was a huge relief.

When he got back to Scotland Yard, Clifford Burge's report had to wait. Marmion was too excited about his own news. He talked about his telephone call with Beatrice Naylor. It had left him feeling certain that Sarah Standish – Irene Peck – was the woman involved in the burglaries in the capital. While he was interested in the information gathered, Burge remained dubious.

'I think that you need to take a closer look at Grace Whittington,' he said. 'I spoke to the store detective at Swan & Edgar who arrested her. She was using the name of Patricia Inigo at the time, and she got herself a silk scarf without having to pay a penny.'

Marmion was fascinated by the story of what had happened but his preference for the other female suspect remained. In his mind, her connection with Ireland was paramount.

'The cottage she bought is not far from Cork. Have you forgotten that she once used the name of Mrs Corkwell when visiting one of the jewellery shops?'

'No, I haven't, sir,' said Burge, 'and I remember that she used two other names – Mallow and Bandon – which are places in the same part of Ireland. But that doesn't mean you have to sweep my suspect aside as if she didn't matter. What if the two women are working together?'

'There's little chance of that, Cliff. The one thing I do know about actresses is that they love the limelight. Each one of them yearns to be the centre of attention. I have a strong feeling that Miss Standish is the criminal. Working with burglars who are happy to leave a dead policeman and an injured detective in their wake points to a special kind of woman.'

'I believe it's Grace Whittington.'

'Then why is she wasting her time stealing a silk scarf?'

'Perhaps she likes silk scarves, sir.'

'Sarah Standish has direct links with Ireland. That's the clinching argument for me.'

'After the mistake we made with Miranda Darnell,' warned Burge, 'we must gather more evidence before we move in. At least we have some idea of where Miss Whittington lives.'

'Do we?' asked Marmion.

'I think so. The only reason she named the vicar of St Luke's is that she must live somewhere near it. How else would she know the Reverend Lockhart's name? He was a lovely old boy, by the way, and very sorry that he couldn't help us.'

'You're right,' conceded Marmion. 'We need to gather much more evidence before we strike. I'm not reporting any of what we've discovered today until we're certain which of these two ladies is in league with the burglars.

'I still believe it will be Miss Whittington,' insisted Burge.

'Miss Standish is my choice.'

'What if it's neither of them?'

Marmion grimaced. 'Then we have a very big problem to solve.'

Alice Marmion was by no means the first visitor to arrive at the hospital. The waiting room was already quite full. She found herself sitting next to an anxious old woman who talked about her husband's heart operation in exhaustive detail.

'It's the second time they've had a go at Bert,' she said, morosely.

'I'm sorry to hear that.'

'They don't always get things right first time, you see.'

'No, I suppose not.'

'It was the same with that hernia of his. Bert was in agony after the first operation.'

Alice became worried. Keedy had had exceptional medical treatment in the military hospital. Had he been moved to somewhere with much lower standards? She stopped listening to the woman's droning pessimism and just offered an occasional nod. The one consolation was that her companion showed no interest at all in why Alice had come there.

When the bell signalled the start of visiting time, everyone got to their feet. Alice was among the first to reach the stairs. Having established which area of the hospital Keedy was in, she skipped up the steps as if she were in a race. A nurse was standing outside the ward with a clipboard, ready to give advice to visitors. Alice hurried up to her.

'I've come to see Joseph Keedy,' she said.

'Ah, yes,' replied the nurse, looking at the list in front of her, 'he's a new arrival. You'll find him in the last bed on the right.'

Alice was shocked. 'Isn't he in a separate room?'

'I'm afraid not.'

Alice needed a moment to adjust to the situation. All hope of privacy had disappeared. Other visitors were already trickling past her into the ward. After thanking the nurse, she walked past the long array of beds on both sides of the ward until she came to the one in which Keedy was propped up on pillows. He could read the sadness in her face.

'I'm sorry about this, Alice,' he said.

She managed a smile. 'It's better than nothing, I suppose.'

'You look amazing.'

'And so do you, Joe,' she said, studying him. 'If they let you sit up, you must be getting better. How are you?'

'Bored stiff, to be honest – until you got here.'

'Mummy sends her love.'

'What about your father? Is there any news about the case?'

'None that I know of, I'm afraid. But they're still after that man who shot you. They won't give up until they get him.'

'I want to be out there helping in the search.'

'There's no chance of that, Joe.'

'Sit down,' he said, indicating the chair beside the bed. 'We can at least hold hands.'

Alice lowered herself on to the chair. He took hold of her hand and kissed it. They smiled at each other. His gaze then shifted to the main door.

'Oh, no!' he groaned.

'What's the matter, Joe?

'We've got company.'

Alice turned around to see his brother, Dennis Keedy, striding towards them. Dressed in funereal wear and carrying his top hat, he sailed along between the beds with an expression of intense solemnity on his face.

CHAPTER NINETEEN

Eamonn Corrigan hated inactivity. His friends were happy enough to relax at the house in Aston all day, but he had the urge to keep busy. Having explored the Jewellery Quarter, Corrigan had bought a map of the city and its environs, then spent all his time gathering information about shops that might be worth considering as targets. Like all major industrial cities, Birmingham had suffered from repeated enemy air raids. Wherever he went, Corrigan saw clear evidence of the damage that had been wreaked. The population was not disheartened, however. War might have wearied them but there was still an underlying belief in victory.

When he got back to the house in Upper Thomas Street that evening, he sat down with his friends and took out his notebook. He held it up.

'I've got half a dozen certs in here,' he boasted. 'The one in

Yardley is tempting, but my favourite is in Erdington. That's not too far away from here.'

'I'm still not sure about this,' muttered Regan. 'What if she finds out about it?'

'No chance of that happening, Tom.'

'Oh, yes there is. That woman is uncanny.'

'But she's not here, is she?' argued Corrigan. 'She's well over a hundred miles away in London. How could she possibly know what we're up to?'

'I agree with Tom,' said Orr. 'It's too risky.'

'Yes,' added Regan. 'Why can't we just obey orders and do nothing?'

'That's what she told us to do, Eamonn.'

'Stop going on about her!' yelled Corrigan, banging his fist down on the table. 'That bloody woman is not even properly Irish – whereas we are. We came to this country together on a mission. Let's stick to it.'

'We were also told to report to her,' Orr reminded him. 'Be fair, she did a lot for us. She took chances. Without her, we couldn't have burgled those shops so easily.'

'But they were only shops in poor areas of London. We should have been setting our sights a lot higher. Face the truth. We need every penny we can get. Let's be more ambitious,' he urged. 'Get your coats on, lads. I'll show you what I mean.'

The arrival of Dennis Keedy had threatened to ruin Alice's visit to the hospital. He was the last person she wanted to see while she was enjoying precious time alone with his brother. The undertaker, however, was in a more subdued mood. Having learnt that Keedy had been moved, he had come to the other hospital to make sure that his brother would be looked after properly there. To Alice's amazement, he asked her to pass on his apologies to her mother for being too assertive during his telephone call with her. Dennis told her that he had now accepted that his brother would be right to move into the Marmion family house when he was discharged. After half an hour or so, he wished Keedy well, gave Alice a token kiss and then left.

'That's a relief,' said Keedy.

'It wasn't as bad as I'd feared,' confessed Alice. 'I thought he'd spend the whole hour giving you a lecture and ignoring me. It was kind of him to come, really.'

'Dennis has his good side.'

'Let's forget him now, Joe. While I'm still here, let's make the most of it.'

'Of course,' he said, stroking her hand. 'It's so lovely to see you again. What have you been up to all day?'

'Nothing special, really.'

'Weren't you lying on the sofa and dreaming about me?'

'No, I helped Mummy with odd jobs, then we did some shopping.'

'Ah, so you're in training to be a housewife, are you?'

'Not exactly,' she said. 'I'm not ready to stay at home yet. I'll have a job to do, remember.'

'You're definitely staying in police uniform, then.'

'I think so. I miss the routine.'

He lowered his voice. 'Tell me about this talk we're supposed to have with the vicar.'

'He needs to explain things to us, Joe.'

Keedy grinned. 'It's a bit late for that, isn't it?'

'Be serious for once, will you?' she scolded. 'Marriage is a big step to take. Some people don't realise the full implications. They're just so desperate to be together that they rush into it.'

'Well, we can't be accused of doing that, Alice.'

'No, I've had plenty of time to get to know you properly and see your weaknesses.'

'What weaknesses!' he protested. 'I don't have any.'

'Yes, you do – but this is not the place to discuss them.' She looked around then spoke in a whisper. 'Does everyone here know what a hero you are?'

'No, they don't, Alice, and they're not going to know either. I made that point to the sister. As far as everyone else is concerned, I'm in here after a stomach operation. If the other patients knew the truth about me being shot while trying to arrest burglars, they'd be pestering me with questions all day long.'

'Don't you enjoy being admired?'

'Not in this case.'

'Then I think you've done the right thing, Joe.'

'Instead of being a hero,' he said with a grin, 'I'm the villain of this ward.'

'Why?'

'It was because of me that my brother turned up here.'

'You didn't invite him, Joe.'

'I'll still get the blame.'

'Why?'

'Most of the patients here have had serious operations,' he said. 'They know only too well that they're lucky to be alive.

Didn't you hear that buzz of alarm when Dennis walked in here? He terrified them. When they saw an undertaker, they all wondered which one of us he'd come for.'

Left alone that evening, Ellen Marmion took the opportunity to finish the latest novel she had borrowed from the library. It had helped her to defeat time, but she was now back in the real world. Since her daughter would not return from the hospital for a while, she decided to continue clearing out various items from Paul's room that would be in the way. In due course, as he began his convalescence, Keedy would be their guest. It was important to make his temporary home as clean, comfortable and uncluttered as possible. While he was living there, she and Alice had agreed, they would say nothing to him about the work they had done at the new house. The surprise would only be revealed when he was well enough to visit the property.

Before she could even go upstairs, however, the telephone rang. She picked up the receiver.

'Hello . . .'

'It's me,' said Marmion. 'I just wanted to warn you that I may have to go to Ireland.'

'When?' she asked in alarm.

'Some time in the next few days.'

'Is it safe?'

'It's a lot safer than going to a war zone in France, Ellen. That's what Joe and I did last December – and we came back alive, unhurt and having solved some very nasty crimes.'

'Yes, but you won't have Joe at your side this time.'

'Cliff Burge will watch my back. He won't let me down.'

'I can't pretend that I'm happy about this, Harvey,' she said.

'That's why I wanted to give you a warning so that you'd get used to the idea. We have a lot of questions to ask and the only place we'll get answers is in Ireland. Trust me, Ellen. There's no real danger for us.'

'Have you forgotten what happened to Joe? One of those Irish burglars shot him.'

'Catching them is my priority,' he promised, 'and the way to do that is to find the person giving them orders. I'm doing exactly what Joe would want me to do. How is he, by the way? Is Alice back from the hospital yet?'

'No,' she said. 'I'm expecting her any minute.'

'Well, tell her that I'd appreciate a word, please. I'd like to hear how Joe is getting on.'

'So would I, Harvey. I want to be told that he's completely safe. He doesn't have the army guarding him any more. That worries me. The burglar who shot him obviously wants to kill him. What if he finds out which hospital Joe has been moved to?'

'There's no chance of that happening, Ellen.'

'Yes, there is,' she said, fearfully. 'Joe could still be in danger. He'll have no defence at all against that murderous Irishman.'

Occupying a corner site, the pub was in Digbeth. It had been built at the turn of the century in a style typical of the area. Tile and terracotta dominated. Corrigan had taken his friends there because it was an Irish pub. They felt at home in its warm, rowdy atmosphere and enjoyed hearing so many Irish accents. They had just returned from appraising a jewellery shop near the city centre. Corrigan waited until they'd each had a first sip of their pints of Guinness before he put his question to them.

'Well, what do you think, lads?' he asked.

'It's twice the size of the places we burgled in London,' said Orr, grinning. 'That means there'll be double the value of the jewellery inside. I'm tempted, Eamonn.'

'Good.'

'Well, I'm not,' said Regan. 'It's far too dangerous.'

'Not like you to be scared, Tom,' said Corrigan. 'I thought you'd like a challenge.'

'We've no idea what the place looks like inside.'

'Then we'll have to find out, won't we? I can do that. I'll pop into that shop and ask to look at a selection of pocket watches. I may even buy a cheap one to show that I'm a genuine customer.'

'But you'll have nobody to distract the jeweller the way that she always did.'

'Don't even mention her,' snapped Corrigan. 'This burglary is all ours. There's no rush. First, we get to know the area around the shop. Then we find out if there are any patrols at night.'

'We need a safer escape route than last time,' insisted Orr.

'We'll have it, Pierce.'

'Then you can count me in.'

'No,' said Regan, 'there are too many dangers. And what if we do burgle the shop? What happens to the stuff we steal?'

'I take it up to London,' said Corrigan, 'and turn it into money in the usual way.'

'But we're supposed to hand over everything we get to her.'

'We'll go above her head, Tom. I'll take it to Ireland and hand it over in person. That way we'll have proved ourselves.

We'll have shown that we don't need her at all.' He leant in closer to Regan. 'There'll be no more demands from her. She'll be out of the picture altogether.'

'That suits me,' said Orr.

'What about you, Tom?' asked Corrigan.

After a few moments, Regan nodded. 'I agree,' he said.

'Then let's drink to it.'

They raised their glasses, clinked them, and took a long, satisfying drink.

It had not taken long for Keedy to realise that he'd lost the luxury of silence he'd enjoyed in Mile End Military Hospital. It simply didn't exist in the one to which he'd been moved. Noise was constant. Patients never stopped talking to each other, sometimes raising their voices to reach a person on the opposite side of the ward. Then there was the loud squeal of trolleys being pushed up and down as the meals were doled out. But it was during visiting time that the din was loudest. There had been moments when Keedy could barely hear what Alice was saying to him.

Even when the lights were switched off, noises continued. There was the snoring of the man in the bed next to Keedy, the persistent coughing of the patient opposite, the involuntary grunts and wheezes and, from time to time, the patter of feet as nurses came up and down the ward. How he managed to fall asleep Keedy did not know, but it eventually happened. Sheer fatigue sent him off into a nightmare. He was back at the siege in Limehouse, begging to lead the charge into the house, taking a gun from someone, then waiting while the door was battered down. Primed for action, he went fearlessly into the house and saw the face of the man on the stairs.

Everything then happened in slow motion. He saw the gun in the man's hand, watched it being aimed at him, then heard the weapon go off. After what seemed like a full minute, the bullet hit him in the stomach, burrowed deep inside him and knocked him to the ground. Keedy let out a silent scream of agony and woke up to find that he was sweating all over.

Before he went to the café that morning, Giles Underhill walked along Shaftesbury Avenue to the theatre where he would be acting in due course in a production of *Misalliance*. His name would be in large letters on the advertising boards. A list of his many theatrical credits would be printed in the programme along with his photograph. He would be alive as an actor once more. After indulging his vanity for a few minutes, he walked to the café in Frith Street, sat down at an empty table and waited for his friend to arrive.

But she did not come. He sat there for the best part of an hour, rehearsing what he was going to say to her, but his efforts were in vain. Was she ill? Had she forgotten the arrangement? Was her absence deliberate? Had he offended her in some way? Why had she let him down? Underhill had no answers to the questions. He was simply left with the uncomfortable feeling that she had disappeared completely from his life.

Marmion was grateful once again to Special Branch. They had supplied both the names and photographs of Eamonn Corrigan's known associates. Claude Chatfield had brought the new information into Marmion's office. The superintendent put the two photographs on the desk. Marmion studied the faces of the men.

'Pierce Orr and Tom Regan,' he said. 'They were involved in that burglary in Limehouse and in the siege that followed. They look like real villains to me.'

'What I see is two Irish thugs.'

'Be fair, sir. One of these men has got great skill. Opening a safe under pressure is a difficult exercise. While the younger one acted as a lookout, the other one helped Corrigan empty the safe and the window display in seven consecutive jewellery shops. My guess is that Regan once worked for a firm that manufactured locks and safes.'

'Don't ask me to admire criminals,' said Chatfield. 'They're vermin to me. Find them.'

'There's no proof that they're still in this country,' said Marmion. 'Corrigan has a charge of murder hanging over his head and his friends are equally culpable. Most people in their position might find it safer to move back to Ireland immediately. It's one of the reasons I need your permission to go there myself.'

'We need you here, Inspector.'

'But I've picked up the scent of that woman who works with them.'

'You and Burge thought that you'd identified her once before. You were embarrassingly wrong. The one thing I do accept is that the woman lives in London – so why do you want to go across the Irish Sea to find her?'

'What I need to discover is who this woman is and for

which organisation she is working. Corrigan and his cronies are not here on holiday, sir. Jewellery they steal in this country is funding a group of terrorists in Ireland. They're obsessed with the idea of Home Rule.'

'It's a pathetic dream. Look what happened during the Easter Rising in 1916. They were ill-prepared and badly led. The so-called Irish Volunteers and other militia groups seized the post office in Dublin.'

'I remember it well,' said Marmion. 'Patrick Pearse read out a proclamation declaring that Ireland was an independent republic.'

'We soon put an end to that nonsense. Martial law was declared, and the rebels were crushed in less than a week. Pearse and the other six men who signed the proclamation were executed. Almost two thousand supporters of the Rising were sent to England and imprisoned.'

'Without trial,' recalled Marmion.

'For God's sake, man!' exclaimed Chatfield. 'Whose side are you on?'

'I'm on the side of justice, sir, not arbitrary arrest.'

'They got what they deserved.'

'There's no point in arguing the toss,' said Marmion, reasonably. 'The simple fact is that the Rising was crushed but the desire for Home Rule is still very strong among some Irish people. I'm determined to arrest four of them. That's why the search must move to Ireland.'

'I'm still not persuaded that you need to go.'

'Perhaps I should ask the commissioner for his opinion.'

'Don't you dare!' howled Chatfield. 'You report directly to me.

I'm the person who makes the decision about allowing you where to go.' He drew himself up to his full height. 'My first instinct is to refuse the request because you'd be putting yourself at risk. There are still German submarines in the Irish Sea, remember.'

'Convoys have weakened their effect considerably. I'd sail to Dublin without any fears of being torpedoed.'

'Why there? I thought this woman has connections with Cork?'

'I'll certainly visit the estate agency that had dealings with her,' said Marmion, 'but my search will begin with the Royal Irish Constabulary in the capital. They'll have a strong interest in our quartet of Irish republicans.'

'How long do you intend to stay?'

'That depends on how much we find out.'

Chatfield started. 'We?'

'Detective Sergeant Burge will come with me. It will be good experience for him.'

'Keedy would be far more use to you.'

'I agree, sir, but he's out of action.'

'What's the latest news?'

'He's been moved to Shepherd's Bush hospital and deprived of the close attention he received in Mile End. My daughter told me that he's in a general ward now. Hopefully, it's a sign of the improvement he's made.'

Chatfield pondered. Evidently, he still had doubts about the proposed visit to Ireland. Marmion waited patiently until he was given a curt nod of assent. He smiled inwardly.

* * *

During the morning visit, Keedy's ward seemed to be even louder than before. He and Alice had to raise their voices to hear each other. Concealing the fact that he had had a disturbing nightmare, he told her that he had slept well and awoke feeling much better. Keedy admitted that he would have preferred his private room back in Mile End but had now adjusted to the new situation.

'I've got real companionship here, Alice. Everyone is so friendly.'

'But not quite as friendly as Nurse Bell, I fancy,' she teased. 'I'm sorry,' she went on quickly, 'that was cruel. Tell me what happened after I left yesterday. Did anyone complain about your brother?'

'Oh, yes,' he said. 'Several patients told me that the sight of Dennis walking in here gave them a nasty shock. I couldn't help having a brother who was an undertaker. They were relieved when I promised that he wouldn't be coming back with his tape measure.'

'I passed on his apology to Mummy.'

'How did she take it?'

'She was very grateful but she's still wary of him. It's that lofty manner of his.'

'Let's not waste time together talking about Dennis,' he said. 'I want to hear what you've been doing since yesterday evening – and if you spoke to your father about the case.'

'I didn't but Mummy did. He rang from Scotland Yard.'

'Did he give her a progress report?'

'No, he just wanted to warn her that he might be going to Ireland.'

'Oh,' said Keedy with a note of yearning, 'I'd love to go with him. What could be nicer than a trip to the Emerald Isle? I've always wanted to see the Giant's Causeway.'

'Daddy will be going there on police business. In any case,' she added, 'I think that the Giant's Causeway is somewhere up in the north. My father mentioned something about going to Dublin then on to Cork.'

'See what else you can find out about the case.'

'It might be safer if you don't know. You were advised to take a complete rest. Forget all about the incident that put you into hospital. Concentrate on your recovery. We're getting married in April, remember. I want you to look at your best, Joe.'

He tapped his chest. 'I'll be bursting with energy by then.'

'Only if you take things at the right pace. In other words, do what the doctors tell you.'

'I will,' he promised, stifling a yawn. 'Have you sent out the invitations yet?'

'I posted them earlier this morning. Most of the guests still think we're having a June wedding. It's only fair to warn them that it's been moved to April.'

'They're bound to wonder why.'

'It's because of what happened to you, Joe.'

'But they don't all know that,' he said. 'Some of them will be shocked by the sudden change of date. They'll think it's because of what happened to you.'

'Joe!' she exclaimed, blushing.

'We wouldn't be the first couple forced to get married because you'd become—'

'That's enough!'

'Imagine how that doddery old aunt of yours will react.'

'Aunt Winifred knows me too well to think badly of me,' she said. 'Besides, there was a report of the siege in all the newspapers. You were hailed for your bravery. One of them said that you should get an award.'

'I've got one,' he said, fondly. 'She's sitting next to my bed.'

'And she's starting to get very cross with you.'

'Why?'

She frowned. 'Let's talk about something else, shall we?'

'What's more important than our wedding day?'

'I'm starting to feel . . . embarrassed.'

He grinned. 'Imagine how embarrassed I'll feel when the vicar tells me the facts of life.'

'Behave yourself, Joe Keedy!'

Alice put a hand to her mouth to suppress her laughter.

Even if he had seen her, Giles Underhill would not have recognised his friend. In addition to wearing a wig and some old clothing, she leant heavily on a walking stick as she went past the café in Frith Street. It was a sentimental visit. Her conversations with Underhill had often been the most enjoyable part of her week. With his help, she'd gone back into the past when the only thing that mattered to her was performing in a theatre. She led a very different life now. Had he found out the truth about her, he would have been deeply shocked. It was another reason why it was time for the friendship to stop.

Meanwhile, she had pleasant memories to enjoy. As she hobbled past the café on the opposite side of the road, they came flooding back into her mind. She went on for a few minutes, then paused as she felt a sense of profound loss. There would be no more meetings in Frith Street. The time had come to end that chapter in her life. She was about to continue her walk when she realised where she was standing. It was outside a small jewellery shop.

'Ireland!' said Burge in delight.

'I had a feeling you'd like the idea.'

'Getting out of London will be a relief, sir. I know it's the command centre of the country but it's also a place under continuous enemy attack. Ireland will be much safer.'

'I wouldn't be too sure of that, Cliff. There are enemies of a different kind over there. The men we're after may well have retreated there to escape arrest.'

'What about the woman?'

'According to you,' said Marmion, 'she's right here in London. I agree with you. Where we differ is that I don't believe she's passing the time of day by stealing silk scarves from Swan & Edgar. The woman controlling those burglaries – Sarah Standish – has bought a house near Cork. Until she moves there, she's hiding somewhere here in the capital. Did Miss Naylor give you any idea where that might be?'

'No, sir. It's not for want of trying, mind you. She's worked hard on our behalf, but she's come up against a brick wall.'

'That's not her fault. What she's discovered so far is invaluable.'

They were in Marmion's office. Burge had difficulty controlling his excitement.

'When do we set off for Ireland, sir?'

'Tomorrow morning. We're catching a ferry from Holyhead to Dublin.'

'Did you get the superintendent's approval?'

'Eventually,' said Marmion. 'Chat thinks it's a waste of time, but I managed to persuade him in the end. It will put a lot of pressure on us, of course. It's not a pleasure trip. We need to come back with solid evidence.'

'What if we manage to find the burglars there?'

'That's when we have an argument with the Royal Irish Constabulary. We'll be on their patch, Cliff. They'll want to make the arrests and claim full credit for doing so. It's important to get them on our side from the start. Of course,' he added, 'it may be that Corrigan and his friends are still hiding somewhere in this country – and they won't be idle.'

When he entered the jewellery shop, Corrigan was wearing an overcoat that he had stolen from Harrods. It gave him both respectability and a hint of wealth. When the manager welcomed him, he asked to see a selection of pocket watches. While the man went to get them from a display cabinet, Corrigan let his gaze drift casually around the interior of the shop.

CHAPTER TWENTY

When her visit to the hospital had finished, Alice Marmion made her way to the house where she and Keedy would begin their married life. Sad that he no longer got the attention lavished on him at Mile End Military Hospital, she was pleased to see that he'd adjusted to a new routine and, despite its shortcomings, had learnt to accept it. Her mother was waiting to welcome her at the house and had even prepared a scratch meal for them. When Alice had changed into some working clothes, they sat down to eat.

'How was Joe?' asked Ellen.

'He said he felt much better – though he did yawn a few times. I'm not sure he's getting a full night's sleep. There's always somebody who needs a bedpan or who calls the nurse for some other reason. Anyway,' said Alice, 'at least there was no sign of his brother. The sight of Dennis gave some of the patients the jitters.'

'He has the same effect on me.'

'Joe says that he's mellowed quite a lot.' She tasted her tea. 'This is nice, Mummy.'

'I stiffened it with a drop of turps,' said Ellen, laughing at the expression of horror on her daughter's face. 'What do you want to tackle today?'

'I'll make a start on the main bedroom. That will mean stripping off some more wallpaper, I'm afraid, but I want to do the job properly.'

'You're turning into a very good painter and decorator. Mind you, when you were at school, you loved art. You were so proud of the paintings you brought home. They were wonderful.'

'Paul didn't think so. He kept teasing me about them.'

'I think he was jealous because you had obvious talent. Besides, younger brothers always tease their sisters. It's in their blood.'

'I did my share of baiting him,' confessed Alice. 'That made us quits.'

'What would Paul say if he saw what we've been doing here?'

'He'd think that we were mad. Painting and decorating are man's work to him. He'd ask why we didn't wait until Joe could do it.'

'Then he hasn't seen the hours that Joe works. That goes for your father as well. If he's been on duty until late in the evening, he's too tired to do anything but flop into a chair.'

Alice was pensive. 'Do you think we've made a difference?'

'Yes, of course – the living room looks lovely.'

'I wasn't talking about us, Mummy. I was thinking of women in general. Since the war first started, we've rolled up our sleeves and got to work. Look at munition factories, for instance. If it wasn't for female workers, many of them would have to close.'

'You're right, Alice. I remember that murder investigation led by your father. Five munition female workers were killed in an explosion at a pub called the Golden Goose.'

'Yes,' said her daughter. 'They were called canaries because of the way chemicals turned their faces yellow. The women were having a birthday party when that bomb went off. They stood no chance.'

'All five of them did their share towards the war effort, working in conditions bad for their health. Lots of other women have done the same – including you, of course. The Women's Police Force is doing an important job.'

'We tell ourselves that every day before we go on duty. Even with its dangers, I like the work. It's been an education. But will the WPF and all the other working women get recognition for what they've done when the war is over? I doubt it,' said Alice, pursing her lips. 'Politicians have short memories.'

Ellen finished off her sandwich and washed it down with tea. She rubbed her hands.

'Right, let's get started, shall we?' she said, getting up. 'Let's turn this house into a lovely home for Mr and Mrs Joe Keedy.'

On any day, Scotland Yard was dealing with a wide variety of cases and deploying its officers accordingly. Sir Edward Henry's main interest, however, was in the investigations that attracted robust criticism in newspapers. He came into Chatfield's office with a copy of the early edition of the *Evening Standard* in his hands.

'Have you seen this?' asked the commissioner, holding the newspaper up.

'Yes, Sir Edward. It's very unfair.'

'We're doing our best to fight crime in the capital day after day and all this reporter can do is to mock us for our inefficiency. I think a stern word with the editor is in order.'

'Exactly, Sir Edward. We need support from the press – not constant criticism.'

'Inspector Marmion has been in the line of fire again. Don't they understand that murder investigations take time?' asked Sir Edward. 'What's the latest news on the case?'

'Marmion is sailing to Ireland tomorrow to gather evidence there.'

'Will it be reliable evidence?'

'I hope so. Detective Sergeant Burge will go with him.'

'Do they believe that those burglars have fled back to Ireland?'

'It's a strong possibility, Sir Edward.'

'When are these possibilities going to turn into certainties?' demanded the other. 'The only way to appease the press is to get results. A serving police constable was shot dead, and a detective sergeant was badly wounded by the same gunman. No arrests have been made. Think of the effect on the criminal community. They'll believe they can get away with anything.'

'I'm very conscious of that, Sir Edward.'

'As commissioner, I have to shoulder the blame for our failures.'

'We haven't failed,' argued Chatfield. 'We are just taking a little longer to solve this case than we'd hoped. Inspector Marmion is confident that this trip to Ireland will bear fruit.'

'The press will only call off their attack dogs if we have the villains in custody.'

'It will happen, I promise you. May I ask if you have read the whole newspaper?'

'No, I haven't. I got no further than this undeserved criticism of Scotland Yard.'

'In that case,' said Chatfield, 'you missed an item about Sergeant Keedy. They even included a photograph of him.'

'Surely, they're not blaming him as well. Keedy tried to tackle those men. He's a hero.'

'The article acknowledged that, Sir Edward. It praised him for his bravery. Then it did the most stupid thing possible.'

'I don't follow.'

'It revealed that Keedy has been moved from a military hospital in Mile End to a hospital in Shepherd's Bush. We can only hope that those burglars have gone back home to Ireland,' said Chatfield, anxiously. 'Otherwise, they'll have learnt where the sergeant is now being kept. He's a much easier target now. They may decide to kill him out of sheer spite.'

Corrigan was familiarising himself with Birmingham. After walking around the city centre for a couple of hours, he went back to New Street railway station to take a train back to Aston.

The station had been heavily bombed by German aircraft and the roof had had to be replaced. Scaffolding was up everywhere, and workmen were still remodelling a public footpath over the station. As he walked across the concourse, Corrigan saw passengers from an incoming train streaming through the barrier towards him. One of them tossed a newspaper into a wastepaper basket. Corrigan moved swiftly to retrieve it. He was pleased to see that it was a copy of the *Evening Standard*.

On her second visit to the hospital that day, Alice went up to the second floor at a more leisurely speed. When she reached Keedy's ward, she saw something that made her stand and gape. At the far end of the room, Keedy was propped up on pillows, talking to three of the other patients. The men were hanging on to every word he uttered. As Alice got closer, she could see the admiration on their faces. The patients became aware of her arrival, muttered their apologies, and withdrew to their individual beds. Alice turned to Keedy.

'What's going on, Joe?' she asked.

'Can't you guess?'

'They found out why you're in here.'

'They did more than that, Alice. Apparently, there's a piece about me in today's *Standard*. It makes me sound like the bravest detective in Scotland Yard. The word has spread. One of those men just asked me for my autograph.'

'Have they been annoying you?'

'Not really. I'd rather have remained anonymous but it's nice to be able to put a smile on people's faces. They're treating me like a celebrity of some kind.'

'You are a celebrity in my eyes,' she told him. 'And I'll want your autograph soon as well. After the wedding, I'll stand over you in the vestry until you've signed your name alongside mine.'

'But your name will have changed.'

'I'll be Mrs Keedy and proud of it.' She kissed him on the cheek. 'How are you feeling this evening?'

'Oh, I feel much better, thank you.'

'Have you been examined?'

'Yes, the doctor did his rounds this morning after you'd left. He was very impressed with the surgery I had in Mile End. All I need to do now is to rest and recuperate.'

'And fight off your fan club,' she added.

'Some of them are far worse off than me, Alice. They'll be in here much longer. Anyway,' he went on, 'let's forget about them. Tell me about your day.'

'There's not much to tell,' she said. 'By the time I got back home, Mummy had lunch ready for me. We spent most of the afternoon going through the guest list and working out the seating plan for the wedding breakfast.'

'Keep my brother well away from me.'

'Dennis will be at the far end of the top table.'

'Make sure that he doesn't give a speech,' said Keedy. 'If he does that, I'll feel as if I'm about to be buried. I want to enjoy the occasion.'

'So do I,' she said, squeezing his arm. 'Every second of it.'

'You will, Alice. That's a promise.'

'I can't wait.'

'When is your father off to Ireland?'

'Early tomorrow morning.'

'I hope he finds out what he's after. The sooner those men are behind bars, the better. Corrigan is the worst of them. He's evil.'

'Try to forget what happened, Joe. Those burglars have disappeared from your life. You must simply relax in here and get steadily better.'

Alice was about to add some more advice when she was interrupted by an old man in pyjamas and a dressing gown. He had shuffled across the ward with a newspaper in his hand.

'My missus has just brought the *Standard*,' he said, giving it to Keedy. 'There's a photo of you in it. See for yourself.'

'Thank you very much,' said Keedy, taking the newspaper.

'You're welcome to it, Sergeant.' After beaming at him, the old man shuffled off.

Alice glanced at the photograph. 'It makes you look so handsome, Joe.'

'I am handsome,' he said, laughing. Then his face tightened. 'Oh no!'

'What's up?'

'It's this article about me, Alice. It explains exactly where I am. I thought I was completely safe in here.'

'Let me see,' she said, taking the newspaper from him.

Keedy was worried. 'What will happen if Corrigan finds out?'

Eamonn Corrigan waited patiently in the queue at the ticket office until it was his turn. After travelling the short journey to Aston to tell his friends what he'd learnt from the *Evening*

Standard, he was back in New Street railway station. He moved forward to the hatch.

'A single to London, please,' he said.

'First or second, sir?'

Corrigan sniggered. 'First. It's for a special occasion.'

Knowing that he had to leave early that morning, Marmion had resorted to his alarm clock. His bag was already packed so that all he had to do before departure was to wash and shave. Not wishing to wake his wife, he reacted instantly when the alarm went off, pressing the button to kill the noise. After rubbing his eyes, he looked up and saw a ghostly figure in the gloom.

'Good morning, Harvey,' said Ellen. 'I've brought you a cup of tea.'

'I was going to sneak away without rousing you.'

'Drink this, then go to the bathroom,' she said, putting the teacup on the bedside table. 'When you've got dressed, there'll be breakfast waiting for you in the kitchen.'

'You're a gem, Ellen, do you know that?'

'I'm not sending you off with an empty stomach. There's no rush. Your car won't be here for almost half an hour.'

'Thanks for telling me.'

She moved to the door then paused. 'Oh, Alice had a message for you.'

'What is it?'

'Bon voyage!'

Keedy had a troubled night. When he was deep asleep, he was assaulted by the same dream. He felt the same uprush of determination, taking the gun and waiting until the door was battered open. As soon as he could, he dashed into the house, then stopped to stare up at Corrigan. He could see murder dancing in the man's eyes. When the Irishman's gun was fired, the bullet came in slow motion, gliding through the air until it hit his midriff then lodged in his stomach. The pain was indescribable. Keedy came awake with a silent scream, then realised he was dripping with sweat again. It was frightening. The man who'd tried to kill him was still at liberty. More to the point, he knew exactly where his target was.

Her life was governed by a strict routine. It was the reason she remained so healthy and active. After eating her breakfast and drinking a pot of tea, she went into the living room and sat down to plan her day. The warmth from the fire heated the entire flat. The one luxury she allowed herself was the use of a maid who let herself in at seven in the morning, put the ashes from the previous day in a bucket, laid and lit the fire, then slipped silently out. Her employer was never lonely. Her mind was filled with so many happy memories. There were prayers to say, speeches from her favourite plays to declaim, letters to write and a series of exercises to perform. Her body was fit, her mind alert and her commitment to Ireland deeper than ever.

Recent events had disturbed her, but the danger had passed. The three burglars were in Birmingham now, safely out of the way. None of them would stir until she ordered them to do so. For the time being, she could forget all about them.

* * *

Carrying an umbrella to ward off the rain, Corrigan took a first look at the hospital. As he went past the main gate, he glanced up at a board that told him the visiting times and the telephone number of the hospital. He memorised the details instantly. There were no armed soldiers on sentry duty as there had been at the military hospital. Keedy was unprotected.

Though the idea of a trip to Ireland had appealed to them, they had not anticipated the discomfort of getting there. Seated in the compartment of a train, Marmion and Burge had to endure a journey of almost three hundred miles to Holyhead in bad weather. There was worse to come. When they finally went aboard their ferry, they were warned that the crossing would be subject to high winds, heavy rain and choppy water. It meant that there was no possibility of going up on deck. Instead, they sat in a crowded restaurant, listening to the teacups rattling and feeling sick.

'I wish I hadn't eaten anything,' said Burge, ruefully. 'It's upset my stomach.'

'Try to think about something else,' advised Marmion, 'and hope the pain will go away.'

'What happens when we get to Dublin?'

'We go straight to police headquarters. They are expecting us. I rang Inspector Doyle.'

'How much does he know about the case?'

'He seemed a little confused at first, then he found Corrigan's name in their files and realised what we were up against. Corrigan is not only a prolific burglar, he's wanted for a string

288

of other crimes. Doyle described him as desperate – the kind of man who'll stop at nothing.'

'We know that.'

'If he'd had access to the sergeant, he'd have killed him. That's why we had an armed guard assigned to him while he was in Mile End Hospital.'

'What about now?'

'Oh, he's perfectly safe where he is. Corrigan doesn't have a clue that he's been moved. In fact, since we stepped up the search for him and his associates, he's probably left London altogether. Who knows?' said Marmion with a grin. 'He may be travelling back home on this ferry.'

'Then I hope he's even more seasick than me!'

Corrigan had booked a room in a hotel within reasonable walking distance of the hospital. He used the hotel telephone to speak to a woman on the reception desk there. She had a pleasant manner and a readiness to help.

'My name is Alan Keedy,' he told her. 'I believe that you have a cousin of mine in your hospital. His name is Joe Keedy.'

'Just a moment, sir,' she said. 'I'll have to check.'

'I'm in Manchester right now but I've got a business meeting in London tomorrow. If possible, I'd like to find time to drop in to see Joe. Will that be possible?'

'I think so, Mr Keedy.' There was a pause. 'Ah, here we are. I've found your cousin's name. He's in Maynard Ward.'

'Doesn't he have a private room?'

'No, I'm afraid not,' she replied. 'They are reserved for patients in the most critical condition. Mr Keedy is in a bed at the far end of Maynard Ward. As he gets better, he'll move steadily up the ward until he's near the doors.'

'I'm very grateful for that information.'

'Is there anything else you need to know, sir?'

'No, thank you.' he said with a sly grin. 'You've told me everything I wanted.'

Dun Laoghaire was the busiest port in Ireland. By the time they docked there, the weather had improved, and their discomfort had eased considerably. Marmion and Burge stepped ashore in Dublin and took stock of their surroundings. Burge noticed something.

'There seem to be two different police forces on duty here,' he said. 'The one looks very much like our own force, but the other has more of a military air. Also – they're armed!'

'Most of the men on duty here are in the Dublin Metropolitan Police. They're an unarmed urban force. They look after the city. The others are members of the Royal Irish Constabulary. They're more important. I'm hoping that one of them will be here to welcome us.'

They were in luck. When they had gone through customs, they found a driver waiting to transport them. He was a solid man in his forties with a weathered face and dark eyes filled with suspicion. He saw the two detectives and moved forward to intercept them.

'I'm to take you to Phoenix Park,' he explained.

Marmion was surprised. 'How did you know we were from London?'

'You stick out a mile, sir. Everyone else on the ferry is Irish. I can see it in their faces. They look glad to be in Dublin.'

'And so are we,' said Marmion with feeling. 'The crossing was an ordeal. We're grateful to be on dry land again.'

'That doesn't make you Irish, sir.'

'Who cares? It makes us feel safe.'

'I second that,' said Burge.

After looking from one to the other, the driver led the way to a police car, unlocked the doors and watched them get into the rear seats. Closing the door after them, he got into the driving seat and started the engine. The police car drew away from the kerb. They noticed the way that other vehicles treated it with respect. The driver was not conversational, only speaking to answer their questions and doing so tersely.

'How long have you been in the RIC?' asked Burge.

'Long enough,' grunted the driver.

'It started as the Irish Constabulary,' said Marmion to Burge. 'It earned the title "Royal" by virtue of conspicuous bravery in suppressing the Fenian Rising of 1867.'

'My father was involved in that,' the driver told them. 'It's the reason I joined the police. He brought me up to know where my duty lies. The Fenians were crushed that day – and good riddance to them!' he snarled. 'I'm just sorry I wasn't there myself to join in.'

He drove on in an uneasy silence.

Alice got to the hospital early for the morning visit. She was worried about Keedy. Until he had been rushed to hospital with a bullet inside him, Keedy had never shown fear of any kind. Having come close to death, however, he had been forced to accept that he did not, after all, live a charmed life. He was as vulnerable as any other man. There was another factor to consider. Keedy was about to get married and take on responsibility for a wife. It was his duty as a husband to remember that discretion was the better part of valour and temper his urge for action.

On her previous visit, Alice had seen the worrying effect that the item in the newspaper had had on him. His face had been drained of colour and his eyes had lost the glint of self-confidence that she knew so well. Keedy had felt cornered. Without any concern for his safety, a newspaper had blithely told its readers exactly where he could be found. The man who shot him during the siege had been seen hanging around the first hospital where he had been. The present one had nothing like the security of the military hospital. Alice could understand his apprehension.

She was still anxious on his behalf when the bell rang. She joined the surge for the staircase and went quickly up two flights. Striding along the corridor, she was the first to reach the ward and go into it, desperate to have the reassurance of his smile of welcome. But he was not there. She stopped in horror and her throat went dry. Keedy's bed was empty.

When they met him in his office at the Depot, the visitors were impressed by Terence Doyle. He was a tall, slim, elegant man in his fifties with a lilting voice that entranced them. After waving them to a seat apiece, he offered them refreshments and the three of them were soon enjoying tea and biscuits. Doyle had put Marmion and Burge at ease.

'I won't bore you by talking about the structure of the RIC,' he said. 'All I will tell you is this. Where you have a commissioner, we have an inspector general who is senior to him. As for inspectors themselves, we have a wide selection – county inspectors, district inspectors, et cetera.'

'Sounds like a recipe for confusion,' said Marmion.

'Indeed, it does – yet, oddly, the system seems to work. Anyway, it's good to meet you, Inspector Marmion. I'm sorry if my last telephone call was a trifle unhelpful. Now that we're face to face, I hope to be of more use.'

'Were you able to make enquiries?'

'Eventually, I was. I say "eventually" because we've been very busy with real crimes. Regarding the purchase of a house near Cork, I can't see that a serious crime has taken place.'

'Yet this woman is reported to have taken a policeman with her to the estate agency.'

'That may have been simply for show. People are cheated out of houses from time to time if a buyer comes in with a higher offer, even after contracts have been signed. It's sharp practice, but not necessarily grounds for litigation. There's another point,' added Doyle, shrewdly. 'This woman was an accomplished actress. Could it be that this "policeman" of hers was simply an actor in police uniform? Impersonating a policeman onstage is not illegal, of course, but it's a crime in real life. Would this woman resort to such a trick?'

'I believe that she would resort to anything,' said Marmion, opening his bag and taking out a magazine. 'This is a photograph of her, taken a few decades ago.' He handed the magazine to Doyle. 'In those days, the theatre was her life. She has now dedicated it to securing Home Rule for Ireland.'

'Then why is she living in London?'

'It's a question I'll put to her when we arrest her.'

Doyle was firm. 'If she moves to Ireland, it's the RIC who should make the arrest.'

'Let's not argue about it,' said Marmion. 'We came to establish that the woman involved in the purchase of that house really was Sarah Standish. It means a visit to an estate agent in Cork.'

'That's something with which we can help you, Inspector,' said Doyle, taking a long look at the photograph before handing Marmion the magazine. 'I can put a car and a driver at your disposal. Is that agreeable to you?'

'Yes, it is. Thank you very much.'

'This is a beautiful country. You will have an opportunity to see some of it on your journey south. Cork is a fascinating city. If you had time, I'd suggest a visit to the Ring of Kerry as well.'

'We didn't come here to see the sights,' Marmion reminded him.

'Quite so. If this woman, Sarah Standish, has connections with Ireland, I can understand why she should wish to retire here. She'll be welcomed with open arms. However,' Doyle went on, voice hardening into a growl, 'if she's coming back to cause us more strife under the banner of Irish Home Rule, we'll lock her up in prison for a long time.'

While her daughter was visiting the hospital, Ellen continued with the job of cleaning the room in which Keedy would be sleeping in due course. She used a sweeping brush to fish out some boxes from under the bed. They contained toys bought for Paul when he was a child. She remembered how happy he had been when he played with them. They were no use to him now, yet she hated the idea of getting rid of them. Still on her knees, she held a well-worn teddy bear in her arms and let fond memories seep back slowly into her mind.

Ellen stayed on the floor until cramp set in, forcing her to struggle to her feet. She tried to continue her work but was unable to do so. Something was holding her back, freezing her muscles, blurring her vision, and numbing her mind. What disturbed her the most was that she had no idea what it could be.

CHAPTER TWENTY-ONE

Alice Marmion was at once relieved and frightened. While she was delighted to learn that Keedy was still alive, she was alarmed to hear that he was still under threat. He had been moved to a single room on the third floor. When she was taken here, Alice saw that a man was standing outside it. Taken into the room by a nurse, she found Keedy sitting up in bed. He understood the look of panic on her face.

'I'm sorry if you had a shock,' he said, grasping her hand.

'Your bed was empty, Joe.'

'Someone was supposed to stop you going into Maynard Ward. They moved me here for safety reasons. Luckily, there's a young woman on the reception desk who was kind enough to pass on the news that my cousin, Alan, had rung to say that he'd visit me today. There's only one problem.'

'What is it?'

'I don't have a cousin named Alan.'

'Who was this man?' gasped Alice. 'Could it be the one who . . . ?' Keedy nodded. 'That's terrible, Joe. He's stalking you.'

'The superintendent came to my rescue. I got the sister to ring Scotland Yard to tell him what had happened. Chat was here in a flash. He not only had me moved out of that ward, he brought Detective Constable Younger with him to stand outside my door. That bulge in his coat was a gun, by the way. Barry Younger owes me a good turn. When I beat him at snooker, I never demand money – just a pint of beer.'

Alice was puzzled. 'How can you be so relaxed about it?'

'I'm only relaxed on the outside, Alice. Inside, I've had a few tremors.'

'What if that man finds out that you're in here?'

'The staff have been warned not to speak to anyone looking for me. If, by chance, he does work out where I am, he'll have no chance of getting past Barry Younger. He's a lousy snooker player but a genius with a gun in his hands.'

'If only Daddy could catch this man!' she sighed.

'He will do in time. Meanwhile, I hear your father's gone off to Ireland.'

'Yes, he left the house in the small hours. He's probably in Dublin by now.'

'Then let's hope that he gets the answers he's after,' said Keedy. 'Right, no more fears, okay? I'm alive and kicking, as you see, and I intend to stay this way until someone walks up the aisle towards me early in April. Okay?'

'I'm bound to be worried, Joe.'

'I'm safe and sound.'

'Then why don't I feel sure of that?'

'It's because you're one of nature's worriers, that's why.' He stroked her hand. 'Everything is under control, Alice.'

She took a deep breath. 'Yes, of course,' she said. 'I'll do my best to believe it.'

Eamonn Corrigan felt thwarted. When he had reached Maynard Ward, he had put his head inside to look at the beds at the far end. One of them was empty. The patient in the bed opposite was not his quarry. Corrigan was vexed. When he asked the sister where Joe Keedy might be, she refused to tell him. She would not even admit that the patient was still in the hospital. Corrigan had withdrawn at once. The hospital staff had probably been warned not to speak to someone posing as Keedy's cousin. There was no point in staying there so he left the building at speed.

On the walk back to his hotel, he was angry. Keedy was being kept hidden. There had to be a way of getting to him. He went through all the possibilities. When it finally dawned on him how he could reach Keedy, he grinned broadly and slapped his thigh in triumph. The problem was solved. Corrigan stepped into a pub to celebrate.

The drive to Cork was a delight. The rain had stopped, the clouds had cleared and – most important of all – they had a far more amenable driver. As they wended their way south, they enjoyed the views of the rolling countryside. There was little sign that there was a war on. Having come from London, where the impact of war was highly visible, they were overwhelmed by a sense of relief. The journey was over a hundred and sixty miles, so they stopped in Waterford to stretch their legs and relieve themselves. They were soon back in the car, driving on towards Cork. Since the driver was well versed in the problems of policing the country, they fed him endless questions to improve their knowledge of Ireland.

'What's your view of the demand for Home Rule?' asked Marmion.

'I don't have views, Inspector,' said the man. 'I just take orders.'

'How strong a party is Sinn Fein?'

'It's been steadily building up its support. There's a branch in Cork. I daresay that the Irish Brotherhood is active there as well, calling for Home Rule. First, of course, they're looking forward to the day when this war is finally over, and we can start to pick up the pieces. Everyone here wants peace.'

'So do we,' said Marmion, 'but there's no sign of it. And there's no guarantee that we will emerge as victors. Some people are already predicting a German victory.'

'That would be a disaster,' said Burge.

'Let's hope and pray that it never happens.'

They were still discussing the outcome of the war when they finally arrived in Cork. The driver brought the car to a halt at the first police station he came to. He went into the building to get directions to the estate agency.

'We've got here at last,' said Burge. 'I hope it was worth the effort.'

'I'm sure it was, Cliff. I've got this feeling.'

'I wish that I could share it, sir.'

'Look at the facts. We know this woman is keen to return to her home country. Nothing is stronger than patriotic feeling. It informs everything that Sarah Standish does. Don't be fooled by her age. She's clearly capable and decisive. Time hasn't blunted her belief in Irish independence. If anything,' said Marmion, 'it's sharpened it.'

'What are we hoping to hear from the estate agent?'

'I want him to confirm that the buyer of the property really was Irene Peck, the woman's real name, and what London address she gave when she signed the contract. All we need to do then is to board a ferry back to Holyhead and start the journey home.' Marmion chuckled. 'When we tell him what we found out, the superintendent will be delighted with us.'

'Chat has finally done something useful,' said Keedy. 'He deserves three cheers.'

'Once he knew that you were in danger,' said Younger, 'the superintendent moved quickly. He had me on sentry duty outside your room in a flash.'

'You were a sight for sore eyes, Barry.'

'I'm keen to keep you alive so that I can beat you at snooker for once.'

Keedy laughed. 'Not a hope in hell of you doing that.'

'Oh, yes there is.'

Barry Younger grinned. He was a big, barrel-chested detective in his thirties with a pencil moustache. He'd stepped into the room to have a brief chat. Keedy was grateful.

'I feel as safe as houses with you outside my door, Barry.'

'I was glad to be assigned here. It's a privilege to look after you, Joe. When I get home, I can tell the wife that I've been protecting one of the bravest officers we've got.'

'I didn't feel very brave when I saw that the *Standard* had told everyone in London what hospital I was now in. To be honest, it made me shudder. If you hadn't turned up, I might have had a visit from the man who put a bullet in me.'

'We've frightened him off.'

'That's very comforting.'

'What sort of man is he?'

'Persistent,' said Keedy. 'Far too bloody persistent.'

Alone in his hotel room, Corrigan made a list of the items he needed to buy. Since the police had a description of him, he would have to change his appearance completely. They had somehow learnt of his visit to the hospital and whisked Keedy away from Maynard Ward. It probably meant that he was being guarded day and night. But there was another way to reach him if Corrigan was bold enough to take the option, and it would not involve searching the hospital. All that he had to do was to watch and wait. Then he could strike.

Keedy was a handsome man. He would certainly have a woman in his life. It might be a wife, or a girlfriend and she would certainly visit him every day. Corrigan simply had to wait and watch. Once he identified the woman, he could intercept her. She would know where Keedy was being kept in the hospital. With a gun pointing at her head, she would tell Corrigan exactly what he asked her. It would be that easy. He allowed himself a smile of congratulation.

When they tracked down the Dempsey & Howe estate agency, they found it near the centre of Cork. Situated on a corner, it had a rather quaint appearance. There was nothing remotely quaint about Vincent Dempsey, however. Invited into his office, they were confronted by a corpulent man in his fifties with an expensive tailor who had somehow managed to disguise most of his bulges. Dempsey had a bald head trimmed by white hair. Assuming that they were new clients, he was disconcerted to discover that they were Scotland Yard detectives. The moment they raised the topic of an unfair sale, he went straight on the defensive.

'You've been misled, I fear,' he said, waving a chubby hand. 'There was no problem with the sale. It went through without any difficulty.'

'That's not what we've heard,' said Marmion. 'Before we go any further, can I ask you to take a look at a photograph of a woman who bought the property under discussion?' He showed Dempsey the magazine photograph. 'Please allow for the fact that it was taken many years ago.'

The estate agent needed only a second to recognise her. He nodded vigorously.

'That's her without a doubt. Her face is so memorable.'

'Her stage name was Sarah Standish,' said Marmion, 'but I daresay she would have used a different name when she signed the contract.'

'I'll tell you what it was,' promised Dempsey, moving to a filing cabinet, and opening a drawer. It took him moments to extract the correct file. 'Here we are,' he went on, opening it, 'I have a copy of the contract right here.'

'Which name did she sign?'

'Miss Irene Nora Peck.'

'And how did she conduct herself?' asked Marmion.

'She was a trifle upset when she arrived,' said Dempsey, 'but she calmed down when I explained that there had been an unfortunate mistake. We were not going to cancel her contract with us.'

'She obviously thought that you were.'

'Yes,' added Burge. 'I don't believe that the lady would have made a long and uncomfortable journey here unless she had a very good reason.'

'It was to challenge the legitimacy of what you were trying to do,' added Marmion. 'Why else should she bring a lawyer and a policeman?'

'Neither of them had much chance to speak,' recalled Dempsey. 'Miss Peck did most of the talking. It was more of a performance than anything else. She had clearly lost none of her histrionic skills. To tell you the truth, she was rather intimidating.'

'Don't expect any sympathy from us, sir.'

'I'm not asking for any, Inspector.'

'When she first signed that contract,' asked Marmion, 'was there a deposit involved?'

'Yes,' admitted Dempsey, 'and it was quite a substantial one. Before I could repay it, the lady descended on me with two companions in tow. Naturally, I apologised for the inconvenience caused and offered to pay any costs incurred in travelling from London.'

'That brings us to her address. Do you have it in the file?'

'Of course, Inspector . . .'

As the address was read out, Burge jotted it down in his notebook.

'And was that the first time you met the lady in person?'

'Yes, it was. Miss Peck had a lawyer acting for her. She knew the cottage in question and had coveted it for years. When it came on the market, she ordered her lawyer to make an offer for it.'

'So, as far as you were concerned, the deal had been done.'

'Indeed, it had. The sale was quick and remarkably painless.'

'That was until a second buyer stepped in,' Burge reminded him.

'There was another enquiry about the property – that much was true. But I assured the buyer that we had already accepted an offer and that the cottage had been sold.'

'Miss Peck seems to have a different version of what occurred,' said Marmion. 'To be frank, I prefer to believe hers. You sought to increase your profit on the sale.'

Dempsey winced. 'I was happy to accept . . . the amount that the lady offered.'

'Trust is vital in your profession, sir. To avoid making expensive mistakes, you must be a good judge of character. When you met Miss Peck,' said Marmion, 'what was your assessment of her? Was she fit, healthy, clear-minded? Please give us as much detail as you can. We have a very special interest in this lady . . .'

Alice and her mother had just finished working at the new house and were clearing up. With the smell of paint still in their nostrils, they looked around with pride. It had been another productive afternoon. On their walk to the bus stop, Alice was curious.

'Have you managed to work out what it must have been?' she asked.

'No, Alice. I'm still none the wiser.'

'Something you saw in Paul's room must have stirred a memory for you.'

'Lots of things did,' said Ellen, 'especially those toys.'

'What exactly did you feel?'

'I didn't feel anything, Alice. That's the point. I sort of . . . well, seized up somehow. It was minutes before I could move again.'

Her daughter was decisive. 'You need to go to the doctor, Mummy.'

'It's not a physical thing. If it had been, how could I have worked so hard this afternoon? It's all in the mind. That's what's so worrying.'

'You could discuss it with the doctor.'

'What's the point? There's no medicine he can give me. I'd be wasting money if I went to him. Anyway, I feel so much better now. Getting out of the house was a tonic.'

'What will happen when we get home?' asked Alice. 'Will

you have that same kind of paralysis again?'

'No,' insisted Ellen. 'I'm certain of it.'

'How can you be?'

'Because I'm not going near Paul's room again.' She saw a vehicle approaching. 'There's our bus. Let's hurry or we'll miss it.'

Marmion and Burge were happy. It had taken them a considerable effort to get to Cork but they felt that their journey had been worth it. By confronting Vincent Dempsey, they had got information that would have been impossible to glean any other way. On the drive back to Dublin, they were able to discuss what they had learnt from the adipose estate agent. Burge did not mince his words.

'Dempsey is a crook,' he said. 'He tried to increase his profit by lying to a customer who had put down a large deposit. In her case, she challenged him and got her cottage back. How many other customers has he tricked out of a house they thought they'd bought in good faith?'

'Irene Peck was definitely not the first.'

'She's certainly got some spirit. Very few women of that age would have the strength and determination to make a journey across the Irish Sea. We found it bad enough ourselves. It must have been agony for her.'

'I admire what she did, but I have no sympathy for her.'

'Why not?'

'I'm fairly certain that she's been working hand-in-glove with those criminals.'

'It's beginning to look that way, sir,' conceded Burge.

'Do you remember what Inspector Doyle told us?' asked

Marmion. 'He wondered if the policeman she took into the estate agency might have been an actor. It's a plausible suggestion for a woman whose whole life revolved around the theatre.'

'Pegasus Costumes have a wide selection,' said Burge, 'but I doubt if they'd have been able to supply the correct uniform for the Irish police.'

'Costume hire is available in Ireland, you know. The Abbey Theatre in Dublin will probably have a wide selection as well. Sarah Standish would know that because she's performed there. It said so in that magazine article about her. That leads me on to another idea.'

'What is it?'

'I'm wondering if the lawyer who went with her to that estate agency was also an actor in disguise. Remember what we were told. The two men hardly did more than introduce themselves. They left it to her to do all the talking.'

'So, in other words . . .'

'Yes, Cliff. I do mean that. Dempsey told us that she put on a performance for him. He didn't realise that the policeman and the lawyer had also rehearsed their parts.'

Burge was shocked. 'The woman is as much of a crook as Dempsey.'

'The difference is that she's far more deadly.'

'I agree.'

'He got what he deserved. Now, who are you voting for?' asked Marmion, turning to him. 'I believe that we've found the person we're after. Do you still stand by the lady with the silk scarf?'

* * *

Corrigan had changed his appearance completely. Instead of the hat he'd worn on his earlier visit to the hospital, he bought himself a cap. A crumpled old coat had been found in the market where he'd also acquired a walking stick. When he entered the hospital, he was bent over so that his face was largely concealed. In the waiting room filled with visitors, someone stood up and offered him their seat. He was grateful, especially as the seat was a vantage point from which he could scour the whole room. She had to be there, he told himself. Whether she was Keedy's wife or girlfriend, the woman was certain to turn up. Corrigan prayed that she had come alone.

He let his gaze run along the rows of seats. Most of the women there were too old for someone of Keedy's age. Of the younger ones, few were attractive enough to appeal to someone like the detective. Corrigan whittled the possibilities down to three. Two of them, however, had come with a friend. Only one of them – the prettiest by far – was on her own. When the bell rang, she was on her feet at once and was among the first to depart. He remained in his chair, happy to stay there until the young woman was ready to leave.

They had decided to stay the night in Dublin and catch an early ferry back to Holyhead in the morning. Their hotel was near the docks. It was quiet, unpretentious, and meticulously clean. More importantly, it had a small restaurant. Marmion and Burge settled down for the first meal they had had since reaching Ireland.

'It's so good to feel hungry again,' said Burge, studying the menu.

'Yes,' agreed Marmion. 'We can't expect those biscuits we had with Inspector Doyle to keep us going indefinitely. I'll send him a report of what we found in Cork. If, by chance, Sarah Standish slips through our fingers and comes here, the inspector can have the fun of arresting her.'

'Only if the woman really is the person whom we're after.'

'I thought you'd accepted that she was.'

'So did I, sir, but I'm having second thoughts. Sarah Standish – or Irene Peck – may simply be an Irishwoman who wishes to live out the remaining years of her life in the place where she was born. That's understandable. Apart from anything else, it's much safer here than in London. The German air force is concentrating its bombing raids on us.'

'So?'

'She's finally decided to come here before the enemy launches its spring offensive. The papers have been full of reports about it. They don't want to spread panic but they're not exactly very reassuring. An article I read the other day said we should "prepare for every eventuality". That's a polite way of warning us that we could lose.'

'I prefer to believe that we're going to win,' said Marmion.

He broke off as a waitress came up to take their order. The first thing on their list were two pints of Guinness. When they had made their selections from the menu, she went off.

'To return to our case,' resumed Marmion. 'I'm now convinced that Sarah Standish is the woman we must find. She's obviously a very tough woman. Dempsey admitted he found her scary. She's a real fighter.'

'Grace Whittington may be equally tough.'

'That's irrelevant.'

'Why do you dismiss her so easily?'

'It's because she has no apparent connection with Ireland,' said Marmion. 'Look at our other suspects. Miranda Darnell was married to a man born in Dublin and Sarah Standish grew up in Cork. All that we know about the other woman is that she's a clever shoplifter.'

'She may well be capable of more serious crimes.'

'We have no evidence of that.'

'Bea Naylor may come up with more information about her.'

'We're the detectives, Cliff,' said Marmion. 'We can't rely on untrained amateurs.'

'That's unfair. Miss Naylor worked hard for us. But for her, we wouldn't be in this country.'

'You're right. The woman deserves credit.'

Burge went on to heap praise on Beatrice Naylor, suggesting that – in the event of an arrest based on her information – she deserved an acknowledgement of some kind. He broke off as the waitress returned with a tray bearing two pints of Guinness. Both men reached for a tankard.

'What shall we drink to?' asked Burge. 'Victory on the battlefield?'

'I suggest something more pressing,' said Marmion. 'Let's drink to the possibility of an early end to this case.' They tasted their pints of Guinness and gave smiles of approval. 'We finally discovered the real reason why we came to Ireland.'

'I've just had another thought about Grace Whittington . . .'

'Keep it to yourself, Cliff. The woman is irrelevant. We

already have our prime suspect. You can join me tomorrow when I go to her home and arrest her.'

'I'll leave that pleasure to you, sir.'

'What will you be doing?'

'I'll be continuing the search for that other retired actress on our list.' He took another sip from his tankard. 'Just in case.'

Tom Regan and Pierce Orr were also enjoying a pint of Guinness. They were in the Irish pub in Digbeth, wondering how their friend was getting on.

'Where d'you think Eamonn is now?' asked Orr.

'He's doing what he told us he'd do and that's kill Sergeant Keedy. He hated that article in the *Standard* about how brave Keedy was. What about us? Didn't we show bravery as well? It took guts to set fire to that place in Limehouse then shin down a rope in the dark and escape.'

'She thought we should never have been cornered there.'

'Bugger what she thinks!' exclaimed Regan. 'I hate taking orders from a woman.' He smirked. 'Hey, shall I tell you something? It's about afterwards. Just before we set off, Eamonn swore that when they met, he'd have his way with her.'

Orr was shocked. 'But she's old!'

'Many a good tune played on an old violin,' said Regan with a cackle.

'Not if the strings are broken.'

'Be fair, man. She's kept her good looks. Eamonn was tempted.'

'What happened?'

'She threw him out of that flat of hers and warned him

never to come back. Eamonn had really upset her. That's why he wants us to break away.'

'I'm not happy about that, Tom,' confessed Orr.

'Let's trust in Eamonn. He knows what he's doing.'

Corrigan had been patient. Seated in the waiting room, he read a newspaper and waited. When the bell rang, he got to his feet at once. Visitors began to stream out from the various wards. He stepped out in the entrance hall and waited for them. When they appeared, they went past him in groups, and he was afraid that he might have missed her by mistake. Towards the end of the exodus, she finally appeared, but there was a problem. She was talking to an older woman, who seemed to be in distress and was dabbing at her eyes with a handkerchief. The two of them left together and headed for the bus stop.

Corrigan went after them, keeping well back. Still chatting, the two women waited for some time until a bus finally came along, and they climbed into it. He followed. The bus was quite full, but the women managed to find an empty seat upstairs that allowed them to sit side by side. Alice put a consoling arm around the woman's shoulders. Corrigan was a few rows behind them, straining his ears in vain to catch what they were talking about, but there was far too much noise elsewhere. He could hear nothing above the general babble. All that he could do was to hope that the two women eventually parted company.

Alice had met her in the lift as it descended. Noticing the tears running down the woman's face, she immediately offered her some sympathy. The woman confided that her husband was close to death. It was only a matter of time before she would stop coming to the hospital. Alice felt sorry for her, offering her words of comfort. When they caught the same bus, the woman was still talking about her fear of becoming a widow and leading an empty life. It grieved her that she had no children to help her through the ordeal ahead. Alice eventually stood up as the bus approached her stop. The woman grasped her hand and thanked her for listening. The bus slowed to a halt and Alice went down the stairs with a few other passengers. Getting off, she began the journey home, thinking about the pain the woman had been suffering and wondering how she would have coped if told that Keedy would soon die. It was too frightening to contemplate.

Other passengers from the bus had been walking ahead of her but they turned off into a side road. It was then that she became aware she was being followed. Endless hours of padding the streets in her police uniform had given her a heightened sense of danger. Even though she could hear no footsteps, she knew that somebody was there. Alice was still some way from home. If she turned and saw a man behind her, she might not be able to outrun him. It was better to pretend that she was unaware of him.

She had one advantage. Having been born and brought up in the area, she knew it well. Alice had to act quickly before the man moved in. Turning the next corner, she ran ten yards or so then dived into a gap in the hedge and crouched down. Moments later, she heard footsteps as a man ran past her and started looking in doorways. Alice crept behind the hedge until she reached the corner. She then sprinted all the way home.

* * *

313

Corrigan was furious. He was certain that he'd identified someone who could tell him where Keedy was hiding. Having trailed her patiently, he'd been waiting for the best moment to strike. But she knew that he was there and tricked him. The woman was clever. Certain that she would visit the hospital on the following day, he was equally certain that she would not be alone. There would be somebody with her to offer protection. He had failed.

After running all the way home, Alice was breathless as she unlocked the front door and went into the house. Closing the door behind her, she bolted it as well, then leant against it to catch her breath. Ellen came into the hall and saw her.

'How was Joe?' she asked.

'I'll tell you in a moment,' gasped Alice, moving to the telephone. 'I need to make a call first.'

'Who are you ringing?'

'The police.'

CHAPTER TWENTY-TWO

They were alone in the restaurant, enjoying a cup of coffee after the meal. Marmion and Burge felt restored. They'd forgotten all about the discomfort of the crossing earlier that day.

'What have we learnt by coming here?' asked Marmion.

'I hope that we've learnt enough to make the superintendent smile for once.'

'Chat is never happy unless he can harass us.'

'It's worse than that in my case,' said Burge. 'There's a hostile look in his eye. He simply doesn't believe I'm good enough to be a detective sergeant.'

'Well, I certainly do,' Marmion told him. 'I've been impressed by everything you've done, Cliff. I'm glad I had the sense to recommend you. Joe Keedy agreed. You were an ideal choice.'

'I don't feel ideal sometimes.'

'You're still finding your feet. It could be worse. Imagine working in the RIC.'

'What do you mean?'

'Well, the British public has finally learnt to accept that a heavy police presence is necessary during a war. It's different over here. Most Irish people see the police as a symbol of foreign oppression – especially the ones we're after.'

'I can see why Corrigan and his friends despise us, but what about this woman?'

'She wants freedom from British control,' said Marmion. 'That's why I'm certain she's Irish. You saw the place where she was born. It's worth fighting for, in her opinion.'

'Do you think she condones the way that Corrigan shot that policeman?'

'Ask her when we arrest her.'

'You're certain it's Irene Peck, aren't you?'

'Yes, of course. I can't understand why you don't agree with me.'

'I do and I don't,' admitted Burge. 'When that estate agent described her, I could see what a formidable woman she must be. She sounds more than capable of winning the confidence of a series of owners of jewellery shops.'

'So why don't you accept that she must be our target?'

'Once bitten, twice shy.'

Marmion nodded. 'Ah, I see.'

'I was convinced that Miranda Darnell was working with those burglars. Everything pointed to her. I made the mistake of feeling certain she was our woman. And what happened?'

'You ended up with a red face.'

'I've never felt so stupid,' confessed Burge.

'You can make amends,' promised Marmion. 'Unlike the other one, this suspect is neither blind nor infirm. She got the better of Dempsey and that's not an easy thing to do. You may have failed the first time, Cliff, but you can put that disappointment behind you. The best way to do that is to make the arrest. Irene Peck – or Sarah Standish – is all yours.'

There was a time when she drew immense pleasure from looking through the photograph albums that recorded her career in the theatre. It was heartening to be reminded of her triumphs onstage. She had also loved to thumb her way through old programmes and wonder what had happened to the other actors with whom she had worked. But she was in no mood for nostalgia now. The album she flicked through contained reports and photographs clipped out of newspapers. It was a means of boosting her resolve to carry on with her work. When she reached the photograph of a corpse at the feet of British soldiers, she had to snap the album shut.

It hurt her too much to look at the man she'd loved. Revenge was her only pleasure now.

It was some time before the police car eventually arrived. The two uniformed constables listened to Alice's story and clearly thought that she was an excitable young woman who had imagined a danger that might not have existed. It was only when she explained that she was in the Women's Police Force that they began to take her seriously. When she told them who her father was and why she had been visiting the hospital, their manner changed completely. Inspector Marmion and Sergeant Keedy were names that immediately aroused their respect. With Alice also in the car, they drove back to the point where she had shaken off her stalker.

The three of them got out and walked back to the bus stop where Alice had alighted earlier on. They then traced the route she had taken and searched the whole area. Nobody was about. When they drove Alice back to the house, she thanked them and went inside.

'Any luck?' asked Ellen.

'I'm afraid not, Mummy. The man is long gone.'

'Do you still think that he was on the same bus as you?'

'I'm certain of it,' said Alice. 'Because I was trying to comfort that old lady, I was distracted. When I found myself alone, I was much more alert. I just wished I had some sort of weapon with me to defend myself. I've been on night duty many times, but we always have a policeman with us in case of trouble. I'm never afraid – even when drunks spill out of a pub and jostle us.'

'But this was different. You were completely alone.'

'That wasn't what worried me, Mummy. It was the fact that the man might have been waiting for me when I left because I had something he wanted. He must have guessed that Joe would have a visitor and he picked me out somehow. What if he was the man who tried to get at Joe in the military hospital? That thought terrified me.'

'He knew where Joe had been moved because it was in the paper.'

'But he didn't know where they'd put him for safety,' said Alice. 'I did. I had the information he needed. Oh, I don't

318

know,' she went on, shaking her head. 'Maybe I'm wrong. He might have been after me for the obvious reason. I was a young woman on my own. He wanted to assault me.'

'I'm afraid that your first guess was right,' said Ellen. 'You must never go there alone again. I'll come with you.' She lowered her voice. 'Are you going to tell Joe what happened?'

'Of course, I am.'

'But he's not in danger, is he? You told me that he has an armed guard.'

'That's not the point, Mummy. If I didn't tell Joe what happened, he'd never forgive me. Also, if this man is hanging about the hospital, there's a chance of catching him. Oh!' sighed Alice. 'If only Daddy was here right now. He'd know exactly what to do.'

After an early breakfast, Marmion and Burge left the hotel and made their way to the ferry. The forecast was more promising this time. The weather was fine and the sea far less choppy. Much of the force had gone from the wind. It encouraged them to venture up on deck to take a last look at the Irish capital, even though it was shrouded in darkness. Burge felt sorry to leave.

'We had no chance to explore Dublin,' he complained. 'It's such a lively city.'

'I agree, Cliff. But there's something you haven't noticed.'

'Is there?'

'We're on duty again,' said Marmion. 'That means we have things to do and places to go. Besides, doesn't the thought of seeing Chat gladden your heart?'

'Frankly – no!'

'At long last, there's good news to report. We've not only identified the woman involved in those burglaries, we have her address in London.'

'I'm schooling myself not to expect too much.'

'Good advice. We shouldn't make assumptions.'

Burge pondered. 'How long is Sergeant Keedy expected to stay in hospital?'

'Oh, he'll be there for some time yet, I'm afraid,' said Marmion. 'Abdominal wounds can be very tricky. The main thing is that he's safe and having the best possible medical attention.'

'What about that burglar who's been trying to get at him?'

'His name is Eamonn Corrigan and he's the kind of man who bears a grudge. He and Joe have clashed before. Apart from anything else, Joe once arrested a wild Irishman named Niall Quinn and sent him back to a prison camp in Wales.'

'Why should that upset Corrigan?'

'Quinn was his nephew.'

'Ah, I see.'

'Corrigan wants retribution.'

'How far will he go to get it?'

'As far as it's necessary, Cliff. Men like Corrigan don't have boundaries. Danger means nothing to them. They feed off it. Once he's set his mind on something,' stressed Marmion, 'nothing will divert him. In other words, Joe Keedy will never be completely safe until Corrigan and his associates are safely behind bars, waiting for their turn with the hangman.'

* * *

It was still dark when Corrigan arrived at the hospital. He was able to keep to the shadows and watch members of staff arriving. An ambulance arrived and a patient was lifted out of the rear of the vehicle. Male orderlies came out with a trolley. Corrigan saw his chance. As the newcomer was wheeled into the building, the Irishman slipped in behind him as if he was a concerned relative of the patient. Once inside the hospital, he darted off down a corridor. Somewhere on the ground floor, he reasoned, there had to be a changing room for the male employees. He knew that he looked like an intruder. In a white coat, however, he would be invisible.

Superintendent Claude Chatfield was known for his stamina, arriving early at Scotland Yard, and staying late into the evening. When he got to his office that morning, the telephone rang by way of a welcome. He snatched up the receiver and discovered that he was talking to Alice Marmion.

'I'm sorry to disturb you,' she said.

'No apology is needed. Only an emergency would make you contact me this early.'

'It's about a visit I made yesterday evening to the hospital.'

He was worried. 'I hope you're not about to give me bad news about Sergeant Keedy.'

'It's the worst possible news, Superintendent,' she told him. 'That's why I had to get in touch with you. What happened was this . . .'

* * *

Corrigan's search was thorough. He soon discovered the changing room. When he slipped inside, he found an unexpected bonus. On the wall was a large chart, showing where every ward and room in the hospital was located. After studying it for a few minutes, he opened one of the cabinets along the wall and took out a white coat. He then dived into the toilet to take off his coat and hat, hanging them on the peg behind the door. The white coat was slightly too large for him, so he turned up the sleeves. His gun was in its holster, but he did not expect to need it unless he was cornered. Corrigan intended to use the knife in a sheath attached to his leg. One thrust into Keedy's heart might not be enough to kill him. He would therefore slit the man's throat for good measure. The patient would be unable to defend himself.

The first time that Claude Chatfield turned up unexpectedly at the hospital, Keedy had been surprised. He was frankly alarmed by the second visit. Told about Alice's experience on the previous evening, he was torn between anger and remorse. Because he'd been unable to defend her, Alice had been put through a terrible ordeal. She'd been stalked by a man who would have shown no pity for her. Keedy could not bear to think what he might have done to Alice. He was writhing with a sense of helplessness.

'I need a weapon, sir,' he said.

'Don't be silly,' replied Chatfield. 'You're not in a fit state to defend yourself. Besides, you have Detective Constable Younger outside the door, and you know all about his prowess as a marksman. I've also brought additional support.'

'How many of them?'

'Three. One of them is in the waiting room to watch for anyone suspicious turning up for the morning visit. Another man is guarding the stairs to watch everyone who comes up and down them, and the third officer is in the lift. All three are armed. If Corrigan tries to get up here by that means, he'll be spotted. In other words, you're well protected.'

'Then why don't I feel safe, sir?'

'It's because you're still in shock after what happened to you.'

'My mind is completely clear,' argued Keedy. 'I know how cunning this man is. Corrigan escaped from us when we had dozens of men surrounding that house. If he finds out where I am, he'll get to me somehow.'

'Stop fearing the worst,' advised Chatfield. 'There's a strong possibility that this man will stay well away from the hospital. He must realise that the young woman he trailed yesterday would report the incident to the police. As a result, security here will have been tightened.'

'That won't stop him, sir.'

'We'll see. I need to return to Scotland Yard now but I'm leaving you in the capable hands of four well-trained officers. That should put your mind at rest.'

Keedy glowered. 'Well, it doesn't,' he murmured.

When the ferry docked in Holyhead, they were pleased to find that there was a police car waiting to take them to the railway station. Marmion and Burge climbed into the rear of the vehicle and listened to the driver's weather report. It seemed that they might well encounter rain on their journey to London. As they set off, Burge looked through the window.

'Home at last!' he said. 'Superintendent Chatfield – here we come!'

Corrigan had completed his search. Having found a trolley in the corridor, he used it as an additional part of his disguise. It enabled him to search the ground floor before exploring the next level. As he stepped into the lift, a man was standing quietly in a corner. One glance told Corrigan that he was a detective. The police were taking care of Keedy. He continued his search floor by floor until he came to a room with someone standing on guard outside it. All the other individual rooms had a card on display outside with the name of the occupant typed on it. This one was the exception to the rule. After nodding to the detective, Corrigan moved on with a smile. He had found Keedy.

It was time for Alice and her mother to get dressed for the morning visit to the hospital. Both were going with a sense of trepidation. Despite the assurances from the superintendent, Alice was not entirely persuaded that Keedy was safe. She was desperate to see him with her own eyes and to tell him about the frightening experience she had had after her last visit. When they left the house and headed for the bus stop, Alice pointed out the hedge behind which she had hidden from the man stalking her.

'Thank goodness it was dark!' said Ellen. 'In daylight, he'd probably have seen you through the branches.'

'I've never run so fast in my life, Mummy.'

'You've always kept yourself fit.'

'It's an important part of being a policewoman. Gale Force keeps telling us that. Very few crooks allow you to arrest them. They make a run for it. I once chased a shoplifter for over a hundred yards before I caught her.'

'I'm so glad that you always have a beat partner.'

'Iris is even faster than I am,' said Alice, 'and she's quite fearless. I wish I'd had her with me when I was on my way back yesterday.'

'You'll have me looking out for you today. Will I be able to see Joe at the hospital?'

'Of course, Mummy, but I'd rather see him alone first, if you don't mind. He'll want to know exactly what happened when I was followed. But, yes, you must pop into his room yourself. Joe will be pleased to see you.'

'I do hope that awful man doesn't turn up again.'

'So do I,' said Alice, nervously. 'The mere thought of him makes me shudder.'

Corrigan knew that preparation was vital. Having established where his quarry was, he had to plan his escape. He therefore went up to the top floor and found the emergency exit, running up and down the steps to see how fast he could get away. He then went in search of a storeroom and found what he wanted on the third floor. It was full of cardboard boxes and old newspapers. Some broken wooden chairs were also pressed into use. Corrigan began to build himself a bonfire.

* * *

Noise was continuous inside the hospital. Some patients were so vulnerable that they wore earmuffs. Nursing staff took care not to spoil the relative calm. Then the fire alarm screeched aloud in every ward and threw the entire hospital into a panic. The sound was deafening. Desperate patients tried to clamber out of bed and reach for their dressing gowns. Nurses went running to see where the fire had broken out and how serious the blaze was. There was pandemonium in every part of the building.

Having set his bonfire ablaze, Corrigan watched from a vantage point. He waited until the detective outside Keedy's room went off to find out where the fire had started. Rolling up his trouser leg, he pulled the knife from its sheath and ran down the corridor to the room where his victim would be cowering in fear. Having disabled him with a bullet, he could now finish him off with a sharp blade. Corrigan was burning with satisfaction.

As he flung open the door, however, he saw that he had a problem. Keedy was not there. The bedclothes had been thrown back and the patient had flown. There was no time to wonder where Keedy had gone. Corrigan had to put his own safety first. Sprinting to the fire escape, he went down the steps at high speed, colliding from time to time with others who were also in flight. When he reached the ground floor, he joined the surge of bodies going out through the main exit. He kept running until he was well clear of the building and the deafening hysteria.

* * *

When their bus pulled up outside the hospital, Alice and Ellen were confronted by a terrifying sight. Smoke was billowing out of a window. Patients and staff were still pouring out of the building. They could not hear the fire alarm, but they could see its dramatic effect on those who had been inside the building.

'The fire is on the third floor,' cried Alice. 'That's where Joe is.'

'Don't jump to any conclusions,' said Ellen, trying to soothe her. 'It will soon be under control. It doesn't seem to have spread to any of the other floors.'

'This is his doing, Mummy – the man who followed me. He couldn't get at Joe any other way, so he's set the whole hospital on fire.'

The bus was starting to empty now. They followed the others out on to the street and heard the approaching fire engine. Ellen was frightened but Alice was completely distraught. She ran towards the hospital, desperate to find out if Keedy was still alive.

For reasons they could not understand, the train journey back to London was much faster than the journey to Holyhead on the previous day. Marmion and Burge went straight to the superintendent's office to give him their report, but he silenced them with a raised hand.

'There's an emergency at the hospital,' he told them. 'It's on fire.'

'Heavens!' exclaimed Marmion. 'That sounds like Corrigan's work.'

'They have it under control, but you can imagine the effect it had.'

'What about Joe Keedy? Is he safe?'

'I'm afraid that I don't know, Inspector.'

'Then you must excuse me, sir. I'll get over there at once.' Marmion moved to the door. 'Sergeant Burge will tell you about our trip to Ireland.'

Once the fire had been put out, staff and patients were allowed into the hospital again. After another wait, visitors were brought in as well and sent off to their respective wards to see how their loved ones had coped with the disaster. Alice was relieved to find the detective on guard outside Keedy's room. More importantly, she saw the patient sitting up in bed.

'Are you all right, Joe?' she gasped. 'When we saw that smoke coming out from this floor, we were horrified. I was afraid that that dreadful man had burnt you alive.'

'He didn't get the chance, Alice. The moment I heard the fire alarm, I knew that Corrigan was here. During that siege we attended, he used a blaze to distract us while he and his cronies escaped. He tried the same trick again, but it didn't work. I struggled out of bed and crawled under it.'

'Did he come in here?'

'Yes, he did. I heard the door being flung open and he rushed in.'

'What did you do?'

'I held my breath and waited,' said Keedy. 'Thinking they'd moved me to another room, he ran off and, I suppose, made his escape. I knew that Corrigan would try to kill me. Luckily, I managed to dodge him.'

Alice burst into tears of relief. He put his arms around her and pulled her close.

'As long as that man is at liberty,' she wailed, 'you'll never be safe.'

'Yes, I will. Corrigan won't dare to come back now.'

'How do you know?'

'He's shot his bolt,' said Keedy. 'And he knows that the search for him will be stepped up. My guess is that he's probably on his way out of London right now.'

With his head in a newspaper, Corrigan sat in a train taking him back to Birmingham. Nobody in his compartment seemed to notice that he was wearing a white coat.

When he got to the hospital, Marmion was intercepted by his wife who told him how their daughter had been followed by Corrigan when her visit came to an end. Marmion was duly appalled and glad that Ellen would accompany Alice on her visits from now on. The two of them went up together to Keedy's room and heard how he had escaped from the intruder by hiding under the bed.

'You might have caused yourself damage, Joe,' said Marmion.

'I didn't care if every single stitch popped apart, Harv. I just wanted a hiding place.'

'I don't blame you.'

'But what's your news?' asked Keedy. 'Alice told me that

you'd gone off to Ireland in search of evidence. Did you find any?'

'We found the one thing we wanted most – the name of the woman who has caused us so much trouble. Even as we speak,' he added, 'Detective Sergeant Burge is on his way to arrest her.'

Clifford Burge had to control his overconfidence. On his way to the address he'd been given, he kept reminding himself that he had been in this position before, so certain that he was about to make an important arrest that he never even considered that the woman in question was innocent. It had been a serious blunder and he had no wish to repeat it. When he got to the block of flats, however, he could not suppress a faint tingle of excitement. He went into the entrance hall and looked at the list of occupants of the various flats. His eye fell on the name of Irene Peck. The actress was no longer using her stage name. Burge found that significant.

He went inside the building and located the flat. He pressed the bell beside the door. There was a long silence. After pressing it a second time without a response, he used his knuckles to rap on the door. He heard movement inside the flat. The door was opened a few inches before a chain stopped it. Burge found himself looking at an elderly woman and caught a whiff of her perfume.

'What do you want?' she snapped.

'I'd like a word with you, Miss Peck,' he said, producing his warrant card. 'I'm Detective Sergeant Burge from Scotland Yard.'

'How do I know that?'

'Because I have no reason to lie to you. If you refuse to let me in, I'm afraid that I will have to summon help and have this door smashed open.'

She was outraged. 'Why on earth would you do that?'

'It's because we have been tracking your movements over recent weeks. We even visited the estate agent from whom you bought a house near Cork.'

'There's nothing illegal in that transaction,' she said, tartly. 'Can't a woman buy a cottage near the place where she was born without being pestered by someone from Scotland Yard?'

'I'm afraid that there's more to it than that – as you know only too well.'

'Stop talking in riddles, young man.'

'You have been working with three Irish burglars,' he said, 'to steal jewellery from a series of London shops. I have come here to arrest you for those crimes. Please don't waste time on pointless denials.' She burst into laughter. 'Mockery will get you nowhere, Miss Peck. We've gathered enough evidence to link you to Eamonn Corrigan and his friends.'

'I do beg your pardon,' she said, controlling her mirth. 'Let me open this door properly so that you can come in. I'll be most interested to hear about this "evidence" of yours.'

Closing the door, she removed the chain so that she could open the door wide. Burge saw that he was talking to a striking woman in a multicoloured robe. She had an air of self-possession that was unnerving. When he stepped into the flat, she shut the door behind him. Burge was already beginning to realise that he had made a mistake for the second time. As he began to rehearse his apologies, she drew herself up to her full height.

'Now, then,' she said. 'How much money will I get when I sue you for wrongful arrest?'

Tom Regan and Pierce Orr were playing a game of cards when there was a thunderous bang on the front door. Regan went off immediately.

'That sounds like Eamonn,' he said.

When he opened the door, Corrigan pushed past him and went into the kitchen. He opened a cupboard, took out a bottle of Irish whiskey and poured a sizeable measure into a glass. Only when he had had a first taste did he turn to his friend.

'And before you ask,' he warned, 'no, I didn't kill him. Keedy escaped somehow. Mind you, I did come close to burning the whole hospital to a cinder.'

'What's that?' asked Orr, joining them. 'Did you start another fire?'

'It was the only way to get near him,' said Corrigan.

'Tell us what happened, Eamonn. It's not often that you make a mistake.'

'It wasn't a mistake,' insisted Corrigan. 'I was just unlucky.'

'Will you go back for another crack at him?'

'No, I won't, Pierce. I'll stay here with you two until things quieten down a little.' He took a long sip of whiskey. 'Then I'll take another look at that jewellery shop near the city centre.'

'We could do with some action,' said Regan. 'All we've

done here is to sit on our arses and wonder how you were getting on.'

'I gave Keedy a nasty fright. That's something to be proud of.'

'You should have taken us with you. Sure, we could have helped.'

'My business was personal. It's strictly between me and him.' He smirked. 'Mind you, I tried to involve her as well.'

'Who are you taking about?' asked Regan.

'Keedy's woman, as pretty a piece of skirt as I've seen in a long time. The pity of it was that she gave me the slip. It would have been a lovely way to give Keedy another wound. If I'd got my hands on her,' he boasted, 'it would have hurt him far more than that bullet in his belly.'

Though they were safely back home, Alice and her mother were still deeply upset. They could not cope with the thought that someone was so desperate to kill Keedy that he set fire to a hospital in which Keedy was a patient. Corrigan had somehow escaped. It meant that he was free to make another attempt.

'I'll never feel safe until that horrible man is caught,' said Alice.

'I'm as anxious as you are,' admitted her mother. 'The only consolation is that you managed to escape him when he followed you home.'

'Forget about me, Mummy. Joe is safe. That's the real consolation.'

They were seated either side of the kitchen table. Ellen had poured each of them a cup of tea, but they were too jangled to drink it. Alice kept thinking about how close Corrigan had come to killing Keedy. For a matter of seconds, they had been alone together in the same hospital room. Keedy must have been holding his breath under the bed.

'Your father will sort it out,' said Ellen. 'He's going to have Joe moved to somewhere safer. And this time, the information will be kept from the *Standard*. That man, Corrigan, will have no idea where Joe is.' She sipped her tea and pulled a face. 'This is cold.'

'We've been too busy talking about what happened at the hospital. In any case, I'm not in the mood for a drink. My stomach is still churning. Anyway,' said Alice, 'let's talk about something else. I've been meaning to ask you if you'd been into Paul's bedroom.'

'Yes, but I didn't stay long. I felt scared.'

'Why?'

'I don't know, Alice. There was something . . . unsettling me in there.'

'Would you like me to come in there with you?'

'No, no, it's my problem and I must . . . solve it my own way.'

'But there must be a reason why you're afraid to go into that bedroom. Most of Paul's things have been taken out of there. What is it that frightened you?'

'I wish I knew.'

'In due course, Joe will be moving in there.'

'That's why I was so keen to get it ready for him but . . . well, you know what happened.'

'I want to understand why, Mummy. I mean, it's so unlike you. Do you think you I should go in there and take out the last of Paul's things?'

'No, Alice. It's my job. When I feel better, I'll go in there and do it.'

Cliff Burge and Marmion were in the inspector's office. Marmion wanted a report.

'Did you manage to track the woman down?'

'Oh, I found her easily enough and I tried to arrest her. But there was a problem.'

'Go on.'

Burge shrugged. 'She wasn't the person we're after.'

He described what had happened when he called on Irene Peck and how he left her feeling that he'd made a complete fool of himself. After a second failure, he was more determined than ever to find the right person to arrest. His first step was to call on Beatrice Naylor at Pegasus Costumes. He wanted to find out if she could tell him anything more about Grace Whittington.

'And could she?' asked Marmion.

'Oh, yes. She remembered meeting her at the stage door when she was waiting to get her autograph. Miss Naylor recalled how beautifully dressed she was. The actress was wearing a small crucifix on a silver chain. That rang a bell for me. I remembered what Miss Whittington had told that store detective at Swan & Edgar. She gave him the name of a vicar who could vouch for her.'

'You had the sense to track him down. He'd never heard of the woman.'

'That was because she deliberately gave the name of the wrong church. If she's consorting with Irish criminals to further the cause of Home Rule, the chances are that she might be a Roman Catholic. I looked at a directory of London churches.'

'That was enterprising of you. What did you find?'

'The Catholic church of St Alban's. It's close to the Anglican church she mentioned to that store detective. When I got there, I met Father O'Brien, a very helpful old gent. He knew Grace Whittington well, except that she was using her real name of Peggy Dark. She came to church every Sunday. He was happy to give me her address.'

'Where exactly is it?'

'Not far from Baker Street,' said Burge. 'When I said I thought this woman might be our main suspect, you dismissed her as a mere shoplifter. I think you underestimated her, sir.'

'Let's go and find out,' said Marmion, getting to his feet.

'I'm going to ask you a favour.'

'What is it?'

'Could you make the arrest this time, please?'

The fire had been quickly extinguished but the patients at the hospital remained in a state of alarm. Keedy was more frightened than he cared to admit. He'd been alone in the same room as a man determined to kill him. Next time Corrigan got that close to him, Keedy might not be so lucky. When there was a knock on the door, he tensed. It opened to let Barry Younger into the room. The newcomer had a broad smile.

'Good news,' he said. 'You're getting rid of me.'

'But I need someone to guard the door.'

'Oh, you'll be well protected. They're moving you to a safer location.'

'Where is it?' asked Keedy.

'Edmonton Military Hospital.'

'We solved the murder of one of the surgeons there.'

'That's why Inspector Marmion chose it,' said Younger. 'When he explained the situation that you're in, they were happy to find room for you – and they guaranteed armed guards around the clock. How does that sound?'

'I can't think of a better place to go.'

'You'll be transferred after dark. Nobody will know about your move this time.'

Keedy grinned. 'My future father-in-law is a genius.'

'He just wants to keep you alive long enough to marry his daughter,' said Younger.

When they entered the building, they were amused by the notice saying that male visitors were not allowed after six o'clock in the evening. Marmion turned to Burge.

'What is this place?' he asked. 'A nunnery?'

'According to that list,' said Burge, pointing to a board on the wall, 'her flat is number four.'

'Then let's pay her a visit, shall we?'

Marmion led the way along a corridor until they came to the right door. He rang the bell. There was a shuffling sound from within, then the door was opened to reveal an elderly woman with more than a few vestiges of an extraordinary beauty. The fact that she was exquisitely dressed added to her impact on her visitors. They both noticed the silver crucifix she was wearing. Her poise was remarkable.

'Well?' she asked, pointedly.

'Miss Whittington?' asked Marmion.

'Yes, that's right. Who might you be?'

'I'm Inspector Marmion of the London Metropolitan Police and this is my colleague, Sergeant Burge.' They produced their warrant cards for inspection. 'I wonder if we might have a word with you, please?'

'What does it concern?' she asked, her voice remarkably calm.

'The theft of a silk scarf from Swan & Edgar.'

She laughed. 'It was a dreadful mistake on the part of a store detective. The manager apologised and told me to keep the scarf. But why should two detectives take an interest in a crime that never took place?'

'If you invite us in,' said Marmion, 'we will explain.'

'Oh, very well,' she replied. 'If you must, come on in – but don't expect to stay long. I'm expecting visitors.'

'That suits us, Miss Whittington,' said Burge.

They stepped into the flat and waited until she closed the door. She led them down a corridor and into the living room, indicating two chairs. They sat down and she lowered herself into the armchair opposite them. They noticed how much heat the fire was generating.

'You have a charming flat, Miss Whittington,' said Burge.

'Don't tell me what I already know,' she replied. 'Now, why are you bothering me?'

'Do you know a man named Eamonn Corrigan?' asked Marmion, bluntly.

'I've never heard that name before. Who is he?'

'He's a person of more than passing interest to me, Miss Whittington. Earlier today, he started a fire in a hospital in Shepherd's Bush to create a distraction. Corrigan was there to kill a colleague of ours, Sergeant Keedy, a man he shot during a siege some days ago.'

'This is all very unfortunate, Inspector, but it's of no interest to me.'

'There's something I didn't mention,' said Marmion. 'Sergeant Keedy is due to marry my daughter early in April. In short, I have a very good reason to keep him alive and an equally good reason to arrest Corrigan along with his associates, Thomas Regan and Pierce Orr.'

'I wish you well in your search for these dreadful individuals,' she said without betraying the slightest discomfort, 'and I hope that nothing stands in the way of your daughter's marriage.'

'That depends on you, Miss Whittington.'

She was insulted. 'Me?'

'The three men I mentioned take their orders from you,' said Burge. 'The inspector and I have not long returned from Dublin. Someone in the RIC confirmed that Corrigan, Regan and Orr are wanted for multiple crimes.'

'That may be so,' she said, evenly, 'but how dare you link their names with mine.'

'You had an illustrious career as an actress,' recalled Marmion, 'but your talents have been put to a more sinister use of late. Evidently, you love to appear before an audience.

I therefore invite you to appear before a private audience of eight people. Each one of them is the owner of a jewellery shop in London and each one of them will be certain to remember a performance you gave to win their confidence.' He saw her face twitch. 'Yes, Miss Whittington, the game is up. As you well know, Corrigan shot dead a policeman. He and his accomplices will hang for the murder.'

'I had nothing to do with it,' she insisted. 'He was forbidden to carry a gun.'

'Clearly, he disobeyed you. I'm certain that you didn't tell him to set fire to a hospital either,' said Marmion. 'He acted of his own volition. He even dared to stalk my daughter one night. It's another reason why I want to arrest that man.'

'All we need is the address of where we can find him.' said Burge.

'How the devil would I know it?' she said, her voice still controlled.

'It's because you control those three men – or, at least, you did.'

'They've started to operate without you, Miss Whittington,' said Marmion. 'There'll be no more money coming to you to fund your activities. The play is over, I fear. There'll be no curtain call this time.' He held out a hand. 'Give me the address where I can find Corrigan.'

Her head bowed. 'Yes, of course,' she conceded. 'I was fool enough to trust that madman.' She got up to reach for a handbag and opened it. 'This is what you want, Inspector,' she went on, holding out a small notebook, then drawing it back immediately and tossing it onto the blazing fire. She laughed aloud. 'Oh dear! That was so clumsy of me.'

Seated nearest the fire, Burge reacted quickly, grabbing the tongs, and using them to lift out the notebook before dropping it on the hearth and stamping on it. The smoke from the notebook was soon dispelled. Her face was a study in hatred and defiance.

'You'll never find them,' she yelled.

'Have more faith in us, Miss Whittington,' said Marmion.

'We found you, didn't we?' added Burge.

She winced. 'Only because that fool, Corrigan, disobeyed my orders.'

'He won't be allowed to disobey the hangman's orders,' said Marmion, coldly. 'Now, then, Miss Dark, it's my duty to tell you that you are under arrest . . .'

Since they had been told that Keedy was about to be moved, there was no opportunity to visit him that evening. Alice and her mother began to prepare the evening meal. It was not long before the telephone interrupted them. Ellen picked up the receiver. Alice could tell from her voice to whom she was talking. She waited until her mother came back into the kitchen.

'What did Daddy have to say?' she asked.

'He's about to go to Birmingham.'

'Why?'

'He believes that the men they're after will be there.'

'Does that include Corrigan?'

'Oh, yes,' said Ellen. 'He's the one your father really wants.'

'How did he get hold of the address?'

'It was in a notebook owned by the woman who gave those men their orders. Your father rang the Birmingham Constabulary, and they offered him all the help he needs. He'll be on the way north within minutes.'

'I just hope that Daddy catches them all,' said Alice. 'I want some good news to pass on to Joe when I visit him tomorrow in his latest hospital.'

The transfer from Shepherd's Bush to Edmonton went without a hitch. Keedy was grateful to be going somewhere completely safe. It meant that he missed seeing Alice but that was unavoidable. She would be able to visit him on the following morning and bring the latest news. He now had the consolation of a good night's sleep, guarded by armed soldiers.

When their car arrived outside Ansells Brewery, a uniformed inspector was waiting to welcome them to Birmingham. He had already deployed his men in key positions around the house in Upper Thomas Street. Marmion was delighted with the man's thoroughness.

'Do we know if the three of them are inside?' asked Marmion.

'Yes, they're all there,' said the inspector. 'One of my men spotted them rolling back home. From the way they walked, it looked as if they'd been drinking.'

'Good. A few glasses of Guinness will slow their reactions.'

'I did as you requested, Inspector. I've brought six armed officers and six additional men. The house is surrounded.

We're ready for the signal to move in.'

'I'll be at the front,' said Marmion, turning to Burge. 'You go round to the rear, Cliff. And remember that Corrigan has a gun. No heroics, please.'

'I'll bear it in mind,' said Burge before trotting off towards Upper Thomas Street.

Marmion followed with the inspector, hoping that this siege would end more happily than the one in which Keedy had been injured. Inside the house was the man who had shot the sergeant. Marmion put the capture of Corrigan at the top of his list. When they reached the house, he checked to see that everyone was in position. He then signalled to the two policemen with shotguns. They used the butts of their weapons to smash the door open, then led the way in. Marmion was on their heels. Regan and Orr were in the living room, too drunk to do anything more than put up a token resistance.

'Where's Corrigan?' demanded Marmion.

'Gone to the privy,' said Regan.

Marmion heard a roar of anger from the tiny garden. He rushed out to see Corrigan in the gloom, emerging from the privy with trousers around his ankles, then wrestling with two policemen. A third officer came up behind him and struck the back of his head with a truncheon. Corrigan soon slumped to the ground. Marmion was delighted.

'Wipe his arse and put some handcuffs on him,' he said. 'Well done, everyone!'

Over breakfast with his wife and daughter next morning, he missed out the coarser details of the arrest. Marmion was soon picked up by a police car and driven to Scotland Yard. He was going to give a full report to Chatfield but was letting his daughter tell Keedy the good news about the arrests in Birmingham when she visited the hospital.

'Once I've done that,' said Alice, 'I'm going to report for work.'

'Are you sure that you feel up to it?' asked her mother.

'Oh, yes, Mummy. I'm raring to go. And while I'm away, I want a promise from you that you'll go into Paul's bedroom once more.'

'I did that first thing this morning. It was . . . an effort, but well worth it.'

'Did you feel upset again?'

'Yes, but I also understood why. Things have gone, Alice. Most of Paul's stuff is in the attic but there were odds and ends I left in that room. They'd all gone. In fact, they were worthless and yet they'd been stolen. That's when I had this strange thought.'

'Go on.'

'I'm sure I'm wrong. It's the reason I never mentioned it to your father. If those things were taken from Paul's bedroom, was there anything else missing?' She took a deep breath. 'I haven't dared to look. Would you come with me?'

Alice understood. There was a wall cupboard in the living room that contained a jumble of objects. One of them was a large mug in which the housekeeping money was kept. Leading her mother into the room, she opened the door of the cupboard and reached for the mug. Alice brought it out and showed it to her mother.

'It's empty!' cried Ellen.

'Are you sure that there was money in it?'

'Of course, I'm sure. Your father put it in there days ago.'

'Then where has it gone?'

When she realised what must have happened, Ellen's face turned white with alarm.

'Paul has a key to the house,' she said, wincing. 'He's back.'

Claude Chatfield was delighted to hear a full report of the arrests from Marmion. He even had the grace to congratulate Burge for his part in the operation. The fact that Corrigan was now in custody had given him great satisfaction. Chatfield had made a point of ringing the police station in Limehouse to pass on the good news, knowing that it would in turn reach the parents of Constable Meade, the officer shot dead by Corrigan. What interested the superintendent most, however, was the woman who had planned the burglaries from the jewellery shops.

'How could any self-respecting woman associate herself with such scum?' he asked.

'Miss Whittington saw them in a different light, sir,' explained Marmion. 'To her, they were fellow believers in Home Rule for Ireland.'

'But according to you, this woman was not Irish.'

'She'd been converted to the cause by a man with whom she had a close friendship. Miss Whittington spoke about him with fierce pride. He took part in the Easter Rising in 1916. Days after it collapsed, he was hunted down by British soldiers and shot dead.'

'That had a powerful effect on her, sir,' said Burge, taking over. 'When her friend was killed, she vowed to continue his work and use the remarkable skills she possessed as an actress. Three men were assigned to her. They burgled seven jewellers' shops in succession. We had the pleasure of arresting them yesterday evening.'

'I'm eternally grateful that you did,' said Chatfield.

'Sergeant Burge deserves credit for finding out the woman's address,' Marmion pointed out. 'When he learnt that the woman wore a crucifix, he traced her through St Alban's, the Roman Catholic church at which she worshipped.'

'How can anyone involved in serious crimes claim to be a Christian?'

'She did not see them as crimes, sir. They were blows struck on behalf of Ireland.'

'Yes,' added Burge. 'She spoke with great passion about it.'

'Thanks to both of you,' said Chatfield, 'that passion has now been silenced. I must say that I commend your determination. You've both worked tirelessly to achieve these important arrests. What drove you on?'

'In my case, sir,' said Burge, 'it was fear of failure.'

'I had a more personal reason to pursue these people,' said Marmion. 'One of them shot Sergeant Keedy and became obsessed with trying to kill him. I wasn't going to let anyone deprive my daughter of a husband. But there were drawbacks along the way,' he confessed. 'On more than one occasion, we were in danger of defeat by these men. I'm so grateful that we were able to secure an advantage over them in the end.' He smiled broadly. 'I will have great pleasure in being present at their trials.'

'What about the trial of that woman?' asked Chatfield.

'Oh, I think she will be looking forward to it, sir. It will be an opportunity to give a last performance. When she stands up in court,' said Marmion, 'there will be no sense of shame or repentance. She will be intensely proud of everything she has done on behalf of Ireland. In her eyes, she has fulfilled her mission.'

EDWARD MARSTON has written well over a hundred books, including some non-fiction. He is best known for his hugely successful Railway Detective series and he also writes the Bow Street Rivals series featuring twin detectives set during the Regency; the Home Front Detective novels set during the First World War; and the Ocean Liner mysteries.

edwardmarston.com

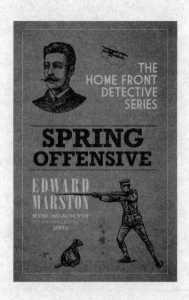

London, March 1918. British newspapers carry the disastrous news that the German Spring Offensive has begun, with thousands of British lives lost. Detective Sergeant Joe Keedy eagerly awaits his release from hospital and is anxious to resume the fight against crime on the Home Front.

Against this sombre backdrop, further mayhem strikes in the capital when a fire provides the diversion needed for an audacious bank robbery. The gang of criminals escape with a sizeable haul and leave one police officer dead and another gravely injured in their wake. For Detective Inspector Harvey Marmion, the investigation has a personal connection, but the task of bringing the culprits to justice will prove to be an uphill battle without Keedy, his detective partner, at his side. And nothing in this case is quite what it seems . . .